LEVELUP

AN 8-BIT NOVEL

MICAH JOEL

An 8-bit Novel

Micah Joel

Copyright © 2018 Micah Joel. All rights reserved.

I love to hear from readers. Your feedback matters. Reach me at http://micahjoel.info/lu

This is a work of fiction. Names, characters, organizations, places, events, and incidents are either products of the author's imagination or are public figures used fictitiously.

The author greatly appreciates you taking the time to read this work. Please consider **leaving a review** wherever you bought this book or telling your friends about these geeky stories.

Cover design by Sherwin Soy

Published by Geek Thoughts, Sunnyvale, CA
http://micahjoel.info
http://8bitnovel.com

❦ Created with Vellum

8-BIT NOVEL?_

What's an 8-bit novel?

- **80s nostalgia** (like **Stranger Things**)
- geeky retro gaming (like **Ready Player One**)
- interactive text adventures (like **Zork**)
- with a touch of **Mr Robot**.

Join my mailing list!

Get These Free Books

As an indie publisher, I don't have the resources of the LevelUP megacorporation to help me promote my book. I rely on enthusiastic fans like you. Visit **8bitnovel.com** and sign up for my mailing list, which includes geeky behind-the-scenes peeks at upcoming projects and free books:

- Damage, a prequel to LevelUP

- Minds and Machines, a short story collection
- Totally '80s: inspirations for the LevelUP universe

P.S.: Uncover the mystery at levelupcorp.online for a special bonus....

In memory of Le Guin and Hawking

Do one thing each day that scares your inner grue.

LEVEL 0_

PROGRESS

0-1: LOCKHEED SUPERFUND_

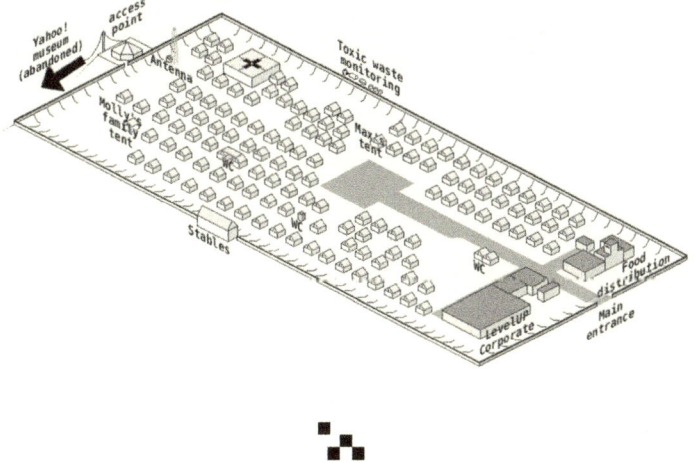

IF ASKED, MAX WOULD SAY LIVING IN THE CAMP ISN'T THAT bad—well—not completely soul-crushing. At least it's *stable*. Nothing ever changes. Except that, today something in or around Max's tent keeps beeping, and it's driving him out of his head.

Camp sweet camp. One-hundred-and-twelve residential tents huddled on an enormous pile of garbage, a thin stratum of earth covering decades of heaped military research waste. "Superfund" is a polite way of saying 'too expensive to clean up.' Here, the whipping wind is an everyday companion, carrying with it the stinging dust and the fetid stench of the salt marshes below

And life goes on. Every legally-mandated necessity one could hope for in exchange for sixty hours of "voluntary" labor at the conveniently-located sweatshop.

Oh, and nobody enters or leaves without getting scanned. The camp runs on equipment that used to line museum displays[1]. That's right, museums. Once upon a time, people used to be well-off enough to collect their old junk behind glass simply to be looked at. Now those things were far too valuable to sit unused—which suits Max just fine. As far as he's concerned, all technology's ever done is throw gasoline on the smoldering fires of injustice.

The flutter of a tent flap announces a visitor. In rushes Maria, one of Max's regulars, every year of her age etched into the lines of her face. She speaks in her usual urgent tones, as if she were already deep into conversation. "Five minutes." She checks her battered watch. "No, three minutes, is all I need, to make sure my nietos are okeydokey," she says.

"I don't want to make you late for the drop," Max says.

Maria waves the objection away. "I'm not even hungry." She produces a ration chit and presses it into Max's palm.

"That's a *week's* worth. I can't take—" Maria fixes Max with a glare that shuts down any hope of argument. He steps back. "Okay, okay, okay. But I need to be there when the delivery arrives. If we hurry, I can sweet-talk Nolan into giving you a few minutes on the a-line before then."

Then it happens again. *The beep.* "Did you hear that?"

"That's not the delivery truck," Maria says.

Come again? Max cranes his ear, but the sound of spitting gravel isn't subtle. A spray of pebbles pelts against the threadbare canvas of Max's tent. *What the?* "No, that isn't a truck at all," Max says. "Stay here."

Max emerges into a fog of dust, the stiff breeze wicking it away from the source, a cheap knock-off sports car in the gaudy neon blue of the LevelUP corporation. The gullwing door hisses open. The driver is a gangly guy with greasy black hair and an equally greasy naugahyde vest.

"Vic. Vic Vertex," he announces, while flashing a broad thunbs-up sign. "Personal assistant to the CEO."

A crowd begins to gather around the visitor. This is Hemera's right-hand man. Rumor is that he had his middle named changed to an emoji just to be more like her.

"Where's our food?" asks Josiah from tent C-8.

"Good news, bad news," Vic says, still grinning. "Which do you want first?"

"Bad," says Molly, not looking up from her video game console, firmly grasped in her good hand. As Nolan's kid, Max sees her constantly in the IT tent, but the two of them have hardly exchanged more than a dozen words, despite being close to the same age. In fact, Molly hardly talks to anyone at all. On account of her disability, she's exempt from work quotas too.

"Bad news it is," Vic says with far too much excitement. "Due to logistic issues outside of LevelUP's control, this week's delivery of Soylent feedstocks will be delayed. If anyone's literally dying of thirst, I've got a few bottles of water here though." He tosses one into the crowd. A fight nearly breaks out over it.

"What do you mean, delayed?" Max asks, carefully laying down each word.

"That's where the good news comes in," Vic says. "Effective immediately, LevelUP is instituting Saturday work shifts." He spreads his hands as if he's just bestowed a valuable gift.

The chatter from the still-gathering crowd rises in volume and pitch. Max senses the rising anger in the crowd; feels the collective tightening of the noose around Vic.

"How is that good?" Molly asks, still without looking up from her console. The bent piece of wire that takes the place of one of her hands taps against the controller buttons.

"It's good," Vic pronounces, "because, that's how you're going to get food. Complete a extra shift, and the drop will be cleared for delivery."

Molly looks up, a confused look on her face. "I don't think that's actually very good," she observes. No wonder nobody in camp likes her. Strange girl.

Vic's phone beeps. Since it runs on 80s technology, it's approximately the size and weight of a brick, and yet he keeps it clipped to his belt. "Well, look at that. Ten A.M. sharp. Chop, chop! Off to work you go." Nobody moves. "Off you go, little volunteers." Max spots several balled fists dotted throughout the crowd.

"You heard the man!" It's Lora Baines, who took charge of the camp since Isidore Morris, the original admin, disappeared without a trace. "I don't like it any more than you, but if those are the rules, then those are the rules. Let's move!"

Her voice slices through the irate trance, and clumps of people split off toward the factory building. Vic slams the door of his car and peppers the crowd with gravel as he peels out.

Max's stomach rumbles. So much for things never changing. He turns toward the factory building, but stops. *Maria*. He pivots on his heel and heads back to his tent.

"Thank you, Max, you're my *salvador*," Maria says before he's even all the way inside.

They squeeze through the narrow divide between tents and descend a worn footpath toward the access point, a platform precariously perched on the steep descent of the hill. At some point, someone carved a terrace into the slope, making the ground more level. The construction exposed a cross-section of crumpled gray metal—something left over from the Superfund era. Nolan set up shop there and carried on as if nothing was unusual about it.

From a distance, the distinguishing feature of the IT department is the thick mass of wires sagging from splintery poles. They emerge through a gash in the tent's side; a bottlenecked connection to the outside world, by way of an ancient building once known by the ridiculous name *Yahoo!*, exclamation mark and all. Upon closer approach, the distinguishing feature is the warmth radiating from the dirty canvas. All those machines inside shed lots of heat.

Max ducks inside the tent, and the smell of hot electronics makes his stomach churn. He can't help but notice Nolan's rash, a little redder than last time, peeking out from behind his salt and pepper beard.

Cross-legged on the floor of the tent, clutching a beeping 1980s-era handheld video game is, Molly. She wears long black braids interspersed with occasional bright purple. Her face and skin are an even mix of both her parents. The tinny sound of her game is familiar, but not loud enough to be the sound Max keeps hearing.

"Max!" Nolan says without looking up. He taps at his IBM PCjr keyboard, and the fifty-pound glass CRT flickers from a spreadsheet to paragraphs of text. "Let's see. ZORK.EXE, still in progress. Here we are. 'To the south across a shallow ford, is a dark tunnel which looks as though it was once enlarged and smoothed. To the north, a narrow path winds among stalagmites. Dim light illuminates the cavern.'"

"Didn't you hear about the new work shift?" Max asks him.

"Of course I did," Nolan says. "I figure they'll wait for me."

Max shifts gears, recalling his journey through the interactive story. His imagination has far better graphics than any computer program could produce. Once again, he's lost in the maze of twisty passages, all alike. "North," he replies.

Nolan taps on the keyboard. "Sorry, compadre," he says. "You have walked right into the slavering fangs of a lurking grue." He slaps his desk, sending the monitor into a precarious wobble. "You sure you're cut out for this game?"

"Maria needs to use the A-line."

Nolan's smile falls away. "C'mon man. You know how expensive analog calls are. What am I supposed to do, interrupt a paying customer's data transfer?"

Max nudges the vintage telephone handset off the desk. The heavy plastic thumps across the floor, dangling on the end of its coiled wire, releasing the scratchy sound of the modem into the tent's stuffy air. The sound makes Max's eardrums itch.

"Hey, what'd you go and do that for?" Nolan asks.

"Looks like you've got an opening right now," Max notes, coolly. "Three minutes. Remember how happy you were after I sourced you that 56k modem? Do this for me and I'll tear up that IOU with your name on it."

"Now we're talking." Nolan flips to another screen and starts provisioning the call, typing rapidly. "You know, people come in here and offer to pay in Maxes now."

"Maxes? Do I really want to ask what that means?"

Nolan looks up, but his fingers continue flying over the keys. "Your legendary IOU-ing has become its own form of currency. Nice touch, writing each one out in rhyming verse."

From the corner, Molly speaks, but not to anyone in particular: "It's going to be a long day." She says and does things like this more often than most people are comfortable with.

In any case, Max isn't sure if inspiring a currency system a good thing or not. Max takes Maria's leathery hand and guides her to the desk chair. "Hurry," he says. "You've got three minutes, then meet us on the floor. You'll be fine." While she's distracted, Max slips her ration chit back into her bag. Not that he can afford it. He can't do this every time. Better to keep people from building expectations. Max barely keeps this little Mercantile afloat as it is, and everyone in the camp depends on his continued services. But, every once in a while, he'll make an exception for those looking after little ones.

Nolan produces an embossed calling card from his pocket. Maria picks up the telephone handset, spinning the rotary dial to work through the long string of digits. The delighted squeal of children hearing their grandma on the phone spills into the tent as Max and Nolan make their way out. They walk together toward the factory floor.

"How am I supposed to keep this place running if I'm giving away time?" Nolan mutters.

"It's called doing the right thing," Max says. "C'mon. She was willing to trade food for minutes. Besides. I know you have an extra stash of A-line access cards."

Nolan has the decency to look at his feet. "There really are no secrets in this place."

THE GREETING CONSISTS of a cheery recorded voicing of 'welcome,' followed by a rough synthesized vocalization of a specific name.

"Welcome…Max Root. Welcome…Nolan Matheson." Ice lines up behind Max and Nolan. She's wearing a ratty Tesla t-shirt (Greatest Hits) that stands out against her dark skin. "Welcome…Ishawna Matheson."

Max passes through the jaunty animated blue arrow that LevelUP corporation inexplicably chose as a holographic mascot, to a screen where the real action is: work assignments for each person entering the factory. It's the same system keeping them prisoners in the camp.

Assignments march across the screen in a jaggy font. Their consecutively assigned workstations are at the far end of one of several workbenches that stretch the length of the building. Max settles in and fires up the soldering iron. By the time the choking fumes of burning flux attack his nostrils, the first workpiece arrives on the conveyor belt, a plastic tray that would normally hold components with pictorial instructions on how to assemble them. The initial set of trays contain only paper.

Nolan groans in agony. "Content moderation."

"Shhh!," Ice hisses.

Ten hours of mindless soldering would be preferable. Sifting through random people's internet postings, Max has *seen things*, even in grainy 8-bit resolution, that have scarred him for life. What could possibly trigger an entire weekend duty roster of sifting through photos? Max slams his iron's power switch off.

The intercom above crackles to life. "Attention volunteer content moderators: Your quota for the day is one-thousand pages per volunteer. Follow all instructions to the letter." That's a not-so-nice way of saying that, just to keep the workers on their toes, the company will deliberately intersperse sentinel images they *expect* to get flagged for something—and pity the poor fool who carelessly passes one of those along without comment.

Max takes a deep breath and flips over his first page. It's not what he expects. It's not a vacation photo from some unimaginably rich person's yacht. Not a crime scene. Not some propaganda tract. There's no blood, or gore, or bodily fluids at all. It's an aerial photo. His eyes scan to the printed instructions: IDENTIFY SUSPICIOUS STRUCTURES.

Suspicious structures? That could mean anything. Max's eyes glaze over for a moment at the prospect of doing this all day. He's about to dismiss this one, when something catches his eye. A small shed, or maybe an outhouse in the middle of a grassy field. It's hard to make out in the low-resolution image. Is that suspicious? Nope. Max colors in the little circle next to the word UNEXCEPTIONAL and moves on to the next one.

And the next, and the next, and the next. It's going to be a long day.

"This is ridiculous," Nolan blurts out.

"Less talking, more working." It's Lora, filling her role as administrator. "The faster we all work, the faster we'll get our food." She's just doing her job, but that doesn't make people resent her less.

Hours crawl past. Mind-numbing stretches of mental effort not quite repetitive enough to get used to. No way to slip into an easy pattern. Max's stomach grumbles loudly enough to get a look from Ice, and he needs to close his eyes for half a minute for each new page, otherwise it's too blurry to see.

"Mom?" calls out a small voice from behind them. Lora swoops out of nowhere to confront the new visitor.

"Oh honey," Ice says, "You can't be in here. We're almost done. Go back to the tent and play on your Game Boy."

"It's an Atari Lynx," Molly corrects. She doesn't look Lora or her parents in the eye, but she holds her gaze at a spot a few inches above Max's shoulder. She seems flustered about something, in a sweetly insistent manner.

"What is it?" Max asks.

"We have a visitor," Molly says.

"FINALLY FOOD!" shouts a volunteer closer to the door. He abandons his post and dashes out. Seconds later, a full stampede is in progress.

---

1. With a few notable exceptions.

0-2 ALERT_

LevelUP corporation's approach to branding seems pretty straightforward on the surface: put an obnoxious shade of blue on *everything*. Especially their corporate fleet. So when the expected vehicle is not a delivery truck, but rather a SUV shellacked with LevelUP's retina-scorching hue, it's equal parts terrifying and exhausting. A visit from corporate is far worse than an extra work shift. It means they want something else.

The vehicle crunches to a stop on the gravel just outside the factory, right in the middle of the circle of harsh light. Two bodyguards uncrimp themselves from the back seat, the cool evening breeze ruffling their ties as the first one begin unloading boxes. The other clears out a perimeter with little more than a look, people tripping over themselves to get out of the way. That done, he barks a word of approval into his neon blue walkie-talkie. The SUV's front gullwing doors hiss open.

Out steps Vic "thumbs up[1]" Vertex, sycophantic grin still in place. He manages to get his picture in every article written about LevelUP. A popular rumor suggests that his middle name got legally changed to an emoji.

Vic shivers in the cool breeze. "Let's get this party started," he says, flashing double thumbs-up signs to himself. Nobody returns his smile.

"Just give us the food," somebody mutters.

Lora Baines, pushes her way through the huddled masses. "What's this about? I've done everything you've demanded. What more do you want?"

Vic grazes Lora with his confused smirk. "And you are?"

Max's never seen Lora this upset. She sputters something that Max can't quite make out. Vic gracelessly snatches Lora's three-ring-binder, the one filled with details of the camp's operation, then turns his attention to inspecting the rest of the gathered residents, making a point of leaving her request hanging.

His gaze settles on Molly, her head down, absorbed in her beeping video game. He swipes it out of her hands. "What have we here?" He unsnaps the back panel to reveal six double-As. "I wasn't aware batteries were permitted in the camp. Where'd you get those?"

Molly says nothing. Her eyes leap from face to face, pleading for support.

Max steps out from the safety of the crowd and grabs the game back, but Vic doesn't let go. Max and Vic lock eyes. "Leave her alone," Max says. He braces his foot and pulls harder. For someone Vic's size, he's surprisingly wimpy. Vic shifts his feet for better leverage. "She's not hurting anyone," Max says, and pries the game toward him. When Vic abruptly lets go, it nearly sends Max tumbling.

From the passenger side of the SUV slithers Hemera ↑. Krapht in the flesh, the CEO with an emoji[2] for a middle initial. Her usual habit, when asked what it stands for, is to simply point upward rather than dignify the question with a spoken response. People usually just pronounced it as "Up." And nobody was quite sure whether the controversial initial came about before or after she took the helm of LevelUP Corporation. It didn't help that in one day—a day that later came to be known simply as *Damage*—nearly every storage device in existence had been destroyed.

Hemera adjusts her sleeve, and Max catches the unnatural glow of a digital display embedded under her skin—a level of technological sophistication unheard of in the camps. Hypocrites like Hemera always deny how deeply technology has infected them.

"…utmost importance," Hemera is saying. Distracted, Max missed the first part. He can't pull attention away from the central question of the moment:

Why is her forehead blinking?

Max rubs his watery eyes, and there's still something there—a flashing pixel. But when he turns his head, the pixel holds position, as if it were floating in front of him. *How?*

Even when he clamps his eyes shut, it's still there—fully revealed as an exclamation point, not just a single pixel. Max opens his eyes, and the symbol drifts until it is centered on Hemera. *What the?*

Hemera raises an eyebrow at Vic. "Contraband," he says. "This guy,"—he aims an accusatory finger at Max—"is bringing in batteries."

Wait, what? Max points at himself and mouths, "me?" Vic is willing to bury him in trouble in the name of petty revenge. Never mind that he was actually correct—Max *had* traded for those batteries, not that Vic had any way of knowing.

Hemera looks Max up and down. "What's your name?"

"Max. Max Root."

"Well, Max, Max Root, you'd better watch yourself." Hemera gestures to the moonlit sea of canvas covering the hilltop. "Which tent is yours?"

The exclamation point blinks more urgently. Max swallows. "C'mon," he says.

Vic looks up from Lora's binder. "That one," he says, pointing.

"Go check it out," Hemera directs, and bodyguard number one obliges, the crowd scrambling out of his way.

"No!" Max stomps toward his tent, but the look in Hemera's eye stops him in his tracks. Without a word, she shows him exactly what the power dynamic is. She could disappear him without a second thought. Just like old Isidore.

Max clenches his fists as the brute shines his flashlight on the tent. As if it's too much trouble to figure out which side the entrance is on, he splits the canvas like paper. He paws through Max's bed, scattering IOU papers from under his pillow. He holds the flashlight with his mouth and hefts Max's footlocker—containing every thing of Max's that he hadn't put in his pockets this morning—on his shoulder before walking back to Hemera.

"Please, no!" Max shouts. He has things from before Damage. Things from his father. Consequences or not, he breaks from Hemera's crushing stare and beelines toward his tent.

All too quickly, Max why this was a bad idea. Before he's out of the floodlit circle, bodyguard number two casually extends an arm, clotheslining Max. In a moment of suffocating clarity, Max marvels that when your trachea is on fire, hitting your head on the ground doesn't even hurt. Well, not for the first second.

Still sprawled out, Max recovers just in time to see the bodyguard, now only steps away, hurl the footlocker to ground, splintering the timeworn plywood. All of Max's belongings tumble into the dust. All the inventory to keep his shop running. Personal effects. Everything that's ever mattered. A golden box from the deepest strata of Max's history lands in front of Hemera's glossy blue pumps. It was one of his earliest belongings, to the point where he can't remember exactly how he got it. Or what it's for.

Hemera picks up the box, turns it over in her hands, then hands it to Vic, who pockets it. "Get rid of this garbage," she says to the bodyguards.

Max scrambles for his belongings. "No! I need that stuff, it's all I have," he calls out, but bodyguard number two threatens to stomp him into the ground while his companion heaps Max's things into the back of the SUV.

With a satisfied look on her face, Hemera puffs on a mini-cig, good for only two or three puffs before it's done. Oddly, Max never noticed her produce a lighter at any point.

"What she says is law," Vic says. "Even stronger than law. Like, *hyperlaw*."

That's not even a word, moron, Max wants to say, but a hand gently reaches to steady him. It's Ice, kneeling alongside, comforting. "Let it go," she says. "Things can be replaced. You can't. We'll get through this." Vic's smirk somehow grows even more irritating. Ice helps Max to his feet.

Hemera turns to the crowd. "Enough of this. I want to speak with the camp administrator. Where is Isidore Morris?"

Silence. Max scans faces around him—full of similar confused looks.

Lora's standing right there. "What kind of sick game are you playing?" she sputters.

Hemera looks her up and down. "I'm sorry, I don't believe we've been formally introduced."

Surprise and indignation battle on Lora's face. Indignation wins. She stomps her foot on the ground, raising a thin cloud of dust that the wind curls across Hemera's elegant legs. Her voice contains a dangerous growl. "*I'm* the camp administrator. After you took Isidore, we had no leader, so I stepped up. I never asked for this this."

"I'm sorry," Hemera says stiffly, "I still didn't get your name."

"Seriously? I'm Lora Baines, Acting Administrator. I've been—"

"Ohhh, *you're* Lora Baines," Vic says. "That was the second thing on your agenda, boss. She hasn't completed a productivity shift in twenty-seven weeks."

"That's because I'm administering the entire camp!" Lora snaps. "You can't expect me…to…" Lora withers under Hemera's glare.

"I expect all such leadership changes to be duly authorized before they take effect," Hemera says. The temperature drops five degrees. "So, regarding Mister Isidore Morris. Surely at least one of you have seen him."

But if Isidore's not here, and LevelUP didn't authorize his exit, how would he get out of camp? The entire perimeter's monitored.

"Very well," Hemera says. "Search the tents. Turn everything upside down." The bodyguards break in opposite directions.

Flashlight beams work their way from one tent to another. The bodyguards manage to avoid destroying anyone else's shelter. The search, of course, doesn't turn up Isidore or any recent evidence of him.

The bodyguards huddle around Hemera, leaning into her ear to say something. Hemera's face colors as she marches back to the SUV. "Get back to work," she screams, even though their bonus work shift is over. She slams the heavy gullwing door behind her—no small feat. The tires spit gravel as the car whisks them out.

The boxes of Solylent bars sit unguarded. Lora rushes over to them. "Max," she calls, "come help with the distribution."

Max ignores her, and instead wanders back to the tattered canvas and bent poles of his tent. He gathers up as many of the IOUs as he can. The ones with boot prints should be fine. The ones that blew away on the breeze will be more difficult to redeem.

So: no livelihood and no shelter for the night, and his head still throbs. A long day indeed. He's going to have to find a new tent somewhere. Maybe Abhinav over in the Moffett camp still has one he'd trade for.

At least all the beeps and blinks are gone, ever since Max hit his head. He rubs the tender spot, where a goose egg rises up underneath his hair.

Max collapses onto his torn sleeping bag and stares up at the twilight sky. There's something hard underneath. After digging around for a minute Max finds it—a loose double-A battery.

He laughs. The bitter kind of laugh that's all the only thing standing between you and a sobbing breakdown. He's always kept a positive attitude through rough times—and there've been a lot of those. This time feels different. Everything's going to end up okay. Right? Even as he thinks it, it sounds stupid in his head.

Max rubs his eyes, suddenly tired as the weight of the day's events settle over him. Nightbirds squawk in the distance, and the rotting vegetation smells less like rotten eggs than it has in a long while. Then the *beep* returns, and with it, a blinking pixel dead center in his field of view.

---

1. ⌁
2. Technically not an emoji, just a boring character on a higher Unicode plane.

0-3 WALK THIS WAY_

MAX MASHES HIS EYES SHUT AND TRIES TO PINPOINT THE faint sounds coming from the Bay. His breathing smooths out until his heartbeat is the loudest thing he hears. It's got the be the stresses of the day wearing down his sanity. Like before, a pixel seems to hang in space in front of him. If anything, shut eyes only make more contrast. In the ruddy darkness behind his eyelids, it looks less like a single pixel, and more like…an icon? Pointy at one end. He can't just lay here and stew.

Max leaves the scraps of his tent and wanders to the edge of camp, overlooking the frontage road that winds its way up the hill. Getting caught outside without clearance is enough of a deterrent that Max has personally never even attempted going AWOL. He's always found it better to work within the system —without much to show for it, he's gotta admit. Now things are different.

Different…the pixel's different. Smaller. As Max turns to the side, the arrow-shape rotates back into view. It's pointing to the far side of camp. Toward the IT tent.

"Max!" Nolan says as Max enters. He doesn't look up from his screen. "Those LevelUP clowns must take classes in mismanagement, amirite? Ready for that new game? Maybe Colossal Cave this time?"

Colossal Cave, also known simply as "Adventure,"[1] is game even older than Zork. Runs great on text-only 8-bit displays. But Max isn't in the mood for games. Nolan looks up.

"Max—" Nolan says, brow crinkled with concern. "You all right? You look like you've seen a ghost."

"Did people used to see things?" Max asks. Nolan looks confused at the admittedly bizarre question. "That didn't come out right. I mean, did people ever put…pixels in their…" he waves his hands struggling for the right words, "field of view?"

Nolan thinks for about half a second before answering. "Sounds like a Heads-Up Display," Nolan says. "HUDs were all the rage by the end of the 2020s. But along with pretty much everything, they quit working thanks to Damage. It's a wonder society survived at all, after seeing how dependent people had become on things like those. You were lucky to be so young, what, around ten? You probably don't remember the worst of it."

Damage. The day had taken on mythical status. According to many, the single worst day in history. How else could you describe the moment in which nearly every computer bricked, worldwide? Nolan was right—Max didn't remember that day. He had memories of before and after, but it was as if his brain had stopped recording during the actual chaos.

Max opens his mouth to say something, then thinks better of it. The next thing he thinks to say also gets caught in a web of tangled questions. "So, these HUDs…were common?"

"Like you wouldn't believe," Nolan says.

"But they all stopped working," Max says.

"Correctamundo," Nolan says. "And all the semiconductor factories stopped working, as did all the computer systems that kept them running, and all the laptops of the folks who knew how to fix the factories, and all the compilers needed to rebuild *those* systems, and so on. The survivors had to start over. Society reboot, rising from the ashes of martial law."

Nolan switches off his CRT, something Max has only seen him do in rare moments when his full attention is required. He leans closer, focusing his watery eyes on Max. "What's bothering you, Max?"

"Just trying to figure out a few things." The pixel winks out, then on again. Great, now it's blinking.

Nolan watches Max for another second, then shrugs and flips his monitor back on with an electronic buzz that makes Max's hair stand on end. Eyes glued to the screen, he says, "Fair enough. Let me know if you need anything."

Max exits to the sound of Nolan's staccato typing, and plops down in the dust. Was he wrong to rebuff Nolan's offer for help? From the narrow terrace on which the IT tent sits, it's not that far down to the gravel access road. Totally jumpable.

Max startles when the pixel reignites in the space right in front of his eyes, bigger and brighter. In fact, it's not even correct to call it a pixel—it's a complete icon in the shape of a pointing finger. And it points to outside the camp. Max creeps as close the the edge as he can manage.

The IT tent sits on a roughly hewn ledge, and underneath there's a video camera is mounted on a steel spike driven into the earth. This is part of the system keeping everyone penned in. But the metal support of this particular security point is corroded and bowed. The camera doesn't get a view of anything more than the dirt two inches in front of the lens. A chink in the armor. The arrow blinks faster. Max jumps across the threshold.

As soon as his feet hit the gravel below, the HUD arrow flips direction, leading him into the set of dirt trails laced across the salt marshes of the bay.

Movement catches his eye: someone else is out here and heading his way. The trails have long sightlines—not much of a place to hide, even at night. Max crouches as unobtrusively as possible and... "Molly!"

She at first seems not to notice, but then, avoiding eye contact, walks up to him.

"What are you doing outside of camp?"

"Walking," Molly says.

"No, I didn't mean literally—never mind..."

"Why are *you* out here?" Molly asks.

"I..." He doesn't know where to start. "It's a long story. There's something going on. Outside of camp, I mean." Max says.

A tiny, lopsided smile appears. "Then I'm coming with you."

The arrow prods him on. The trail loops around an endless expanse of water and emerges onto cracked city streets. Before Damage, these streets were filled with cars scanning the roads with millimeter radar and adjusting their suspension in real-time. Even at his tender age, Max still remembers the silky-smooth feeling of riding in a car. Soothing. Now travel had become more of a roughshod business.

They come to a former industrial park of the Silicon Valley sort, quiet side streets lined with every imaginable tech company. At least now the quiet part is still true.

It's hot, even at night. Despite twelve years of dramatically reduced industrial emissions, the weather seems to keep getting hotter year by year. There's a landfill nearby, and the heat has matured it well beyond ripe. Max's eyes water, though Molly doesn't seem affected.

They pass several abandoned buildings and come to a crumbling overpass. They cross over to what once passed as a residential neighborhood full of dilapidated apartment buildings.

"Is this where are we going?" Molly asks.

"I don't know," Max says. "Ask me again when we get there."

Molly looks around. "Bad neighborhood," she notes. "But it has a secret."

"And you know this how?" Max asks, but as soon as he says it, he knows the answer. "Does Ice know you sneak out of the camp?" Molly ignores the question.

At an abandoned building, the arrow changes into a hand making an OK symbol, then points them toward an entrance. "Looks like this is the place," Max says. "Have you been here before?"

"There's something inside," she says…

---

1. Technically, "Colossal Cave Adventure."

0-4 TROPHY CASE_

THE BUILDING HAD SHOPS ON THE GROUND FLOOR, LOOTED bare, and expensive apartments on the higher floors. The way in leads through a parking garage nestled behind the storefronts. There's no power in this part of town; no streetlights. A metal grate that closes off the garage has been peeled back, leaving a hole large enough for someone much bulkier than Max to fit through.

Just outside the rift, Max notices a curled sign duct taped to the wall. It reads "Entry Forbidden. Consequences for Trespassers." He smooths it out to reveal the symbol of a scarab beetle. "Humans First," Max says. It's a loosely knit group of people who think Damage was a good thing for humanity, and they fight back using whatever means necessary against efforts to reestablish tech. They're obsessive about defending their territory, including this building.

Max peers into the dark. The kind of place where getting mugged would feel like getting off easy. "I don't know about this. Molly, do you hear anything?"

"Yes," Molly says.

"What?!"

"Crickets." Molly cocks her head. "And an internal combustion vehicle on the 237."

Max breathes again. "I mean, not counting the freeway over there, do you hear any people nearby?"

Molly is quiet for a second. "No."

Max takes a step inside, and Molly follows. It's not as dark as Max thought. In fact, the wall nearby glows with an eerie light. Max looks back, and it's coming from Molly's purple braids. "I had no idea glow-in-the-dark hair was a thing," Max says. "Who does that for you?"

"There," Molly says, pointing. Max can't see a thing, but after several steps in that direction, a door comes into view. The handle won't turn.

Max jumps when a gust of cool air washes across his face. But how could there be wind in an enclosed garage? "Did you feel that?" he asks.

Molly shakes her head 'no' but doesn't make eye contact. She does something to the door handle and it springs open.

They're in a stairway (and, judging by the smell, longstanding latrine) littered with the husks of electronic equipment salvaged from the apartments above. Vintage processors sell for a fortune on the open market. Max steps over a Smart Toilet that someone went to the trouble of dragging onto the stairs. It was perched precariously, and a slight nudge topples it, sending it bouncing off every step the rest of the way down, building up to an avalanche of shattered porcelain and printed circuit boards.

Molly covers her ears, even after the sound stops. "It's okay,"

Max says. "It's just a bunch of junk. There's another door at the top, leading to a corridor. The HUD arrow blinks once more. "This way."

The floor creaks as they walk, splintered doors scattered on both sides. They stop at one of the doorways. Inside is dusty, long ago looted and abandoned. These were nice places once upon a time. People used to live a good life, instead of scraping by in tents on top of a toxic waste dump. But now, every single apartment they pass is utterly ransacked.

Until they reach the corridor's end. This apartment has a metal door. Solid and riddled with dents and scratches, evidence of failed attempts to get inside. Alongside the door, some frustrated would-be looter attacked the drywall, attempting to bypass the door completely. The ragged open gash reveals thick steel plating. Somebody built this place like a vault.

Molly runs her finger along a keypad made from some indestructible plastic and it lights up. The sickly green light shines out like a spotlight compared to the purple darkness Max's eyes have adjusted to.

"How can—? There's no power in this building," Max says. His HUD flashes an OK hand sign.

"I know how to get inside," Molly says.

"Really? How?"

"By guessing the code," Molly says.

Max sighs. She's right of course. Zero through nine. How many digits in the code? Maybe six? Eight? That's a hundred million possible combinations. If he had weeks, maybe. "I don't think we can stick around long enough to crack the code," Max says. "We need to find some other way."

Max leans in close to see the key markings better. He runs his finger along the plastic.

KER-THUNK. The lock opens. *What the?*

"Well done," Molly says.

"I didn't do anything!" Max says. "I just touched it and it opened."

"Shhh!"

"What?"

"Voices," Molly says. "People outside."

Right outside? An agonizing moment passes. Max strains to hear. He thinks he hears something far away, on the sidewalk below. "It's okay. They're moving away now."

On second thought, it might be better to lay low here for a little while. Max ducks inside, Molly following and banging the door shut behind herself.

Max cringes. "Shhh. Let's keep it on the downlow here." In the faint glow from Molly's locks, he looks around the space they've entered: an apartment in the prevailing style of the late 2020s. Pre-Damage. Untouched for more than a decade.

The entryway leads to a kitchen on the left, and a living room straight ahead. Spartan but not looted.

"I'm nervous," Molly says.

"*Now* you're nervous?" Max says. "Come with me. Let's look around."

Max reaches for Molly's hand, but he's surprised to grab a handful of bent coat hanger wire. He'd totally forgotten about her prosthetic arm. She must have been only five or six when

Damage happened. Even with the latest artificial arm available at the time, she'd have quickly outgrown it and had to make do with whatever was available. He wraps his hand around the wire and gives it a gentle tug to make sure she knows he's got her.

They take another step deeper inside. A thick layer of dust carpets the floor, and absorbs sound, giving the place a suffocating feeling. They leave footsteps as they go, soft plumes of dust mushrooming up around their feet with each step. Max feels a sneeze building.

First stop, kitchen. Carpet gives way to linoleum, slippery under the dust. The stove has a digital clock, dead as this entire neighborhood. Other than the lock on the outside door, there's not a trace of electricity.

The cupboards are bare of food, and not in the messy already-been-looted way. Max holds his nose and risks a peek in the fridge, but it's empty and musty; no mummified cold cuts or furry stuff. This place was never lived in.

A small dining table and four chars adorn the next open room. Outside windows facing the street and spiderwebbed with cracks. Keeping with the construction theme of this apartment, it must be reinforced glass.

Max gently guides Molly back behind the central wall. He points. "Windows," he says. "In a dark building, you look like a neon sign. We don't want to call attention to us. Can you hold tight here? I'll look around."

Molly nods. When Max looks again, a trick of the light makes her braids seem less luminous. Is he making a big deal out of nothing?

Next to the table is a tiny computer desk with a flatscreen monitor perched atop. Max rubs the dust off the case. "Dell."

Molly leans forward. The brightness increases just a bit more than Max expects. "What year?" she asks.

"Not sure, but it's no use to us. It definitely post-1989." Only computers designed before 1989 remained operable after Damage.

Max can't hold in the sneeze any longer, and the resulting blast knocks a layer of dust off the wall, spreading even more dust into the air. Max jams a knuckle against the bottom of his nose.

"Yeesh, all this dust," Max says. He makes his way to the undisturbed end of the apartment. Molly trails behind, stopping next to the door where they first came in.

Just enough light radiates from Molly's braids to let Max find his way to a single bedroom with its own bathroom, both completely barren. No furniture. Not even a mattress or a shower curtain. Definitely not lived in. No clues.

Max returns to the entrance, where Molly kneels, back to the door, head bent in concentration. "Got it," she says as something tiny plops into the dust. She pockets a tiny screwdriver.

"Uh, Molly, what'cha doing?" Max asks.

She opens the door a crack, reaches to the control pad on the outside, and brings the entire panel inside, still live and glowing. She sets the chain on the door. The skinny, feeble chain, no different from every other one that failed to protect all the other apartments in the complex.

"I really don't think that's a good idea," Max says.

"Hemera said I can't have double-A's." Molly hefts the device in her hand. "This makes electricity, so I won't ever need batteries again."

Hard to argue with that logic. "But looters can walk right in here now," Max says.

"We won't be back, so what does it matter?" Molly says.

"Sure, but I was thinking about a more immediate timeline. What if we get a visitor? Let's get out of here," Max says. He opens the door a crack and listens. It's quiet.

Molly closes the door. "There's still one more room. I want to see it."

The living room. Like the other rooms, it's lacking in furniture, except for the far wall, underneath the windows, where broad trophy case resides. A filthy piece of glass seals off each compartment. It looks like what Max imagined a trophy case would look like; every time he retrieved a treasure in one of Nolan's narrated Zork games, he'd put it in the display.

"That's not a good idea," Max says. "We need to keep low and out of sight, then bug out of here."

"I see something," Molly says.

That dismantled lock leaves Max feeling exposed. The sooner they get out of here, the better. And not arguing will be faster. "Fine."

The carpet is plush enough to be felt under the thick dust. The trophy case is three compartments high and eight across. Max starts at the top row. Pushing on the glass releases a magnetic latch, and the door springs open. Inside is completely bare and dust-free.

"Empty," Max says. Molly doesn't seem to be paying attention, so he works his way across the top row. All empty. *Are we supposed to find treasures and bring them back here on display? That doesn't make sense. We're not in a video game.*

Max works his way through the middle layer, with similar results.

But Molly's attention is focused on the lower shelf. She opens the door revealing a gray box, darker on the lower half, with a black stripe on the right. Max finishes checking the rest of the compartments, finding nothing, and has a closer look. He wipes the dust away before realizing what it is. A piece of 8-bit hardware—worth a fortune. He pulls his hand back from it like from a burning flame.

"Nintendo of America?" Molly gasps. "A game console? I didn't know they made them so big."

"Or that any are left that haven't been scavenged for parts," Max says.

"An actual NES!" Molly shakes her good hand the way someone would after washing. "I've heard of these. I can't believe I'm seeing this!"

"What year?" Max asks.

"Designed in 1983, but didn't reach the US until 1985," Molly says.

"Whoa." Max raises an eyebrow. A complete 8-bit computer. This could be the shot of liquid capital that lets Max rebuild his mercantile—for that matter the whole camp—and keep it running for another year. If it works, that is.

Where did Molly pick up so much history? It seemed like everyone in camp thought of her as a game-playing robot, a fixture lurking around the tents, consuming resources. Knowing trivia about an ancient artifact was a tiny thing, but it hinted at the existence of a wider world. If she knew about this, something that Max himself didn't know after years of experience buying and selling in the camps, what other surprises might lurk behind her smile?

Silence and dust settle between them. Before he can figure out what that means, he feels another sneeze building up explosive energy. "We can't leave this for the looters."

Molly doesn't move.

"What is it?" Max asks.

"They're here."

Adrenaline surges through Max at the words, his heart thumping in his chest. "Who? Right outside? Right now?"

"No, not yet." She turns her back to Max, which momentarily confuses him until he realizes this is her way of indicating to put the goods into her backpack, slung low over her shoulders. He reaches for the deck, and for a moment, he could swear it's powered on. A faint vibration seems to thrum inside the plastic as if there's a spinning fan inside. He listens. Nothing.

He crams the NES into Molly's backpack, including all the wires and controllers.

"Okay, now they're right outside," Molly says. "Four guys. One with steel-toed boots."

"What!? Just fifteen seconds ago you said they weren't here," Max whispers.

"Fifteen seconds ago, they weren't," Molly says.

The doorknob rattles and turns. The door opens an inch until the chain catches. Outside, a voice says, "Hey, check this out."

0-5 RADIOACTIVE_

The door bangs shut. A muffled voice says, "It's chained. From the inside."

"Humans First," Molly whispers, her eyes wide.

"What?"

"*Humans First.*"

There was a time the early days of Damage when the Human First movement had been widely blamed for the chaos. Somehow, the story went, they were responsible for bringing everything down. Of course, that theory didn't explain why older, 8-bit technology continued to work, but angry people looking for someone to blame have never been known for their flawless logic.

"Yeah, I gathered that," Max says. "The sign we saw earlier kind of gave it away."

What Humans First lacks in technology, they more than make up for in seething anger. Threatened by forces they don't understand, which covers a lot of ground.

Molly looks frustrated. "*Humans First,*" she insists.

She's trying to say something beyond the obvious. But what? She sees something. A way out of this? Four angry men just outside the door, driven by overflowing testosterone and testosterone. How will they get out of this one?

Molly changes tactics, and whispers, "Power source." Max shrugs. "Power source, power source, pow-wer soar-sss." Not one to cope effectively with stress.

"There's someone in there," a gruff voice snarls. Sounds like the speaker would outweigh Max and Molly put together.

"Well, kick it in, moron," says another voice.

Max grabs Molly and pulls a few inches clear just as a heavy kick crashes against the door. The chain holds. Outside, a howl of pain.

"Stay here," calls the voice. "I'ma get my crowbar."

"Slow down and explain," Max pleads. "What about the power source?" If she'd have just left the lock in place, they'd be safe now, but Max doesn't see any use in pointing this out.

Quiet settles just long enough for Max to calm down a little, then the door smashes against the creaking chain. A crowbar swipes through the open space and works its way upward until it snags the chain.

Adrenaline fire surges through Max's veins. The world creeps in stuttery slow motion in between each strobe of his heart, every nerve cell in his body on highest alert. He seems to float above the apartment, every room visible at once.

In the space of a single heartbeat, Max considers several plans. He could make a last stand holding the door shut with all his strength until overpowered. He could go out in a blaze of glory, taking the intruders one-at-a-time, using the closest, heaviest object—maybe that beautiful flat screen monitor. But it's awkwardly big to use as a weapon. And that would only be a surprise to the first one to enter. Or he could make for the windows, but they're high above the ground, and had survived a decade of thrown rocks, bricks, and who knows what else. Those were not meant to be opened.

So, no good options.

The crowbar finds purchase. The thick bolt securing the chain gives way with a metallic shriek. Max and Molly stumble backward as the door bangs open and four men stomp through the entrance. One of them has a flashlight, shining through fresh plumes of dust and blazing splotches on their dark-adjusted eyes.

"Scrawny little things," the lead bully says. He grabs Max's collar and lifts him into the air. "Let's toss 'em off the roof."

Max's pulse throbs in his temples. He's ready to explode. His throat is still bruised from the earlier encounter, but that seems like a distant memory. The best he can hope for is to protect Molly.

Too late. The lead bully looks Molly up and down. "What's in the backpack?"

The rectangular bulge of the NES stands out. Max tries to unscramble memory of the earlier moment where he stood up against Hemera's muscle men, even though that was barely an hour ago. He did it before—he can do it again. Right?

It's difficult to get words out. "You wouldn't like it," Max croaks. "It's a portable handi-vac. Take you a week to get through all the dust in here. Pretty sure it's not even HEPA filtered."

Pressure on Max's collar eases. His feet touch the floor again.

The lead bully looks uncertain. "Comedian, huh?" he says. "So was that scientist who wouldn't stop working on his brain-in-a-box. Didn't work out so well for him." He bats Max aside, sending him sprawling into the dust.

Whoa. Brain emulation? That's not what you'd expect to hear from the mouth of an ordinary street tough.

Then Max finally realizes what Molly was saying all along. These are *Humans First* bullies. They have a baseline distrust of anything they don't understand. An active superstition against technology. Like, for instance, that power source that Molly scavenged. *Pow-wer soar-sss.*

Max scrambles back to his feet, putting himself between Molly and the leader. The effort combined with the dust makes him sneeze again. "Curious about that backpack?" Max says, waving away plumes of dust. "It's no vacuum cleaner. That would be kind of silly, here in a place with no power, right?"

The leader looks confused, quickly yielding to anger.

"No," Max continues. "This is something much more special. Let me show you." He slowly reaches for the backpack, keeping his hands in view while he slides it off Molly's shoulders and onto the floor. "I don't know how often you gentlemen get a chance to wander through these parts, but you probably noticed that this particular residence was set up with some extra... what's the word? My pre-Damage vocabulary isn't so great. Ahh, right. Nuclear Radiation Shielding."

He pronounces nuclear carefully; all three syllables of it. The

Humans First leader flinches at the words and subtly shifts weight back onto his heels.

"Here, let me show you," Max says, as cheerfully as he can muster. He opens the zipper and smoothly works his hand to the bottom, finding the electronic keypad.

"Ever seen a nuclear reactor up close?" He suddenly pulls the device free, letting the sickly green light illuminate his face from below. He sticks it in the leader's face. "Here, look."

The leader takes a stumbling step back.

"Eeeew, hold on, it's leaking something sticky. Yikes! This stuff kind of tingles when it gets on your fingers." Max takes a forceful step toward them. "Here."

The leader matches his retreat, bumping against his companions huddled behind him.

"What's wrong?" Max says. "This is the future. Pretty soon everyone's going to have one." And that's all the Human First crew can take. They turn and struggle to be the first out the door. Heavy steps clomp down the stairway, outer door slams hard enough for Max to feel it all the way upstairs.

"Huh," Max says. "Your loss." Then he sinks to the floor, drained. It feels good to just breathe, even if the air is clouded with dust. Instantly, another sneeze starts to build. "That was close. And by the way, thanks for the hint."

"Atari," Molly says.

"Slow down, you lost me again," Max says. "You're not talking about your Atari Lynx again, are you?"

"This room was built here for a reason. There used to be an Atari building on this spot[1]. It was demolished in the year 2000."

"So what? A different building was on this spot forty-one years ago."

"That's why. For us to find," Molly says.

"You're not making any sense. Look, let's get out of here and figure out the details later."

---

1. http://www.atari.io/atari-world-headquarters/

0-6 EQUINE AMITY_

SAFELY OUTSIDE HUMANS FIRST TURF, MAX HAS A NEW problem: he has nowhere to go. Technically he's still a camp resident, but there's nothing for him there. The longer he's away, the more the thought of going back feels like returning to a past life. Molly, at least, still has a place to call home.

His second-most-immediate problem is finding somewhere to keep something as valuable as a vintage piece of 8-bit hardware. Maybe at sunrise he can trek over and unload the merchandise on Abhinav …

Molly remains silent until they approach Lockheed. "Nice move back there. I thought you hate tech."

After getting used to Molly's context-free pattern of speech, full sentences feel extravagant. He only said the glowing panel made his fingers tingle because that's what would maximally freak out the Humans First goons. But it wasn't only words. His fingers really were tingling, just from being that close to modern tech. There was more in common between Max and Humans First than he'd like to admit.

"I don't hate tech. I think of it like…cancer," Max says. "Okay, that didn't sound very favorable. It's not good or bad—it just is. I'm totally fine with trading artifacts. But there's something about tech, especially modern tech, that corrupts people. I just can't bring myself to trust anyone in control of so much of everyone's lives."

"So that's it?" Molly asks. "Trade away the NES. Then back to your usual stupendous life?"

Ouch. "I don't even know what 'usual' would mean at this point."

"Hmm." Molly's silent for another block, but Max can see in her eyes that she's thinking. "There's more to it than that. You were *sent* for the NES. Someone preserved it."

"And that makes me, what, The Chosen One?" Max says. "Not me. I'm just…me." He shrugs. They've arrived back at side of the camp where they originally snuck out. "Wait, how are you going to get back in?"

"Watch," Molly says. She bounds onto the ledge, and just like that, is back inside the camp. By official reckoning, never even left.

She's a pro at this.

"Did you think I can't climb with one arm?"

How often has she been outside the camp? Max wonders. *She could spend all day wondering around while we're working…*

Max makes a placating gesture. "No comment." He scrambles up but loses his footing and needs both hands to keep from tumbling down.

"Huh," Molly says and works her way around the ledge to the

IT tent entrance. A motion sensor light flips on. Max stumbles in behind her. Nolan's not there.

Molly wordlessly turns her back to Max again, and he obliges by removing the NES deck. As if she knows what he's thinking, she asks, "What are you going to do with it?"

"You're going to have to hang on to it until I make arrangements. But be careful. Don't even mention it to anyone." Max sticks his head out of the tent to see if anyone's within eavesdropping distance. Then he rolls down the tent flap.

"What about the lock?" Molly asks.

"Assuming I ever have a tent over my head again," Max says, "I'll need to figure out how to keep my things safe. Er, safer."

"No, I mean *the lock*."

Right. The other piece of tech. Molly spins again, and Max pulls the lock mechanism out of the backpack. He touches the device and it springs to life. Max's fingers tingle again. It feels a little like the creepy sensation he gets when seeing a spider. He sets it down on the desk and shakes his hands. "What *is* that thing? I've been trading for a decade and I've never seen anything like it."

Molly rummages through Nolan's toolbox and produces a voltmeter. She flips the lock onto its face and pokes at it with the leads.

"You claimed it fair and square," Max says. "So, you keep it. See if you can get it to power your Game Boy—I mean, Atari Lynx."

Molly flashes a quick smile at Max's correction.

Max takes a closer look at the NES. His fingernail catches

against a seam in the otherwise smooth plastic. "Wait, what's this?"

"What?" Molly asks, suddenly interested.

The plastic has a nearly-invisible seam along the edge near the side connectors. "I need a little more light. Does Nolan have a flashlight?" Molly hands one over, and Max inspects. "Right. This case has been cut and re-glued on the edge here. See? Fine scratches along the edge. I don't think this is factory standard. This unit has been modified."

"Meaning?" Molly asks.

Max sighs. More bad news. "Probably that the resale value just dropped. Depends on what's been done to the hardware."

Molly frowns. "Are you leaving again?"

Good question. Max himself doesn't know what he's going to do. A fresh wave of fatigue washes over him. If it weren't for that rash spreading across Nolan's face, he might just curl up and sleep here in the IT tent. But he doesn't want to spend a minute more than necessary here.

"There is someone who could tell you everything you want to know about that console," Molly offers. "He's seen it all."

Max's tiredness ebbs a little.

"It's the middle of the night," Max says.

"He'll be up."

"Why would this person help us?"

"I trust him."

Molly turns her backpack to Max, and he carefully packs the console inside. "Follow me."

She leads Max along the southern edge of the camp, behind a long row of residential tents, harshly lit by the ring of floodlights just outside the perimeter. By the time the smell of hay and manure reaches Max's nose, he realizes where Molly's leading them: the stables.

To be honest, calling a frayed bit of canvas stretched out over aluminum poles a "stable" reflects an optimistic worldview. The camp's two horses swivel their ears when they hear Molly approach.

Chen, the stablekeep, appears from a pile of hay, rubbing her eyes, her gray hair pinned into a messy bun. "Molly! What are you doing up at this hour?"

"You two know each other?" Max asks.

"Oh yeah, we go way back," Chen says. Max can't tell how serious she is.

"What brings you here at this hour—ohhh... I get it. Molly, you never told me you had a *special* friend!"

Molly's face flushes to a shade Max had not realized was physiologically possible.

"Oh, my dear, I didn't mean to embarrass you," Chen says. "There are no appointments until morning, but these guys need rest. You're not going far, are you?"

"Library," Molly says.

The library? Why would they go to a library? Chen has a similar thought, judging by the look on her face.

"Max, you know how off-the-books expeditions work, right?"

"Of course," Max says, even though he's always done things by-the-book.

"Okay, then. You get caught, I disavow having even seen you this evening, and all kinds of trouble coming down on your head. But you already knew that," Chen says. Max already has more trouble than he knows what to do with. It's hard to imagine even more.

Molly responds with a gesture that looks a bit like a military salute. Chen saddles up the horses and leads them through the camp. Twenty paces from the path leading to the stables is another path winding its way down the hill without getting too steep.

The horses confidently pick their way down the hill. The path looks like it could pass for a water runoff channel. Just how many secret exits does this camp have?

"What actually happens if we get caught?" Max asks.

"Not much," Molly says. "Besides getting exiled from camp and probably starving on the street."

"Oh good," Max says. "I was worried it might be something serious."

They ride into the dark.

```
0-7 PUBLIC LIBRARY: : LEVELUP
CORPORATE MEDIA CENTER (OPEN TO
ALL REGISTERED CITIZENS AND H6-B
REFUGEES IN GOOD STANDING)_
```

The library building is dark but for a single lit window, and the dimly lit sign out front, which carefully and specifically delineates all who are allowed to enter.

Max dismounts, ties his horse to the bike rack turned hitching post, and rubs his aching backside. For something that's been part of his life so long, horse riding is still pretty awful.

The door's locked, of course, so Max pounds on the window with his fists, yielding no results beyond bruised knuckles.

"You have to get his attention," Molly says. She picks up a stone from the courtyard and bangs it against the window, making a sharp crack that echoes off the brick walls on either side of them. Max is surprised that the window remains unmarked.

A man, perhaps in his eighties, comes rushing from within, hands clapped against his head. "I say for the last time, come back when we're open!" he calls out. He hesitates and peers more closely through the glass. Then he produces a key and unlocks the door.

"Miyamoto," Molly says, and he smiles and waves them in.

"Welcome…Molly Matheson." A pleasant chime. "Welcome…Max Root." Another pleasant chime. They've been made by the standard-issue LevelUP scanner. At least the lack of buzzing alarm noises indicates that they're still in "good standing" with the Visa administration, a government initiative in which LevelUP has their hooks firmly embedded. Once someone reviews the early morning logs from this scanner, that's sure to change.

"Don't worry about that," Miyamoto says, as if reading Max's mind. "I have a bit of a special arrangement regarding the data feed back to the corporate overlords." He turns to Molly. "Molly Matheson, what brings you to these parts, and at this auspicious hour?" He ushers them in.

Just inside the entrance sits a row of crumbling chipboard cabinets—antique mass-merchandise furniture dating to the early 80s—lined with row after row of index-card-sized drawers. The smell of old paper fills Max's nostrils, and with it, the memory of old things. Though this is a library, Max can't see a single computer in the whole place—except, of course, for the LevelUP scanner near the entrance. The librarians' desk is lined with nothing more than neatly-ordered stacks of paper.

"Something to show you, of the hardware persuasion," Molly says.

Miyamoto smiles. "This way." He leads them into his private office, the one they saw lit from outside.

Molly turns the backpack to Max, and he removes the NES. Miyamoto whistles. "My kids once had one of those. So long ago…" He examines the connectors on the back. "Does it work?"

Max shrugs. "We need to find out."

"You'll need a television from that era. Which fortunately we have. Please wait."

He leaves and returns minutes later struggling to push a rattling cart, upon which an analog television set is securely bungeed. The thing is huge, even bigger than Nolan's monitor, and it extends as far backward as it is wide.

Moving to a desk drawer, Miyamoto digs through piles of tangled junk until he locates a colorful cable with the right connectors. He tosses it and Molly catches it mid-air. Her one hand has more dexterity than both of Max's put together.

Molly plugs in the final connector and reaches for the power button.

"Wait!" Molly says. "You forgot something." From her backpack she pulls a controller, with its non-symmetrical connector and plugs it in. "Now, you can turn it on."

"I wonder what games it comes loaded with," Max says. He hits the power button.

The whole room seems to flicker. Max rubs his eyes. He must have gotten dust in them or something. The curved glass screen slowly alternates between solid black and solid white.

At the lower right of Max's field of view there's a horizontal white line. It seems to hover in space, even when he moves his head. It's just there, slowly blinking. Like the cursor on Nolan's DOS prompt.

Max blinks furiously but the artifact doesn't diminish. Max startles as the cursor leaps into motion, as if controlled by someone typing. It leaves blocky pixelated words in its wake:

INSERT CARTRIDGE TO CONTINUE

"Cartridge?" Max asks.

"Ah, yes, these systems don't come with software pre-loaded. You need to provide it separately."

Molly looks up from her game, quickly tucking it away.

Miyamoto demonstrates that the NES has a little door that swings up. There's a space inside for the cartridge. A space the exact size and shape as…

The memory strikes hard and without warning.

RANDOM ACCESS MEMORY: 2029_

A FLASHLIGHT KNIFES THROUGH THE DARKNESS, WIELDED BY A fireman with a helmet and everything. The world feels different—bigger. Purer. Max looks at his hands. Clean, smooth, and tiny. He realizes this is him at the tender age of six. He's reliving the final moments before Damage changed everything.

He could never remember what happened. There had been only a blank stretch of memory. Where did this come from? Concerns about cause-and-effect crumble under the simple immediacy of the moment. He's in the middle of a tour of the fire station and their shiny red trucks. Just him and dad and the firemen.

This was it. This was the day Max's father, Hadley Root, vanished from his life.

"It's all right kids," the fireman says. "Nobody panic. We've had the power go out before. I'm sure at this very minute there are some good folks at the electric company checking their computers to see what happened. They'll send somebody right out to fix it, then the power will come back."

"If the power is out," Max squeaks—his voice is soft and high-pitched—"how can the electric company people use their computers?"

A comforting voice: "That's my boy." Dad! Even though it's dark, dad's hand finds its way to Max's head to ruffle his hair. But joke's on him—Max's hair was already messy to begin with.

"I'm sure this is just a local outage," the fireman says. "And even if not, they've planned for that. They have backup systems for everything. They could run for days without power if they needed to."

Days. The thought of going without electricity for days hadn't occurred to young Max before.

There's a noise outside, maybe an airplane. It gets louder, then louder, then louder still, until it hurts Max's ears. He clamps tiny hands over his ears. If it's this loud inside, he can't imagine what it must sound like outside. The noise draws back a little, then louder again as the building shakes. Metal things fall off shelves in the kitchen and clang around on the floor. The quiet that follows seems startling, cut only by the heavy metal frame of the fire engine creaking as it settles.

"It's okay," dad says. "Just the shock absorbers doing their job." But things sure don't sound okay, especially outside.

Flickery orange light angles into the room as someone opens the door. There's a bad smell, like chemicals and burning.

"This is the chief," a new voice says. This voice is deeper and more commanding. He's the one hurting Max's eyes with the flashlight. "I need all hands on deck. We've got multiple developing situations. And get that kid out of here."

Dad takes Max's hand and ushers him out of the way. Along the edge of the big room, there's a bench. Even there, Max can still hear everything.

"But chief," another voice says, "the computer's down. We've got no dispatch."

Max wonders why the fire station doesn't have the backup for things the fireman was just talking about.

"What do you mean 'the computer's down'?" the chief says. "We just paid a fortune to have redundant everything. What did that guy call them? UPS."

A UPS must be the backup thing, Max decides.

"You don't get it, chief, it's not the power. It's the computers. They're deader 'n a doorknob."

"Well that's just great," the chief says. *While he speaks, another loud explosion shakes the walls and hurts Max's ears. More light comes in as somebody rolls up the big doors.*

"We've got aircraft falling out of the sky," the chief says. "What about cellphones?" *Nobody answers right away.* "Well?"

"Everything's bricked, sir."

The chief lets out a mighty puff of air. "Then I'm your central dispatch now," *he says in a louder voice.* "Red crew, head to points north. Use your judgment and do what you can. Green crew, points south. Yellow crew, points east. White crew, points west—starting with across-the-street. Move!"

More incredible noise as four fire trucks roar to life and speed away, sirens blaring. When they're gone, it's only Max and dad.

"Should we look outside?" *Max asks.*

Dad gently unwraps his arms from around Max and goes to peek. "No, I think we should just stay here for a little bit."

If dad thinks so, it's probably a good idea.

But then from outside, somebody starts screaming. A woman but not mom. A horrible sound. It hurts Max's ears, but in a different way than the explosion. The sound makes him more scared than ever. He can't hold back tears any longer. "Does that lady need your help, dad?" Max asks.

Dad wraps his arms around Max even tighter than before.

Then something strange happens—a beeping sound, coming from dad's pocket. Even though the fireman said everything was bricked, there was something still working. Dad gets that far-away look, the one that means he's looking at something inside his head. Even in this light, Max sees dad's eyes go wide. Then he looks confused. The far-away look is gone.

"Listen, Max, I'm going to go outside for just a little bit. You stay here and be safe. I'll be right back. Don't move."

"Are you going to help that woman?" Max asks.

"No, I need to…yes, Max. I need to go see if I can help her. You stay right here. I'll be just a minute. Stay put." Max's sight gets so blurry with tears that dad seems to melt away.

But he isn't gone yet. "Max, this isn't how I planned it, but I need to give you something important. Take good care of this. When the time comes, you'll know what to do with it." He hands Max a flattish box. It feels like plastic, and in the little bits of light, it shines like fake gold.

"What's this for?" Max asks.

But it's too late to ask. The room seems to get even quieter. Dad was always playing jokes. One time he laughed and laughed after telling Max that his new sneakers had voice-controlled auto-laces and Max talked himself hoarse trying to get them to work. But this time doesn't seem very funny.

In the dark, time passes differently. Max had a wristwatch once, with a digital display and a little light that came on when you pressed a button. But he lost it. Now he wishes he had that wristwatch. Eventually, Max gets lonely and starts to cry. At first it's quiet hot tears, but it gradually *builds up into loud sobs that echo off the bays where the trucks used to park. Dad said he'd be right back. Why was he taking so long?*

It's hard to tell how much time slips past, but it seems like he waits forever, even after the sun comes up again. Max cries out in alarm when another explosion shakes the building around him. More things fell off of shelves and crash noisily on the ground.

When he can't stand another minute alone, Max creeps to the door and opens it. There's nobody around. Everything's wrecked, and a few fires still burn in the distance. There's a stink in the air, like a campfire smell but worse. He's hungry.

But he's so lonely. By the time he runs out of tears, one thing remains with crystalline certainty:

Max will never see his father again.

0-8 RETRO_

SOMETIMES THE PAST STAYS BURIED FOR A REASON. THE crushing sense of loss surges over Max before receding enough for a shuddering breath to escape. He wipes his cheek.

Molly wordlessly asks if he's okay.

She towers above him — he's on the floor. "I…" Max's voice breaks, and it takes several more breaths to compose himself. The smell of musty carpet and old paper fills his nostrils. A fresh torrent of memories threatens to drown Max afresh. He used to come to places like this. With dad. Before Damage.

"I just remembered," Max whispers.

Molly leans down to hear what comes next.

"We need the cartridge." He gestures toward the NES. "It has specific programming. You were right, Molly. There are two separate pieces to be put together." He looks at Molly, who nods solemnly.

"Hemera has it…" Max's thoughts trail into a dead end.

At this, Miyamoto leans in closer. His eyebrows arch in an expression that pleads for the rest of the explanation. Max isn't used to having anyone hang so closely on his words.

"My dad gave it to me, but I never knew what it was for. I'd never even seen a NES before today. The cartridge, it, it was buried at the bottom of my locker." Max sighs. "*Was* being the operative word." He turned to Miyamoto. "Hemera took it. She took everything."

"Now what?" Molly asks.

The look on Miyamoto's face doesn't align with any single emotion Max can recognize. A hint of a smile, perhaps, with an edge of wistfulness set against a dusting of wry twinkle. "Tell me, young man, what would it mean to you if you did have it?"

Bitter anger flares in Max's gut. "What's the use of asking?" he asks. Maybe he's out of sorts from the ripped-off-scab of his dad leaving him, again. He pauses to collect himself, to prevent the spark from exploding into a raging fire. "We don't have the stupid cartridge, so what's the use of talking about what it would mean?"

"Max!" Molly says.

Miyamoto makes a placating gesture, as if to say, *let him go on*. He walks a brisk lap around the room, hands folded behind his back, leaving Max and Molly in relative isolation to talk.

"Did I ever meet him?" Molly asks.

"My dad? Let me think. Yeah, you had to have met him, but you were pretty small."

"What was he like?"

"He was the most important thing in my world," Max says. "He was funny. He had a pun or a joke for everything. Had a unique twist on any imaginable subject. When I was very young, I remember when he lost his job. I could tell he was worried, but in front of me he always stayed upbeat."

"That sounds a lot like you," Molly says. Then, "I'm sorry."

"For what?"

"Sorry for what you had to go through." Molly's eyes widen. "Do you think that's what Hemera was looking for?"

Max can't keep up with Molly's leap in logic.

"The cartridge!"

Max can't account for the excitement in her voice. It's as if she's seeing… Max follows her gaze, and his eyes settle on Miyamoto, approaching, strolling as slowly as he ever does, cradling a gleaming rectangle in his hands. Max needs to look twice to believe it.

Something flat, boxy, and gleaming like gold. Max reaches out, and his finger presses against solid plastic. It's real. He pulls his hand back like from fire. It's tech, but not the kind that makes everything worse.

He turns it over in his hand. There's no question. This is it. Every scratch and worn bit of paint on the edges is exactly where it should be. This is his cartridge. "How?"

Miyamoto's face darkens. "A certain chief executive stopped by here, not long before you did. She brought me this. She was inordinately interested in understanding everything she could about it."

"What did you tell her?" Max asks.

"I told her that I didn't have the hardware to do anything with it," Miyamoto says. "Not that saying so prevented her from stubbornly insisting that I think about it overnight."

A moment passes in silence. Then the three of them seem to come to the same unspoken conclusion at the same time. Max settles the NES on a patch of desk not covered with books and papers. Molly straightens the console, so it's perfectly aligned with the desk's edge.

"Are we ready?" Miyamoto asks.

Max lifts the door covering the cartridge slot, then stops. He hands the cartridge to Molly. "You may have the honor, madam," he says.

A look of concentration in her eyes, Molly slides the cartridge home. She tests the spring action of the connector a few times, then clicks it into place. Max hesitates with his thumb over the power button, then presses it with a satisfying click.

The red LED winks on and the CRT blossoms with crazy blinking rectangles and horizontal bars. Is it a hidden message he needs to decipher? It looks completely random, and it shifts around too quickly to get a sense of some underlying pattern. He'd be hard-pressed to extract any meaning out of it at all.

"Why isn't it working?" Max asks.

Miyamoto lets out an exasperated sigh. "You youngsters have missed out on so much." He powers it down, pulls out the cartridge, blows across the metal contacts[1], and pushes it in again. Max mashes the power button and the game console springs to life.

The title screen lights up, gently quivering as if it were projected onto a screen in a wafting breeze.

The image draws on the screen one line at a time. It's a vicious scarab with imposing black pincers, rendered in pixelated 8-bit glory. Max has seen this before. "What do Humans First have to do with this?" he says.

Letters form below the image.

PRESS ME

"Controllers," Molly says.

"Hang on, it's not done yet," Max says.

More letters animate into place, but with glitches. The display seems unstable, like the whole thing could stop working any second.

STARTTA TO

"It's *is* a secret code," Max says.

More letters:

KEY CONTINUE

Max scratches his head. It almost, but not quite, makes sense. What does it mean?

PRESS ME STARTTA TO KEY CONTINUE

---

1. A narrative necessity, but if you've got NES hardware, never actually do this. The moisture actually helps corrode the contacts.

0-9 START_

AS FAR AS SECRET CODES GO, IT'S NOT A VERY GOOD ONE.

Ignoring the extra junk, it reads: **PRESS START TO CONTINUE**

"Why continue if you're starting for the first time?" Molly asks.

For once, Max is the less talkative one. He's not a gamer. He's avoided this stuff for as long as he can remember. Then why is he so curious?

He mashes his finger on the controller's rubbery start button. There's no electric tingle, no sudden realization of his life's mission. It's just a button. And still, somehow, it leaves him feeling like he needs to go wash his hands.

The screen fades to black, then an 8-bit musical theme swells out of the silence. Max can't quite place it, but he's sure it comes from the ashes of popular culture. The screen fuzzes out with an elaborate wipe and fills with blocky white characters dropping down from above, against a black background.

A message emerges from the chaos, quite different from the

crazed display when the cartridge was fouled with dust. The characters spin like a casino slot machine, gradually slowing and settling on particular values. The text includes spaces like you'd expect to find in written language, but the characters don't make any sense. They're all capital A through Z, in no meaningful order.

"Was this a popular game?" Max asks. "I mean, before Damage."

Miyamoto considers the question for some time before responding. "Ahh, Damage. Hard to forget such a day. The world was very tense, like the string of a shamisen pulled overly taut. It was obvious that something big was going to happen. Except nobody expected it to unfold the way it did. Almost nobody."

What's that supposed to mean? Max wants to ask, but before he can, Miyamoto continues.

"This—" He gestures at the screen, "—isn't a game. It may look like one. But no, this is a message. You spoke earlier about a secret code. That assessment was not far from the mark."

A colorful scarab crawls onto the screen. Molly seizes the controller and navigates the creature around the playfield. It bumps against the letters, and they block its path, but otherwise don't seem to have much effect.

"I don't get it," Molly says.

The letters read:

```
Qngga  mV2Z3  ZhdCB  uIG9i  Ynggd  mYgdW  5lcSB
yYWJo  dHUNC  mp2Z3
```

```
ViaGc  gZ3V2  YXh2Y  XQgaG  MgY2h  tbXly  Zg0KK
HBiYX  Rlbmd

mKSBp  dmZ2Z  yB5cm  lyeWh  jcGJl  YyBxY  mcNCm
JheXZ

hciBm  eW5md  SB0ZW  hyIHN  iZSBu  IGNld  mly
```

Max squints at the screen. He remembers another reason why he hates digital displays so much—they hurt his eyes.

"I've got it," Max says. "It's a cryptogram like they used to put those in the newspapers so people could solve them just for fun."

"What's a newspaper?" Molly asks.

"Every Sunday dad would…" Max wipes his eyes again. "Never mind. That's a distraction from what we're working on here."

"If my theory is correct," Miyamoto says, "then there's an easier way to figure this out."

"What's that?" Max asks.

"There is a sacred incantation that applies in situations like this," Miyamoto says. "It's called a cheat code. Let me see if I can remember it properly."

"Cheat codes," Molly repeats. "Like when I get thirty lives in Gradius?"

Miyamoto smiles. "Yes, exactly like that. Do you remember the code?"

Molly holds the unfamiliar controller awkwardly in her hand and plucks at the buttons with her prosthetic. She taps out a sequence, carefully:

Miyamoto smiles.

Molly follows this sequence with the Start button, and the letters on the screen explode in all directions, swirl around each other with wild abandon, and finally settle into readable text.

```
Our princess is in a maze of twisty passages,
all alike.

It is pitch black. It is dangerous to go
alone.

You are likely to be eaten by a grue.

Take this. (END OF LINE)
```

"At least now it's English, but it still doesn't quite make sense," Max says. The letters flicker again like the console is struggling to keep the display updated. "Whoever sent this message was more into references than clarity."

"I don't believe they had the luxury of being obvious," Miyamoto says.

"End of line?" Max says. "Isn't that from TRON?"

"I thought you didn't watch movies," Molly says.

"I have no problem watching a movie from sufficient distance," Max says.

Molly rolls her eyes. "I don't like that part about the grue."

"The slavering fangs," Max says. "That whole message is one big reference to video games, especially the kind that work over a modem. I'm surprised nobody died of dysentery before it was over."

Miyamoto raises an eyebrow. "Have you even played Oregon Trail?"

"No, but I've seen memes—no wait, I did play it once. So, there's another thing I remember from before Damage."

"Not too many remember such an old game. Even for that era," Miyamoto says.

Max shrugs, but the words land hard. He's not as pure from the defilements of technology as he'd like to think. It's like there's a virus quietly lurking in his bloodstream, waiting for the right moment to…

"Here's what you should be thinking about," Miyamoto asks. "Why did modern CPUs all stop working after Damage, leaving older ones unaffected?"

"Grue sounds like clue," Molly blurts.

Max welcomes the distraction. "Likely to be eaten by a clue? Whoever put this puzzle together wasn't afraid of wordplay."

"Aren't you going to tell me what a grue is?" Molly asks.

Max smiles. "A mythical—some would say legendary—creature from the era of text-based adventures."

Molly says: "Ahhh. Now I remember. Grue from the Middle English *gruen* meaning to feel horror or shudder." She pauses for a moment, a faraway look in her eyes. She shudders.

"Did you memorize an encyclopedia?" Max asks.

"No, only a dictionary," Molly says evenly.

"Never a dull moment when you're around, Molly," Miyamoto observes.

"Okay," Max says. "So, the riddle's decrypted, only to uncover another layer we need to figure out. There's gotta be something we're missing."

Molly works the controller, walking the scarab around the new letters. Until she notices something. "Pixels," she says.

"Yeah, I know," Max says. "This is all very 8-bit."

"No," Molly says, annoyance creeping into her voice, "Look at the pixels."

Max looks. At first, he doesn't see anything. Blocky letters. Crisp horizontal and vertical lines; stairsteppy curves and angles. Straining at the limit of his eyesight, he can make out individual phosphors of red, green, and blue, softly gleaming beneath the CRT glass.

"See?" Molly asks.

Max feels his temper slipping from his grasp, but he counts to ten and looks again. Molly moves the scarab to bump up against the word *grue*. It's an impassable pixel barrier. But in the same sentence, over the word *likely*, the scarab passes part way through, just enough to overlap noticeably.

"Likely," Max says.

Molly nods.

"That word is different. Are there others?" Max asks.

Molly nods again.

Max watches as the scarab edges around the other words in the message. The next aberration is in the word *twisty*. After that, *dangerous* and *Take*.

"That's it? Four words?" Max asks. Molly shrugs.

"Not much of a hint," Max grumbles. "What are we supposed to do with four random words?"

"Not random," Molly says. "They meant something."

An interesting choice of tense, but she's right. The answer comes from the past; not anything Max might be familiar with.

"This is old stuff," Max says, gesturing at the vintage hardware. "Can you think of anything from this era? Anything that makes these four words make more sense?"

Miyamoto peers over the top of his thick glasses. He stares for a long time. "Ahh," he finally says, "I have an idea. It never caught on, but what you have might be an address."

"What do you mean, *address*?" Max asks.

"It was originally proposed by an ambitious company that went by the name Tesseract. Of course, it hadn't been in use for a decade, even by the time of Damage, but nonetheless, it was a fully-formed global addressing system."

"Global addresses? How did it work?" Max asks.

"They carved up the entire surface of the globe into a patchwork of regions, then assigned each one to a name consisting of four words. The idea was to license the lookup tables for a few cents per lookup and make a profit in volume."

"A database," Molly says.

Miyamoto nods.

"I've never heard of Tesseract," Max says. "What happened to the company? Did they go under during Damage?"

"No," Miyamoto says, "Though, in a way, it would've been better. Had they survived until Damage, their assets probably would've been bought out by LevelUP corporation, and a place like this would have access to the database as a matter of course. Alas, that's not so."

"So, what happened to the data?"

Miyamoto flashes a sad smile. "It wasn't Damage that did them in. It was simply lack of marketing skills. They went under of their own accord. When they liquidated, they sold off their data to cover their debts. Even then, they couldn't line up a buyer. Something about liability concerns."

Max groans. "Then we're bricked."

Miyamoto's smile widens. "Perhaps not. Come with me."

He leads them into a stuffy side room lined with shelves of ancient books. A wave of musty and sweet air washes over Max as he crosses the threshold. "Welcome to the reference room," he says. "Not just anybody gets to set foot on this hallowed ground."

They thread down a narrow aisle, pushing through air thick with history. One set of volumes catches Max's eye: *The Art of Computer Programming* by Donald Knuth, a complete set of four volumes.

At the far end of the aisle, along the top shelf, there's a three-ring binder. It's a cheap-looking thing that someone might have picked up in a back-to-school sale two decades ago. Miyamoto pulls it off the shelf, in the process knocking a spider off the edge.

It lands on Max's hand. He screams and shakes it off, but through whatever sorcery spiders possess, it manages to hold tight. Molly gives Max a questioning look, like she's just learned something about him.

Wiping his hand on the carpet, Max says, "I'm not a fan of spiders, all right?"

Molly shrugs, unfazed. "You live in a tent," she says.

Miyamoto seems not to notice any of this drama, and slowly

makes his way back up the aisle. At the front of a room, he has a viewing table with a sloping pedestal made for holding books. He opens the binder on it. The contents are laser-printed pages in a nigh-microscopic font.

"What is this?" Molly asks.

"This," Miyamoto says, pausing for effect, "is *not* the complete Tesseract database. That would require an entire library of printed pages. But some concerned data historians made an attempt. The data was distributed far and wide in hopes that one day it could be reunited and preserved. This is my piece."

Max, still rubbing the back of his hand on his sleeve, looks closer. The text is so small he needs to almost touch the paper with his nose. Miyamoto pulls out a magnifier. "Perhaps this will help."

Every page is divided into ten columns, each about the width of Max's thumb. Each line, in alphabetical order, contains four words followed by two numbers. Latitude and longitude to four decimal points.

"What percentage of the database is this?" Molly asks.

"Only the thinnest sliver," Miyamoto says. "But you are free to look."

Hundreds of pages printed front and back. Molly cuts through the data like a surgeon. In no time at all, she's found it. All four words form an address.

"It's here," she says. "Write down these coordinates. 37.3836, -122.0116"

Miyamoto has paper at the ready, and Max hastily scribbles. "Do you have a map we can look at?" Max asks.

Miyamoto gestures outside the reference room. "You're in a

library. What do you think?" On the wall is a paper map of the entire Bay Area, with latitude and longitude markers spaced along the edges.

Max is about to object that he needs a world map, but the significant digits seem right. The address is nearby.

Molly's a step ahead. "I know that neighborhood," she says. "Let's go!" Before Max can react, she's headed for the door.

"Thank you!" Max says. He grabs the NES and hurries after, wires trailing behind him.

Molly already has her horse unhitched. "Right, backpack," she says and tosses the whole pack to Max to stow the electronics. "Hurry. We need to get out of here as fast as we can."

"It's like one in the morning. Why?" Max says.

"Because of what I saw," Molly says. "Ride."

---

1. The "Wilhelm Scream" of cheat codes.

0-10 ENTRANCE_

Galloping: somehow even more terrible than Max remembers. What's not to like about getting repeatedly punched in the inner thighs by a side of beef? "What…did…you…see?" he asks.

Molly, for her part, seems to hardly notice she's on a horse, much less at a hard gallop. Her voice carries effortlessly over the clatter of hooves. "A phone. I saw a phone, Max. Miyamoto had a phone in his pocket."

That doesn't make any sense. The library's tech dated from the era of vintage plastic handset phones strung along curly wires. Sure, LevelUP has their facial recognition gateway appliance set up at the entrance, but that's true of any building of significance these days. Other than that, the library is simply not a place one would expect to find technology.

"Why…would…" Max never finishes the sentence. He doesn't need to. The only way Miyamoto would have a cell phone was if LevelUP provided it. Hemera had been there before them. Who knows what kind of threats or incentives she might have left rolling around in the back of Miyamoto's mind. The second he left, he must have been on the phone to her. Thus, great urgency to get to the address before Hemera.

The brisk night air slaps him into wakefulness, senses sharpened. Even tiny details in the moonlight stand out. Max digs his heels in, and his horse responds with an extra burst of speed. "Yaw!" he whoops, though the horse is less than impressed.

Molly takes lead. Across a crumbling overpass, alongside a factory building that was the ugliest structure Max had ever seen—and that was before it was abandoned—they arrive at the address. It's a grassy dome standing watch over a barren and cracked expanse of blacktop once used for parking vehicles—back years before Damage, when cars needed people to drive them.

But that's not the most disturbing part of this neighborhood. "Why are we right across the street from a LevelUP building?" Max asks. "Are we safe here?"

"I don't know this place," Molly says.

The LevelUP satellite office looks dead at this hour. They'll be fine. Probably. But then, an electric blue SUV, reflecting light from the LevelUP building, rolls into view a block away.

"This way," Max says, and turns onto the grass. Molly's horse follows course, and they end up side-by-side.

"We need to get these horses out of sight," Max says. The dry grass isn't even knee high. The only structure in sight is a rickety shed near the top of the gentle hill. At least it's out of sight from the road and the LevelUP building.

"No hitching post," Molly says.

Wooden slats lining the shed look older than the shed could

possibly be, faded and gray, even in the pale moonlight. A split in the siding is wide enough to fit the rope through, but with no place to tie off. The splintery wood feels warm against the cool of the night. Max wedges his rope in, and it seems to hold. "Just do your best. I'm sure they won't go anywhere," Max says.

He lets go of the rope and reaches to pat the horse. But the old nag angles its head away from Max, and the rope pops free. He nudges his companion with a friendly snort, and Molly drops her rope. The two horses turn and trot out of grasp. Max could swear that his horse looks back at him with a mocking eye.

"Help me corral them," Max says. "They're attracting too much attention."

"I know those horses," Molly says. "Trying to catch them will raise far more attention."

Fair enough. The horses chase each other down the road and disappear around the corner.

"They know their way back to the camp, right?" Max asks.

Molly's attention is already elsewhere. "This is it?" she asks.

Max tries to visualize the map they had seen at the library. "Yeah, it would be right about in the middle of this field. Top of the hill." Max takes another breath. "Do you smell that?"

Molly's nose wrinkles, and she nods. It's a faint, sweet smell. When Max leans in, it's coming from inside the shack. There's a faint breeze diffusing from between the slats. It smells a little like new electronics, but with a sharper edge.

Max peeks around the edge to get a view of the LevelUP building. The blue SUV isn't in sight. For the moment they're alone.

There's a door on the side of the building, with a scrap of wood nailed in as a handle. Max tugs on it, but it's securely latched, like there's a board across it from the inside.

"Try knocking?" Molly says. She raps on the door, and the sound is strikingly loud; seeming to echo off the buildings around them.

"Not so loud," Max hisses. "You don't know if—"

Something inside thunks, a sound like a piece of wood sliding against another, and the door creaks open. The pitch black inside is broken only by slender threads of moonlight stabbing through gaps in the planked walls.

"Hello?" Molly asks. Her voice is soft and uncertain. It sounds out of character for her. She pushes the door all the way open.

"Nobody's here," Max observes.

"Then who opened the door?" Molly says and walks inside.

"Wait!—"

The interior is bare. If this were a shed, there'd be tools. If this was someone's idea of a house, there's be furniture. Only creaking wood planks, and a fraying rug in the center, covering a slight bulge, as if there's something underneath. Like Lockheed, this place is another Superfund site. Instead of military waste, this one covers huge amounts of pollution left by Silicon Valley chipmakers half a century ago, some of it so pernicious that it was just now breaking down into merely carcinogenic compounds[1].

"What is this place?" Max asks. "A well or something?"

"That rug," Molly says.

Max kicks the rug, releasing a choking cloud of dust. But sure enough, he can tell that parts of it are slightly less dirty than others. It has a pixelated design woven into it: three parallel bars, curving away at the bottom.

"Atari," Molly says.

"Atari as in Atari Lynx?" Max asks.

Molly nods.

"So this is all connected."

The rug looks just out of place enough that Max and Molly have the idea at the same time: they reach together and shove the rug out of the way. Underneath is a rectangular seam in the floorboards.

"That looks unsturdy," Molly says, pressing her full weight against the rectangle.

Something under the floor cracks loudly. The panel Molly's standing on pivots away from her—a trapdoor. Molly plummets, scrambling to hold on to anything she can reach. She gets one hand on the splintered edge of the floor, but before Max can react, her grip falters, and she plunges into the darkness below.

---

1. Technically, California's Proposition 65 was never repealed, even throughout Damage. It's just that people got so used to warning labels on everything, they just tuned it all out.

0-11 COLOSSAL CAVE_

"Molly!"

Max peers into the syrupy darkness. Molly's glowing braids lay spread out like purple rays, unmoving. "Are you hurt? Say something!"

Movement, but not of the comforting sort. The same glitching he saw on the console screen. As quickly as it appears, the distortion goes away. Then the braids tumble over each other in a more organic way.

"Something," Molly says in flat tones.

"Are you okay?"

"Fine," Molly says. She finds her way back to standing. Still too far down for Max to reach. "Whoa."

"What do you see?" Max asks.

"A Colossal Cave," Molly responds.

Molly's only recalling their earlier conversation, yet the absurd thought of a late 1970s text adventure playing out almost makes

Max laugh. Instead, he says, "Can you see a way to get back up?"

"Not cool," Molly says.

"What? What's not cool?"

"The air. It's warm," Molly says. "You need to see this."

Max feels around the frame of the broken trapdoor. His fingers bump against something warm and rusty. A rung. "I think there's a ladder."

He cautiously works his way onto the rungs, testing each before applying weight, and this way descends into the greater darkness. The air grows cooler for several rungs. But then he crosses an inversion layer, and a front of warm, stifling air engulfs him. The sharp sweet smell grows stronger and by the time Max sets a tentative foot on solid ground, he's a bit lightheaded. If it weren't so dark, the walls around him might be spinning.

"Someone's been down here," Molly says.

Well, yeah. When there's a ladder— Pain explodes through Max's skull as a flashlight the size of a coffee stirrer blazes to life in Molly's hands. "Sorry," says the fading blue streaks filling the space where Molly stands.

"Thanks, I guess," Max grumbles. Before them is a long corridor, a clean rectangular passage carved through the earth. The cone of light reveals hard-packed earth, the walls slick with moisture. "Flashlight goes first. Don't touch anything." In the distance, a rectangular door breaks the straight line of the wall.

"Flashlight's dying," Molly says. "No wonder someone threw it away."

"I think it's fine," Max says, seconds before it assaults Max's retinas with a staccato burst of strobes. After hanging on to a final blip of solid illumination for few seconds, it stays dark.

"So, I spoke too soon." Max sighs. "We have two choices. Either we see where that door up ahead leads, or we turn back now." The purple braids bob up and down. "I was hoping you'd say that. Let's keep moving."

Max makes his way down the corridor, and his hand brushes against the side wall. "Careful," he says. His finger tingles. Before long, it's numb.

Maybe his eyes are adjusting to the tiny amount of light here. Max sees faint outlines of the four seams of the rectangular passage, all stretching toward a vanishing point.

They continue until a gap interrupts the line on the floor. The door. Even warmer than the air around them, and the metal faintly vibrates as if machinery lies within.

The door handle is hooked like one might find on a cruise ship or hospital ward. It turns freely.

"Are we likely to be eaten by a grue?" Molly asks.

"I'm pretty sure we'll be fine," Max says, and leans into the door. It doesn't budge. Max puts weight behind it, but it's as solid as a vault. Above the handle, his hand finds a round raised seam with an oddly-shaped hole half the size of his finger.

"Hmm. There's a lock. Got any keys?"

Molly doesn't seem to take the comment in the offhanded way Max intended. "It's got to be hidden somewhere else on this level." She takes a step past the door.

Max reaches out, his hand catching on the bent wire of her prosthetic. Over time, Molly's bent it at a sharp angle suitable for working the buttons on her handheld game. It's not the most comfortable thing to grip, but Max holds on.

Together, they work their way forward. "This level isn't very well-designed," Molly notes.

"What do you mean?"

"It just goes straight on through. It's linear with only one available next action."

It doesn't seem possible, but it gets even darker. The glow from Molly's hair seems to be fading, though somehow the faint outlines of the corridor seem even crisper. Max cranes his head from side to side just to make sure he's not imaging things.

"Do you see that?" he asks.

"It's pretty dark," Molly says.

Max waves his hand in front of his face, but even that has no effect on the faint lines. Ahead, squarely in the middle of the corridor, sits a broken brick. Max *sees* it. Despite the oppressive darkness pressing in from all sides, he sees it. Or at least a schematic wireframe of it, all edges and polygons.

"I don't know what's going on," he says. "But I can see something on the ground here."

A scraping sound as Molly's toe sweeps ahead of her. The brick tumbles to the side, one chunk of it breaking off.

"Ow," Molly says.

"I told you…"

What in the world is going on? "Keep going. Here, since I can see, kinda, let me go first." The corridor doesn't go on much further. Max slows as they approach the end, and Molly bumps into him from behind.

"Hey, careful."

They make their way to the end of the corridor. It's a flat brick wall with a smaller rectangular opening right in the middle. Were it at ground level, it might pass for a fireplace.

"There's something here," Max says.

"If you say so," Molly says.

Max guides Molly's fingers onto the rectangular frame. "See?"

"No, it's too dark," Molly says.

"Figure of speech," Max says. A cursor blips in the bottom-right side of Max's field of view. The HUD is trying to reassert itself.

Suddenly uneasy, Molly says, "We should leave. We're not safe here."

Max swallows hard. Every time Molly has sensed danger, she's been more than right about it. If some of Hemera's goons came down that ladder, there'd be no escaping.

The HUD blinks an arrow, pointing toward the hole in the wall. Second by second, the lines sketching every brick in the wall seem crisper. Is that being generated from the HUD as well? And one of the bricks looks just a tiny bit different from the rest...

Max reaches for the odd brick, and his hand passes clean through. Suddenly he can see inside, floating in the air, a pixelated and slowly spinning rendition of a golden skeleton key. "Tell me you're seeing this," Max says.

"If we don't get out, we'll be trapped in here," Molly says, bouncing with energy.

Max closes his hand around the item and it vanishes with a

musical chime. The exact sound that had been tormenting him for days in the camp. "Tell me you heard that," Max says.

"You're scaring me," Molly says. She pulls away.

A key icon lights up in Max's HUD. "It's your fault—you went off to find a key on this level. Now I've got one. C'mon." Definitely more detail in corridor rendering now. Subtle textures are visible on the walls. "This is incredible," Max says. "It's like being inside a video game."

Back to the locked door, Max puts his hand against the keyhole, and with a ker-thunk noise, the key icon disappears from his HUD. This time, when he pushes against the door, it nudges free.

"Well, this is it," Max says. "Here we go."

He opens it wide.

0-12 √ ROOT TECH_

The door cracks open, and from within a light flickers to life, blinding fluorescent shafts slicing through the darkness. Max shields his eyes from the glare, but not fast enough to avoid afterimages that make his head swim.

Blurry purple splotches fade slowly with each rub of his eyes. From the edges, a room ravels around him. And the lightly sweet smell of new electronics. Max can't help but draw in a huge breath.

This can't be real. So much tech. Max's eye is drawn to one thing in particular—a flat screen monitor. He'd heard about them in stories handed down from before Damage, but he'd never seen one. At it's thickest, it's as wide as his thumb.

None of these were supposed to work anymore. The control circuitry was complicated enough to require a CPU, and all modern CPUs had become useless hunks of silicon. Or were supposed to be. Could someone have repaired these ones? Swapped out the guts with an 8-bit system?

Max had seen technological exceptions before. In the Fairchild camp, one of the traders claimed his brother constructed a 32-bit computer[1] entirely out of loose transistors, and it worked just fine. Of course, the thing occupied several square feet of space, and in rare moments when it wasn't broken, ate through a set of perfectly good double-A's in minutes. Not exactly commercial-grade engineering.

This screen looked *professional*. Slick injection molded plastic casing. No wires hanging out. Someone had put detail into fit and finish, and brought it to market. It wasn't even dusty.

Max runs his hand along the plastic bezel. Smooth. An artifact from a different age.

Max steps back to take in the rest of the room, and notices more hardware based on the same precept. All four walls of this room are lined with desks, each of which is crammed with post-Damage computing hardware. There have been rumors that such things existed. It wasn't possible—so the story goes—for this much advanced manufacturing to be online again and yet be kept a secret from everyone living in the camps.

Except that it was possible.

"There's no bed," Molly says.

"Excuse me?" Max asks, but as soon as the question is past his lips, he gets where she's coming from. This isn't an apartment—there's no place to sleep. No food. Not even a bathroom. Whoever used this place had to come and go as needed.

"What *is* this place?" Max asks.

"You already said that," Molly notes.

Which doesn't make sense, but neither do most of the things Molly says. Max picks at an interesting-looking piece of equipment: a flat box with three lights on the front and two bulbous antennae on the back. "What's this?" Max asks. He looks for a label on the back.

The instant his fingers make contact, the lights above flicker and pop. Then heavy silence congeals over the room.

The light shifts. Instead of harsh overhead illumination, there's light coming from...well, Max can't tell where the source might be. "Molly, are you there?" Max asks, but nobody answers. It's utterly black in the room, but not dark. Like when Nolan's screen shows solid black, but you can still tell that it's on. Only one thing isn't black: Max's HUD. The lines are so faint that Max has to concentrate just to see them. He can make out the general shape of the room, the four corners in particular.

But then the stairsteppy lines sketching the room's edges crumble into tiny pieces and noiselessly crash to the ground, where they shatter further into individual pixels that slide frictionlessly across the floor.

"Molly?" Max asks again, less certain. "Are you seeing this?"

The room is spinning very gently around Max's head[2]. Vertigo brings Max to one knee, just to avoid falling over. Closing his eyes is no is help.

More of the world takes shape around him. A narrow ledge. Far above him, another. Max finds his feet and paces back and forth. He might tip forward or backward, but paling sideways off the edge doesn't seem possible, as if there's an invisible hand constraining him to two dimensions.

Max's sense of proportion seems wrong. Everything seems flattened, and he can't tell how far it is to the ledge above. He stretches toward it, and without warning he launches skyward, effortlessly jumping higher than his own height. He lands roughly, but it doesn't hurt.

What's going on? Max gapes at his hands. But they aren't hands. They're...

A dust of pixels scattered across the floor sweep into a whirlwind. Traces of color peek out from the television static. The swirling cloud grows dense and denser, until it takes on a physical presence, slightly taller than Max, and with arms, legs. A person.

The column of pixels grows denser and brighter, eventually forming into a life-size 8-bit avatar.

The resolution grows sharper, bit by bit, enough that Max can identify who this avatar represents.

It's unmistakable. "Dad?"

Hadley Root clears his digital throat. He looks Max up and down. "Well. I was expecting someone a little more...capable," he says. "Listen up: we have much training to get through, and not a lot of time to do it."

---

1. Kind of like this: http://megaprocessor.com/
2. Or at least it would be if he could see it which he can't.

LEVEL 1_

PROGRESS

1-1 A NEW GAME_

Dizzy. Looking down is all it takes. His shabby high-top sneakers, in a superposition of flat pixels and comforting physical three-dimensional solidity, rest atop a repeating sea of jaggy red pixels. Conflicting signals from his eyes and the HUD give the world an unsteady shimmer as if everything around him subtly vibrates. Taking a cautious step produces an obnoxious tromping sound, and amidst the ensuing shift in perspective, he nearly loses his feet, not to mention his lunch.

Max wrinkles his nose. The air's filled with a sickly sweet chemical aroma, close to that which seeps from the Colossal Cave, though with an edge of clean-air-after-a-thunderstorm. A barrel labeled OIL glows with an uneven orange flame. Smells far better than an oil fire, though. Intoxicating. It even gets in his mouth. Whatever this place is, it assaults all of Max's senses. Beyond that, he can't get a thought out of his head: *how is Dad here?*

His brain wants to declare that this just a dismissible daydream, but he can't bridge the gap reinforced by the tyranny of his senses. Instead, Max focuses on familiar inner sensations;

controlling his rapid breathing, the hammering pulse in his temple. He's *not* going to let himself throw up.

"Why couldn't it have been one of the Muses?" the pixely avatar of Hadley Root bemoans. "Word of advice—never look down. You'll just make yourself wooz out. EYES UP!"

Max's head snaps up, unable to resist the force behind the command. Bright red construction girders stretch into the softly glowing black sky. They creak as if something heavy high above shifts around.

Why all this?

"You are probably asking yourself, *why all this*, blah, blah, blah," Pixel Hadley says, wagging his head. "Well, knock it off. Concentrate, boy!"

"Concentrate on what?" The ground convulses as a huge barrel hisses down the rails of a ladder and bounces off the floor. It pivots and hurtles directly toward Max.

"That," Pixel Hadley says. "Jump!" Hadley launches off the ground, sailing upward until the soles of his feet are higher than his head was. He arcs over the barrel and comes lands smoothly on the other side.

In Max's experience, gaming consists of text-based stories, with interactive commands like, "Take key" or "leap over barrel." And Pixel Hadley called out a verb just before he— "Jump?" Max says. Nothing happens. "Jump?? Jump!"

Zork, this is not.

"Jump, moron!" Pixel Hadley screams.

Just…jump? He thinks about his calves tensing up and letting fly. He thinks about launching skyward. With a *sproing* sound, Max rockets upward, knees nearly grazing the onrushing barrel. The red girder above rushes toward him, laws of gravity and physics flexing like a slinky.[1] Max covers his head, but impact doesn't come. In fact, he sails even higher, landing on the level above. Molly used to talk about platform games. Finally, Max understands exactly what that means.

Pixel Hadley's head pops up from a ladder. "Nice." Bit by bit, the game world grows more familiar, or at least less uncomfortable. The 'real' world—the room where Molly awaits, fades in importance. "Do you know the parable of the caterpillar?" Pixel Hadley asks. Max shakes his head. "He was walking just fine, until one day someone asked him how he managed to keep track of all those legs. He started thinking about it and was never able to take another step again."

"I don't get it," Max says.

"Caterpillars get squished," Pixel Dad says. "Quit trying to think about how to move, or jump, or dodge obstacles. Stop thinking and start doing."

"Wait, obstacles?"

"Can we at least make it to the top without getting pasted?" Pixel Hadley says. "This way." He runs along the upward-sloping girder to another ladder at the far end.

"Climb!" Pixel Dad says. "Don't look behind either."

Before the words completely land, Max glances behind him, and there's a monstrous flaming apparition—the remains of the barrel that he leaped over, now writhing like a flaming amoeba —creeping up the slope toward Max.

Some sliver of Max's mind strains to reconnect with his body back in a cramped room, a solid ceiling not far above his head. So, climbing is an...odd experience. When he first grabs on to the ladder rung, he feels the emptiness of wrapping his fingers around nothing. But the sense of climbing quickly becomes second nature, and Max ascends to the next girder.

Pixel Hadley's already there, but standing still. "I thought you said to hurry—" Hadley cuts off Max with a gesture—*wait*. A massive block of granite the size of a dump truck and studded with ivory spikes crashes down, shaking already-unsteady floor beneath them. *Seriously?* What kind of construction site features...? But then the slab rises slowly back into the air, into a hidden compartment above.

"I thought this was a construction site," Max says. "What's with the big rocky crushy thing?"

"Obstacles," Pixel Hadley notes dryly. "Now!" Hadley dashes through, and Max scrambles behind sticking as close as possible. The trap mashes down again, missing Max by inches.

An actual chunk of rock that size would weigh, what? Somewhere between one and a million tons. What would happen if his pixels got macerated into chunky salsa? Could he actually get hurt here? Could he die in here?

There's no ladder at the end of this girder, only a huge green pipe. Hadley leaps, throwing in a fancy midair flip, sailing right down the middle of the pipe. Max peers into the inky blackness. Behind him, more of the fire creatures approach, unimpeded by the crushing stone trap. He arranges his feet on the flat edge of the pipe. "Here we go," he says to himself, and drops.

Somehow, he changes direction. Rising rather than falling, he emerges thrust forward into a place with a cyan sky, dotted with smiling clouds. The ground, as far as the pixel resolution can depict, is made of sturdy macadam, solid under his feet. The ozone smell is gone here too. Pixel Hadley runs far ahead.

"Wait!" Max says, and hurries after him, taking off so quickly that he launches into the air, again with a cheesy sound effect. His character seems good at jumping. He covers more ground this way, so he jumps again and again, pogoing his way through this strange world.

Square bricks hang in the air, supported by nothing at all. Max leaps without looking up, and abruptly finds one of these structures on a collision course with his face. He tries to shield himself, but the brick shifts upward before snapping back as if attached to a spring.

Something golden flashes through the corner of his eye as a chime rings out of nowhere in particular. A sound all too familiar — Max has been hearing it for days. Words scroll across the lower third of his field of view:

INVENTORY

* COIN

Inventory: this he understands. He even figured out the quirk on the original Zork game where your maximum inventory limit was determined by a random number. If you were holding too much to pick up another item, trying again (and again) would usually work.

A few more leaps and he's caught up. Despite the effort, he's not the least bit winded. "All this," he says, gesturing to encompass the whole world around him. "Why?"

"Consider it training," Pixel Hadley says. "This is just the loading screen. Randomized each time, but ridiculously easy compared to anything you'll later come up against." He stops and listens. Max can't hear anything, but Hadley looks concerned. The way ahead is barred by a locked door, one that looks exactly like the one in the cave. Except filthy black oil's been spattered along the door frame. It drips, pooling along the grainy sand.

"Loading screen?" Max asks. "So I can't really die in here. Right?"

"Interesting question," Pixel Hadley says. "Depends on your definition of *die*. Now help me find a key. There's got to be one around here nearby."

Max kicks a rock out of his way, and a little eight-note jingle plays. A hint uncovered. Pixel Dad looks at him. "Don't just stand there. Pick it up."

The space where the rock used to be doesn't look any different, but Max reaches for it. His hand passes through the ground like it's not even there. Then it closes around a key. The inventory sound chimes again.

"What do you mean, definition of die?" Max asks.

"Death means you go back to the save point, usually at the start of the level," Pixel Hadley says.

"That doesn't sound so bad."

"The thing is, you leave behind all your inventory. If you're carrying something valuable, whoever offs you can just take it. Now hand me the key."

Alarm bells sound in Max's head. "Why? You're just a part of the loading screen, right? I'll just open this door myself—"

Pixel Hadley makes a quick move. It happens too quickly for Max to see, but it ends with a hand holding a long blade a short distance from his chest. It doesn't hurt, but it does take Max's breath away. "You're not ready yet. There are things worse than death," Pixel Hadley says.

The key and the coin tumble out from Max's inventory and

scatter along the ground. Hadley grabs the key. Everything around Max takes on a reddish tint, growing more saturated by the second.

A heavy *ker-thunk* reverberates from the door ahead, which swings open, and Pixel Hadley dashes through it.

Abandoned again. At least the first time, his dad hadn't killed him. Max's world morphs into a silent void of scarlet.

---

1. The toy, not the brand of guitar strings, though that analogy kind of works too.

1-2 BOSS FIGHT_

The uneven flicker of the OIL can marks Max's reemergence at the start of the loading screen. The second time through, it's easier. Climbing seems second nature. Max even grabs the hammer and smashes a few barrels.

He works his way back to the green pipe and emerges in the blue-skied overworld. Despite the warning about randomization, all enemies are in exactly the same as before. Up top, when he smashes the same brick that yielded a coin previously, nothing happens. It's not even a brick anymore, but a bolted down steel plate, hanging in the exactly in the way bricks never do. Another brick, higher up with no obvious way to reach it, reads, 'POW.' Max hurries past, all the way back to the previously-locked door.

The ground where the key was hidden is stained black. A dark trail, like oil poorly scrubbed away, winds through the now-unlocked door. Max peers inside but can't see anything…until he crosses the threshold. As soon as he sticks his nose through, an irresistible force pushes him through. Or maybe it'd be more accurate to say that while he stood still, the entire universe moved past him. From the far side he can't see back, or even re-enter. A one-way passage. The only way out of this loading program is through the exit.

The new level is darker and lined with grey bricks. It reminds Max of the actual tunnel he went through to get here. Despite the lack of an obvious light source, he can still see. Heavier splatters of the black sludge mark the site of a violent struggle. And in the middle of it: a coin Possibly *the* coin, though how could one ever tell for sure? If Pixel Hadley dropped it, that meant that he'd lost a life as well. Max scoops up the coin, and it chimes into inventory. But where was the rest of Hadley's inventory? At a minimum he held a weapon. At the far end of the cave, Max spots something—not a blade, but something cylindrical and yellowing.

Between him and the item, there's a droplet of the black oil, the size of a grape, quivering and straining to stand upright.

"Hey there, blobby little creature," Max says. "Don't mind me. Just passing through." Max takes a step and the slime rears up like a cobra, hissing. Somehow, it's ballooned in volume, not to mention threat.

Max takes another step closer, and the slime doubles again in size, adding a slender lupine snout. It lunges, restrained only by its own elasticity. Max freezes. He's close enough to see the item better. It looks like a tightly-wound scroll. And if Max knows one thing about these games: always pick up a scroll.

His only chance is to outrun the slime. Max abruptly charges ahead, adorable puffs of smoke appearing at his heels. He dives for the scroll. The sudden movement throws the black slime off his scent, at least for the half-second or so needed to scoop up the item. It chimes into inventory.

Max scrambles back to his feet, but a filament of the black

slime wraps around his ankle. Max's arms flail wildly for a moment as he tries to regain his balance, but to no avail. Before he knows it, his legs are hopelessly tangled. His balance topples past the point of no return. The world seems to move in slow-motion as he tumbles. The ground barks against the meat of his palm, a painful jolt shooting through his overextended wrist. He tucks his head under and turns in a complete summersault, keeping his flailing momentum pointed toward the exit still ahead. Max flings his arms forward as hard as he can, taking advantage of every ounce of momentum. Not an elegant maneuver by any stretch. No animator would've done it that way. But it works.

Dad called this training. He was getting the hang of maneuvering through an 8-bit world. Max pushes off and hurls himself toward the exit, so close that the background stops scrolling.

Max tempts fate with a look behind and immediately regrets it. The black slime is at his heels. A doorway's just ahead. Just in reach. As his body sprawls across the threshold, a razor-bottomed metal doorway whooshes down from above, in guillotine-fashion. Max wrenches his body through the doorway, contorting in directions he didn't know his body could bend. He feels the blade graze his ribs, taking with it a section of his shirt. With a horrible screech, it severs the snout of the black slime creature. The bits of it that make it through the door condense into sticky tar.

What happens now? As if in answer to his thoughts, a second metal gate slams shut, leaving him locked in a room with no exits. This place is a battle arena. The armored door adds a dramatic sense of finality. This can only mean one thing.

This is what Molly would call a boss fight.

Given the mishmash of game ideas so far, Max isn't sure what to expect, but—

Max nearly throws up when the creature drops from above—a hairy spider as big around as a kiddie pool, armed with vicious fangs. It hits the ground and springs forward on wiry legs. The thing moves sideways faster than it does forward, its movements unpredictable and menacing.

Stumbling backward, Max doesn't take his eye off the creature, making it quite difficult to attempt darting glances to the left and right, searching for a weapon. *Anything.*

Every one of Max's nightmares converges in the horrific scene that follows as the spider disgorges searing blue laser beams from its maw, in short bursts of three. Max scrambles back until he's pinned against the door.

Max hurls himself sideways—narrowly missing a shower of sparks from a laser blast. The gate glows red-hot where the beam bombarded the metal.

He can't keep this up forever. Or even for a minute. He desperately scans the arena looking for anything useful.

No weapons.

No defense.

Nothing.

No way to escape without going through that *thing* with too many eyes.

Taking his attention off the creature proves to be a mistake. Another laser blast nearly clips his chin. Even the near-miss is enough to bubble his skin.

Max pushes the pain aside and rolls again, in the only direction that avoids imminent bisection. This puts him nearly in the center of the arena, fully exposed. As he rolls, he notices something in the pocket of his jeans. Of course. The coin.

Its yellow pixels form a disk, far larger in his hand than it was in his pocket. It lacks the detail to have a heads or tails side, but one side has white glints suggesting polished metal.

The coin grows even more, to the diameter of a saucer. Reflective side out, Max extends the coin away from his body like a talisman, keeping it between him and the monster's maw.

The attack comes faster than Max can track. He manages to block the next bolt without charring his fingers, and as expected, it reflects it back, though the shot goes wild. Max moves in even closer.

For the next attack, Max lines up better, and the reflected energy bolts strike the spider in the head, whereupon it emit a piercing shriek of anguish, followed by repeated orange blinks, every pixel of the creature flashing in unison like a neon sign. The creature lets out a final whimper and crumples into a heap.

That was easy.

Then it rises, hissing with rage.

Too easy.

The creature rounds for a fresh attack, now moving twice as fast. Seeing the thing skitter across the room makes Max's skin crawl. Energy bolts seem to come at him from all directions, a continuous rain of red-hot plasma without the brief delay Max had been depending on to catch his breath. He's not it the position he'd like, and as he swings the reflective around to protect his head, the energy attack sears through his pixely fingers. His whole arm might just as well have turned into fire, if the waves of pain are anything to go by.

It's not real. Not real. Not. Real. None of this is happening. As hard as he tries, Max can't even remember what it feels like to be in his original body. He left it somewhere, in a colossal cave. Someone else was there with him.

Molly was there. *Is here.* Someone he was willing to stand up for.

Max rises. The coin is fused to the smoldering stumps of his fingers. He lines up the angle, and the next laser blast reflects back into the spider's head. Every hairy segment of the spider's body, then each individual leg, erupts in animated explosions. The gate falls away. Max is free to exit. An item drops down from above—a prize for finishing the level. It's a gleaming trophy, excessively ornate for the resolution in which it's rendered. The inventory noise chimes as he makes contact with it.

Max exits.

There's one more room. A pixel princess is there, dressed in a pink flowing dress and strawberry shortcake hat, but words materialize in the air:

YOUR PRINCESS IS IN ANOTHER CASTLE.

As Max looks on, the pixels fade in intensity, revealing a concerned Molly Matheson underneath.

1-3 [RETURN]_

SCREAMING. CRYING. A BRISK SLAP TO THE FACE.

Molly.

Disorientation surges, washes over Max, then ebbs. Flickering lights around the room gradually resolve into focus. Those aren't pixels.

"Oh, Max, I'm so sorry…are you OK?"

"I…" Max's voice is raspy, like he hasn't used it in a long time. Suddenly, he pats his pockets. "Where is it?"

"What?"

She didn't see any of what happened. "The scroll. I picked it up."

The experience seemed so real. Max groans. What must his jumping and climbing and flailing around have looked like to her? No wonder she was worried.

"Scroll?" Molly asks. "Like papyrus? Cuneiform?"

"Yeah, pretty much." Max recounts his platform adventure.

"Two items," Molly says, "a coin and a scroll."

Max nods. "And a trophy at the end. All captured as inventory."

As the word, *inventory*, crosses Max's lips, information marches across his HUD:

```
INVENTORY:

* COIN

* TROPHY 1

* MYSTERIOUS SCROLL
```

"Whoa, I'm seeing a list of the items right now."

"Items?" Molly says. "What can you do with items?"

Of course. Noun and verb combinations, just like Zork. "Examine coin," Max says.

```
THE COIN IS MIRROR SHINY.
```

"It worked!" Max says.

"What worked?" Molly says.

"Right, I keep forgetting that you can't see this," Max says. "I got a message saying that the coin is mirror shiny. And it was."

"Try something else," Molly says.

"Examine scroll."

```
THE SCROLL IS TIGHTLY WOUND. NO WRITING IS
VISIBLE.
```

"Unwind scroll."

```
YOU UNWIND THE SCROLL AND A WRITTEN PASSAGE
```

APPEARS. IT LOOKS LIKE THERE MAY BE MORE WRITING, BUT THE SCROLL STICKS SHUT, AS IF BOUND BY MAGIC.

"I've got something," Max says. "There's a message in the scroll."

"Read it," Molly says.

"Read scroll." Max reads the text out loud as it scrolls past.

DON'T BELIEVE EVERYTHING YOU READ. YOU MUST GATHER THE FOUR TROPHIES.

"Four trophies. One already. That's good." Molly says. After a brief silence, "That's it?"

"Hmm. Read scroll," Max says.

BEWARE THE POWER THAT BE. CHOOSE YOUR WORLD CAREFULLY. YOU DON'T HAVE TO LIVE LIKE A REFUGEE.

"Shouldn't that be *powers* that be, with an s?" Molly asks.

"Read scroll."

YOU WANT PROOF? YOU'LL FIND IT AT

"Read scroll!"

YOU WANT PROOF? YOU'LL FIND IT AT—

Max makes a frustrated, vaguely profanity-inflected noise.

YOU CAN'T READ ANY MORE OF THE SCROLL UNTIL YOU UNLOCK THE MAGIC SPELL BINDING IT.

"Read scroll!" The message only repeats. "Read scroll! Read scroll! Arrgh!"

Max counts to ten before he can say anything. "I've just been trolled by a scroll."

"Well, that's something," Molly says. "We should get started."

"Started what?"

"Finding the other trophies, of course," Molly says.

"It's not like we have much to go on. We don't even have the tiniest sliver of a hint where to look. I'm not sure I even believe anything written in this scroll. Look...the first line even said not to believe it."

"How did you find the first trophy?" Molly asks, mildly.

"By accident," Max says. "Well, not *entirely* accident."

"The HUD."

"That doesn't count," Max says.

"You don't think there was somebody at the other end, feeding you hints?"

"Look, I'm not somebody's trained puppy. My life consists of more than following the orders of some shadowy presence that's getting way, *way* into my personal space."

"If you mastered the first level, then I'm sure you could handle the next level just as easily," Molly says.

"No, Molly. There aren't levels. This is the real world we're talking about, not a game."

"Says the one reading from a magic scroll."

Touché.

A loud thump rumbles through the ceiling, then the room plunges into darkness. All the equipment in the room powers down, except for a few weakly blinking lights from devices that must have internal batteries. "Time to make our exit," Max says.

Molly's hand finds its way into Max's once again. Max leads them into the even darker corridor. The air feels slightly damper in his lungs, and the wall feels cool when his hand grazes against it. Max remembers where they are—buried deep under an active Superfund site—and wipes his hand across his shorts.

Navigating by the dim glow of Molly's hair isn't going to be enough. "Hold up a second," he whispers. When Molly stops, he pulls out the salvaged lock mechanism from her backpack. It's still emitting a sickly green glow. It's not much, but enough avoid bumping against the walls.

Max leads them back to the ladder, and up. In the darkness, he almost misses a rung, and an alarmingly loud scraping sound reverberates through the narrow space. Max stops to listen.

Footsteps clomp across the room. At least two people up there, one of them in heels. Max hears a voice: Hermera's. He can't quite make out what she's saying, but it's definitely her. That earlier encounter was more than enough for a lifetime, but now he's separated from her by only the thinnest layer of flooring. Her voice fades in and out as she click-clacks across the room.

Across a bare floor—the rug! They had rolled it out of the way to expose the trapdoor in the floor. Once they went through, there was no way to reset the rug to cover their tracks. Which meant that Hemera was staring right at their only way out. Probably deciding whether to go down herself, or to send one of her goons instead—knowing how Hemera liked her bodyguards, probably someone with rippling biceps the size of hypertrophic Rottweilers. That door might fly open at any moment.

Max strains to hear what she's saying. He creeps up a few more rungs, more carefully. By the time he reaches the top, the voices above have gone quiet. Maybe Hemera went to find reinforcements, in which case they've got a narrow window of escape.

"We're trapped," Molly whispers.

"I'm working on a plan" Max whispers.

"A plan?—Sssh!" Max chokes off his response.

A voice. Right on top of them. Hemera again, but Max can't make out most of the words, except for one word that sounds an awful lot like "trophy."

"She has a trophy," Molly says, a bit louder than a whisper. She immediately cups her hand over her mouth.

Max nods. "I knew it." If he knows Hemera at all, she'll insist on validating her suspicions firsthand. After all, she's gone to the trouble of coming all the way out here in person. She doesn't trust anyone else with whatever she might find. Which makes for an opportunity…

"I'm getting you out of here," Max whispers.

"No, together," Molly counters.

"Don't worry about me. I've got a plan for a distraction, but only for a window long enough to get one of us to out of here."

"But there aren't any windows," Molly says.

Based on the voices and footsteps, there's only people up there. A distraction will separate them.

"You need to wait *right here*." Max points at a groove in the wall near the top of the ladder. "If you stand on this little ledge, and keep your hand here to steady yourself, you'll be fine. Don't make a sound. Don't even breathe, and they won't notice you, I promise. Wait until two people move past, then quickly climb out. Silently. Try not to be seen once you're outside."

"No, this is crazy—"

Max thumps the bottom of the trapdoor, bumping it open an inch.

"I told you someone in there," Hemera says, her voice clearer through the open crack.

Max puts a finger to his lips and tucks the green light back into Molly's backpack, plunging the tunnel into darkness. Molly slips on a hoodie to cover her hair. Max slides down the ladder, the rust burning his palms.

Seconds later, the door bangs against the limits of its hinges. Hemera grunts delicately as she lowers herself down, along with the waving beam of a flashlight and the clatter of expensive shoes ticking lower, rung-by-rung.

The piercing light assails Max's retinas. Hemera's flashlight is unconscionably bright, but the beam passes him by. Max is pretty sure he hears the gentle scritch of Molly climbing up and out, and Hemera seems focused on something else, but just in case, he lets out his own grunt in protest.

The light swivels back to him. "What do we have here?" Hemera says. She doesn't wait for an answer, but instead marches down the long corridor and shines her light into the server room. She returns immediately.

"We're too late, there's nothing of use here," she calls to the bodyguard up top. "Have this one brought to my car. We need to have a little chat."

Max doesn't struggle against what happens next.

1-4 THE RIDE OF THE AZURE SUV_

INVENTORY:

* COIN

* TROPHY 1

* MYSTERIOUS SCROLL

Max's aching ribs flare with pain at the sight of the SUV. Somehow the iridescent azure[1] infecting everything inside Hemera's corporate chariot makes everything hurt worse. He pounds against the glass separating him from the bodyguard in the front section. "Hey! You ripped my shirt!" Max screams, but his ursinous captor doesn't react. Maybe the glass is soundproof.

Max crumples against the plush seats. The leather feels cool. Real stuff, not the polymerized synthetic someone would occasionally try to unload as "tent patches" at Max's once and former mercantile. When he closes his eyes, a wave of tiredness washes over him. A tiny vibration catches his attention. He opens his heavy lids, and startles to find Hemera there, on the other side of the glass. They lock eyes.

When Hemera speaks, her voice is startlingly loud, amplified through unseen speakers. "There's something you should know about me, Max, Max Root. I *really* hate coincidences."

There's something unnerving about being closed inside a box at her behest.

"You know what else is a coincidence? That a pitiful refugee camp exists only through the goodwill of a single CEO. Would you say that's a responsible use of investor capital? Would you say that's *moral*?" Silence hangs in the air. Max makes a valiant effort not to respond.

"That's right," Hemera continues. Something in his face must have given him away. Is there a camera nearby? A microexpression analyzer? Without making it obvious, he looks more closely for where there may be any electronics monitoring him. Nothing stands out, though close to the roofline Max spots an antenna very similar to one in the underground server room. He casually reaches his arms into a lazy stretch, and it feels solidly mounted, like it came as standard equipment on the car, rather than something bolted on aftermarket. An exposed metal trimming buzzes under Max's finger as if electric. The inventory sound chimes in Max's ear. He looks around to see if anyone noticed.

Apparently not. Hemera continues, "I could make one call, and before the day is out, bulldozers would raze those filthy tents to the ground. Do you understand what I'm saying?"

Max nods.

"Your only purpose in this conversation is to come to terms with my generosity. If I even suspect that you're lying to me, well, I don't think anyone appreciates getting lied to, wouldn't you agree?"

Max nods again.

"Then we see things the same way. I'm talking too much. Your turn. Tell me something I want to hear."

Ice floods Max's veins. His entire universe compresses into a tiny dot. He might throw up. He needs to say something significant to satisfy her, but he can't say too much. More than anything else, he needs to keep Molly out of this.

"You know," Max croaks. He clears his throat and tries again. "You want to know what's special about this place..."

Hemera doesn't answer. She's patient if nothing else.

"Look," Max says, "you want me to say something you want to hear. But I don't know what you know. Repeating information you already have would waste your time, and neither of us wants that, right?"

"Tell me how long Isidore has been coming here," Hemera says.

Isidore? Hemera knows more than she's letting on. Worse, she assumes Max does too.

"Nobody in the camp has seen Isidore in—I don't know— maybe a month." Max struggles to remember. When *did* he last see Isidore?

Abruptly, the dividing glass descends; nothing but open air between him and Hemera and her bodyguard, who she turns to. "Leave us." He immediately complies. "Make sure we're not disturbed." The hiss of the gullwing sealing, leaving the two of them alone, somehow seems louder and more final than when he first entered.

"You have no idea what you're dealing with, do you?" Hemera says, her voice a whisper. Max resists the urge to lean in closer, just to hear what she says. "Just for associating with Isidore Morris, a known terrorist, I could have you put away for life. The courts are not particularly forgiving these days. Especially…"

Especially what? Max is sure he wouldn't like the end of that sentence, but leaving it hanging is even worse.

"Look, just tell me what you want. Maybe I can help you get it," Max says. Again, he weighs his options for escape. He's quick on his feet. And he gets the feeling that Hemera doesn't know this neighborhood as well as he does. But even if he got away, it wouldn't do much good if the whole camp got bulldozed. For too many families, the camp was all they had. And still there's Molly.

Tap, tap, tap; someone's at the front compartment's side window. Hemera lowers the window a crack.

It's Molly. Whacking the window with…*his cartridge*.

The golden reflection glints in the vehicle's interior light. "Looking for this?" Molly says, her voice distant and muffled.

"Let me see that," Hemera says, unable to contain her blip of excitement. Her hand darts out to grab it, but Molly's too quick.

'Why?' Max silently mouths to Molly.

"Things can be replaced. You can't," Molly says, quoting the earlier words of her mother. "Let Max go, and it's yours."

"Molly, don't!" Max says. That cartridge was one of the few things that linked Max to his dad. Now Hemera was going to take it a second time.

"Fine," Hemera replies, a little too quickly. She mashes a button that hisses open Max's door the width of a few fingers. Hemera snatches the cartridge out of Molly's hand. *Oh, Molly, what have you done?*

Max takes a careful step out, not letting the shaking in his legs show. Hemera's bodyguard appears out of nowhere, and gets in before the SUV zooms away, squealing around a corner.

"Let's get out of here, Molly. I think I need a shower after being that close to human slime," Max says.

"No time," Molly says. "Not safe."

And for once, Max doesn't argue. "Then let's get you home," he says.

"Hold on." Molly pulls out her game console. Dangling from it by wires is the battery from the lock mechanism. She sits. "Just a sec. Need to de-stress."

De-stress? It had never occurred to Max that Molly's game-playing might have been therapeutic. Maybe that kind of escapism was the slender thread helping her cling to hope in a dismal world. Not so different than how Max coped with the world. Or used to. But here and now?

While Molly's occupied, Max checks his inventory to see what he collected from the SUV: A Compact Disc. Max wonders what that could mean.

Suddenly, Molly flips her game off. "OK, let's go." She marches off, in the opposite direction of camp.

"Where are we going?"

---

1. In 2033, LevelUP acquired the assets of Pantone Inc., and immediately trademarked their own particular shade of blue.

1-5 THE MUSES_

INVENTORY:

* COIN

* TROPHY 1

* MYSTERIOUS SCROLL

* COMPACT DISC

In the moonlit shadows of Moffett Field, there's a quiet place, out of sight from streets and overhead surveillance alike. The long-abandoned light rail tracks run at ground level except in one fenced-off area where the line dips out of sight behind a concrete barrier, a roofless tunnel.

Amidst the piles of wind-strewn leaves and trash is a old trampoline, propped up on rocks and covered with enough layers of duct tape to form a crude ceiling. Whoever dumped it here must have been really determined—the fence is at least ten feet high and doesn't have any large breaks for at least a click in either direction. Molly ducks underneath, and Max follows.

"How did you know about this place?" Max asks.

"I made it," Molly says. After an awkward pause, she continues, "I mean, I made it homey. Are you OK?"

"This is homey? Yeah, I'm fine. But Hemera's pure evil. She needs to be stopped before somebody gets hurt."

"Like that's going to happen," Molly says. Max scowls, and she changes tack. "No, wait, that came out wrong. I mean... Ugh."

Max peers at her. She looks away. "Why do you talk that way?" he asks.

"What way?"

"People at the camp call you robot girl. I always thought it was them being jerks because they were jealous that you didn't have to put in factory time. But now..."

Molly makes eye contact, but she turns away after less than a second. "Now you think I'm like that," she says quietly.

"No, not like that," Max says. He expects to see a hurt look on Molly's face, but it doesn't happen. Her face remains neutral.

"It's okay," she says. "It's nice to be seen for once."

"I didn't mean —"

"You always say things the way they sound in my head. You don't jumble up the words when they come out of your mouth, the way they do for me," Molly says. "I like that."

"Thanks, I guess," Max says. He sighs and lets his eyes focus on the far-away stars until a cloud rolls in and blocks their view.

"What do we do now?" Max sighs. "That cartridge was our only clue. Hemera's probably got half the trophies by now."

"You mean this?" Molly asks, producing a circuit board with narrow copper fingers along one edge.

"Is that—?"

Molly smiles. "At least the important parts of it."

"And Hemera?"

"Not exactly a detail-oriented type of person," Molly says. "But she'll figure it out soon enough. We shouldn't stay here." She stops talking, but her eyes flicker with deep thought. "We don't have to live like a refugee. That's what the scroll said. That sounds like life before Damage."

"We need to go back to the camp and help people get out while they still can."

"In the middle of the night? Who'd believe us?" Max asks. "The way we save the camp is by finding the trophies before Hemera does." Max sighs. "We need to get online to see what we can find out. We're going to need a safe place to run searches from. Can't be any of the backbone ISP; Hemera's got her hooks into all of them. We need to find a local operator. Someone we can trust."

"You need an off-book internet drip?"

"Less of a drip, and more of a torrent," Max says.

"OK, let's go then," Molly says. She gets her feet under her and stands.

"Wait, go where?" Max asks.

"To go see someone you need to talk to," Molly says.

"Oh? Where is this?" Max asks. But he thinks he already knows the answer.

"To see the Muses," Molly says.

Sans horse, a trip into the city is less straightforward and more dangerous. But Molly seems entirely comfortable, as if she's made the walk a thousand times. Max was starting to realize that maybe she had.

They enter a part of town that could charitably be called on the edge of abandonment.

Damage didn't much slow down construction, at last not initially, because there were plenty of building materials and strong arms with nothing better to do, so vast swaths of every city got remade in a fashion that better suited the scaled-down economy. Where strip malls might have once lined a busy street, now tightly-packed warrens of one-room apartments took their place.

In the case of the building Molly leads them to, the older storefront wasn't even torn down first. Like a wasp nest in a glass jar, the interior space of a taqueria was lined with claustrophobic corridors and tiny stacked rooms, each not taking up much more space than a coffin.

"This way," Molly says. "The deluxe suite." She leads them around a tight bend toward what used to be a kitchen.

Molly called it deluxe without a hint of irony. It's a slightly larger coffin room, tucked into the far corner of the building, with a door only a child could walk through without stooping.

Molly knocks in a halting pattern:

Knock-knock-knock – knock – knock-knock-knock – knock-KNOCK – KNOCK-KNOCK – knock.

"Morse code?" asks Max.

Molly nods. The door swings open, smooth as a servo.

Max ducks through the doorway. The room is brightly lit with luminous baseboards that run along the edge between the corporate carpet and the battered drywall. But the room's completely empty, not even furniture.

"What is this?" Max asks.

"We're here to see the Muses," Molly says, as if that explains everything. Molly steps past and puts her palm flat against the right-side wall, alongside a full-length photograph of an elderly Japanese man.

The photo frame slides open, revealing another room beyond. A wave of warm, moist air nearly knocks Max back a step. It doesn't stink, per se, but it's clear that many bodies have been in close proximity for a while.

The room is tiny, barely big enough for the three people reclining inside, much less visitors. The inhabitants, feet-to-the-door, wear silvery athletic outfits that flatten their bodies into sleek angular shapes. They have no hair, not even eyebrows. The front of the room holds three screens, one for each of the Muses, and a fourth one unused. And not bulky CRTs, but honest-to-goddess flatscreens, each showing a dizzying array of charts, graphs, and text too small to read from where Max cranes his neck.

"To answer your several questions," the first Muse says, "Yes, this is our home. No, we don't get out much. You may refer to any of us as 'she' or 'her.' The clothing is to help circulation. And we do enjoy helping people, but we are very busy and only do so in return for something of value to us—and there are few things we truly value that we do not already possess."

Max stammers. He hadn't even thought about what he wanted to say, but had he managed to put together questions, those answers would've fit exactly.

"Better let me handle this," Molly says. She addresses the first Muse. "Din, we beseech you—"

"No time for beseeching," Din says. "The Lockheed habitation is in about to fall. You've come here to seek assistance for the four hundred souls living on the hill."

"There is more," the second Muse says. "A key that unlocks a mouldering mystery."

"Are they ready for what they will face?" Asks the third.

Max's mouth makes a sound as it opens and shuts again.

"We're ready," Molly announces.

"What do you offer us in return?" Din asks.

Molly hesitates, then holds her game console out to Din.

That little box means the world to her; Max instinctively feels how much it must hurt her to offer such a sacrifice. There has to be a better way. But Max has no earthly possessions. Nothing at all, except—

Max gently puts his hand on Molly's game and lowers her hand.

"I have something from Hemera's vehicle."

Din's hairless brow arches. "You've been on her personal network." Not a question. "Data." She moves her chin toward Max, and he hears a sound, like the chime of adding to inventory, except played backward. He doesn't need to look to realize his Compact Disc is gone from inventory.

"Approach. Let me get a good look at you."

1-6 IT'S DANGEROUS TO GO ALONE_

INVENTORY:

* COIN

* TROPHY 1

* MYSTERIOUS SCROLL

Max tetrises[1] himself into the cramped room. Even with Molly flattened against the wall, the space isn't wide enough to avoid brushing against Din. She's cool to the touch. What Max initially thought was a flatscreen turns out to be part of a bigger whole—a glorious high-end laptop that the Muse operates through a remote that she cradles in her palm.

Din clicks to conceal a window before Max can see what's on it. She fixes her gaze on Max. He feels like she can see through him. The soft hiss of the ventilation system is the only noise for a seeming eternity. The other two muses' lips move in a silent whisper.

Max glances at Molly. "What's going on?"

Din speaks: "Thank you. That will be all."

"What?" Molly says.

"What do you mean, 'that will be all'?" Max says.

"We appreciate your visit, and we have no need of your services at this time."

Molly tickles Max's ear as she leans in to whisper. "They don't trust you."

Just when he was starting to feel like he might get a clue about what's going on, this happens. And for once, the HUD isn't providing any guidance on what to do. "So that's it? I give you valuable data, collected at great personal risk, and you just take it and send me away?"

A tiny hint of a smile from Din. "You have spirit. Perhaps even enough."

"Enough for what?" Max snaps.

"To endure the sacrifice necessary to continue with this discussion."

"Sacrifice?" Max sputters. Molly puts a hand on his shoulder, and the simple gesture takes him aback. She's not the comforting type. "I already gave you the last thing I had of value. What more do you want from me?"

Din laughs, the soft sound scarcely louder than breathing. "Oh, you misunderstand. I refer not to a mere transactional token, but rather to the inevitable outcomes entailed by your choice here."

Max clamps his eyes shut to think. "You're saying that once I start down the dark path, forever will it dominate my destiny."

"Well…yes," Din says. "Except that we are on the opposite side of the dark path."

"I'll do it," Max says. "Wherever that ends up leading me."

Din clicks to reveal the window she hid earlier.

Even this close, Max squints to read the microscopic text on the screen. He's never imagined a display could have such resolution. There's too much going on—too many windows—information overload. But the new window makes sense to him: a terminal. He's seen Nolan type commands and get immediate responses. He reads:

```
<LevelUP corporation>
```
[2]

corp:archives:oceo Hemera↑Krapht $

Max gasps. The terminal is logged into an internal LevelUP server, in Hemera's private space. "What is this?"

"The key to the next trophy," Din says.

"Sure this isn't a honeypot?" Molly asks.

"Look closer," Din says.

Molly and Max rearrange themselves until Molly can just reach the laptop's keyboard with her good arm. Her fingers fly across the keyboard. She calls up a listing of files. "What's an oceo? Ohhh. Office of the CEO. Why would she—" Wait, there's something else. "Hemera's not big on selfies. So why does she keep a jpeg file in her private sandbox?"

"A photo? Of what?" Max asks.

"Can't look at a photo in a terminal. Do you have somewhere I can download this file to?" Molly asks.

"No. And all trace of this connection will be destroyed once you log out," Din says. "There must not be a single thread linking us to this intrusion, once LevelUP learns of it."

"Maybe it's a mislabeled text file," Max says. "How can we be sure it's an image at all?"

"Points," Molly says, copying Max's favorite phrase. "Let me see if it has EXIF."

"Exif?"

Molly does something else, and a bunch of text streams into the window—line after line of short meaningless words, places in the file where scattered alphabetic characters grouped together. But then:

```
From the graveyard, go N, W, S, W.
```

"Why does that sound familiar?" Max asks.

"That's the way into the graveyard in original Zelda," Molly says.

"So, we need to find a graveyard? Where?"

"If that means what I think, we won't have to go far," Molly says.

"It's dangerous to go alone," Din says.

Molly looks at her expectantly. "Take this," she mouths. Din doesn't react.

"Take this." Max checks to see what just chimed into his inventory.

"Medicine, huh. How's that supposed to work?" Max asks.

"If you get hurt, you can—"

"No, I understand the game mechanic. I'm not a savage," Max

says. He looks at his hands. "But this is the real world. I can't heal a real would with a virtual potion. Can I?"

"We gotta go. It's not far," Molly says.

Not far, in this case, means around the corner, to Room 303 in the same building. Molly punches in the provided access code but stops before entering the last digit. "Something's not right here," she says.

"What?" Max asks.

"The screens," Molly says.

"Well, sure," Max says. "Just like in the Colossal Cave, or whatever that underground lair deserves to be called."

"No, that's different," Molly says. "The cave's screens weren't factory new. They were all models that existed before Damage. The Muses had newly-designed screens."

"Hey, you brought me here. You're the one who's vouched for them. Now all of a sudden you're suspicious?"

Molly frowns, little wrinkles forming at the top of her nose. "Something feels weird this time."

"*Now* it feels weird? What's so weird about new monitors?" Max asks.

"Because there can't be new hardware without functioning factories."

Max makes a gesture for go on...

"Factories are expensive," Molly says. "If and only if they produce useful things, in sufficient quantity, they turn a profit. You know, capitalism. No good to have a factory producing secret goods in limited quantity.

"Technology factories are complicated. They required computers to keep everything running. Once the computers stopped working, they went offline. So, replace the computers, right? Scavenge up old 286 PCs and Commodore 64s and NES consoles to run the factory again. Easy right? Not so fast. None of the software that controlled the factories ran on ancient hardware. So, rewrite the software, right? Nope. Writing software requires software tools. And none of the software-writing-software ran on ancient hardware. Everything needs to start over.

"By the time that gadgets start appearing again, the reboot is nearly complete. Technology is almost ready for the next leap forward."

Max hasn't seen Molly this animated before. "But that's a good thing, right?" Max asks.

"Not if we don't know why Damage happened in the first place," Molly says.

Max knows about the many rumors that continue to spread wildly even to this day. Aliens. Time travelers from the future. Divine intervention. But none of them make as much sense as what Molly's just said.

Max's attention snaps back to the moment. Door 303 clicks unlocked, and Molly pushes it open. This space is barely larger than the Muses' room, albeit with a higher ceiling. It has similarities though: unfinished walls and the cheapest carpet imaginable. On the floor is a NES console, plugged into the wall for power, and twin leads running from the connector ports. But the wires run not to control pads, but to person-sized platforms with guard rails, and long-forgotten VR connectors consisting of bulky goggles and an Ultra Power Glove, something that, up to this moment, Max had heard of only in rumors.

Retro gaming had a huge boom after Damage, though at that

point calling it "retro" was stretching the truth. Games and peripherals native to the refurbished technology of the day went through a renaissance. But even through all that, Max had never been well-off enough to play on a full VR rig.

"Brain Attic," Molly says, a hint of awe in her voice.

Could it be? Once, when Nolan somehow got his hands on a dozen Token Ring network adapters, one of the shadiest characters Max had ever traded with made his way into their camp, and took them off his hands. The payment kept him afloat for a month. Only after-the-fact did Max learn that the buyer was a suspected envoy for the Brain Attic project.

This must be an entrance to Brain Attic, an 8-bit shared reality exclusive to the few folks who could get their hands on the hardware—and entrance fees—necessary to participate. Certainly nobody from the camps had ever played it.

"I love this game," Molly says, and steps onto the platform.

Wait, what? Molly?

The surface under Molly smoothly scrolls as she takes a step. She carefully slides the headset over her face. She's blind to the outside world with that on, but still she reaches for the power glove and slides it into place like a practiced movement.

Max follows suit. Even touching this equipment feels dirty, staining his fingers. Everything about Brain Attic goes against what he stands for. Yet here he is.

The headset, upon closer inspection, is more than just goggles. It feels heavy and unbalanced, like it's about to fall off his face. It's utterly dark inside. Is there a power switch? The display flickers, a split-second of painful white, followed by decaying scanlines.

Then the world materializes.

---

1. Research suggests that playing Tetris soon after viewing traumatic material may reduce the number of flashbacks. Nobody told Max this.
2. http://levelupcorp.online
3.

1-7 THE EIGENTHEIF_

INVENTORY:

* MEDICINE

* COIN

* TROPHY 1

* MYSTERIOUS SCROLL

The scene teeters as Max adjusts his headset. His eyes focus past granulated countryside bounded on one side by sheer stone walls that communicate a boundary more than any sign could. Max faces a tall monument constructed from slate-gray stones and black mortar. A tiny row of red hearts appears whenever Max glances down. He turns to look around, and the ensuing wave of nausea nearly topples him.

Everything about this place assaults the senses. The colors are just a little brighter than anything material. Every object within sight is just a bit too immediate. Even through the pixelation, more real than real. The soundscape is fully modeled too. A small bird flies past, its shrill call carving through space until it's behind him. Max turns his head to follow, and his stomach lurches. *People pay for this?*

A scrawny creature—monkey?—meerkat?—hedgehog?—hard to tell beneath those huge cartoonish eyes—waddles up and tugs at Max's hand. Its fingers have squishy pads, dry and warm to the touch. "Whoa-ho! Take it easy there, pard'ner. This your first time?"

Max ignores the distraction. "Molly? Are you here?" Would they have both been placed at the same starting location? Would she be able to hear him?

He needs to find her, but every second brings a new distraction. It makes sense how people could spend days on end immersed in an environment like this. Soon he can't even notice the pixels anymore, unless he really concentrates.

Another tiny creature, identical to the first, materializes out of nowhere and says something indistinct to someone on the opposite side of the monument.

"No, I've been nauseated lots of times," a familiar voice replies.

"Molly!" Max peeks around the brickwork, but runs into an odd sensation, like he's run against an invisible barrier. The immersion is fragile, especially when he tries to move around. He still has some sense of his real body, the one wearing the VR glasses and power glove against his skin. His actual forehead, bumping against the crumbling sheetrock.

"Careful," Max says, rubbing his forehead. "This simulation doesn't handle moving around too well.

"Working fine for me," Molly says, flexing five working fingers where her prosthetic hand normally appeared. She stretches her arm behind her, producing loud pops from her shoulders and elbows.

"*Is* this your first time in this game?" Max asks.

"Sure," Molly says. Her tone is so neutral that Max can't figure out if she's being sincere or sarcastic.

"Okay. Try walking toward me. Look out, there's a—"

"I don't need practice," Molly says. "I pick up on things quickly. Worry about yourself."

Max carefully plans his next step, and stumbles anyway. Up close, the tufts of grass sprouting from the ground blossom into blurry rectangles.

Better to not think about it too much. Max rises and takes another step, much like he would back in the real world. Smooth. He's got this. Probably. "Where's this graveyard?" Max asks.

"First we need to get a sword," Molly says.

"But we're only here to find what the Muses were talking about," Max says. "Why would we need a sword?"

"Trust me," Molly says. "Always get the sword first."

Max looks around. "What about that cave?" Max says.

Of course. It's dangerous to go alone. They descend into the cave, dark except for two fires burning. The old man who inexplicably seems to live there gives them each a rickety wooden sword, Max's chiming into his inventory.

"Do you know where the graveyard is?" Max asks the old man, but he doesn't veer from his programmed silence.

Back in the overworld, they venture north through a narrow channel in the rock formation, into a forested area. They pass through a boundary where the world seems to pause around them before the next scene scrolls into view. They've just crossed into another screen.

"Watch out!" Molly screams and flings herself out of the way of a wooden club, bigger around than her body, that shakes the earth as it crashes down. Attached to the club is a giant hand, and attached to that an even bigger cyclops, who looks prepared to eat horses (much less adventurers). He towers over both of them.

"You never said there'd be monsters!" Max says.

"I said always get a sword," Molly corrects, then whirls around in an uncharacteristically graceful move, landing a clean slash against the monster's bare chest. It doesn't even leave a mark. "Oh," she says, backing away.

The monster turns on Molly, leaving his back exposed to Max. This is his moment. He drives the sword home with both hands. An explosion of pain rockets through his clenched fists. For a sliver of a moment, the real world seeps back in. In a tiny room, Max just pounded indentations into the drywall of room 303. But in the game world, the wooden blade bounces harmlessly off the cyclops's thick hide, reflecting the full force of Max's strike back into his arms.

"We can't win," Max says. "The monster's too strong."

"No time to level grind," Molly says. "Hemera could be getting the next trophy as we stand here." She ducks, another whistling attack passing over her head.

"Why would they put such a powerful boss character one screen away from the start," Max says. "That hardly seems sporting."

Molly freezes, a faraway look in her eyes. She dances away from another attack. "You're right. There's something we're missing. There has to be a way to defeat the cyclops. I need a second to think. Keep him busy."

Keep him busy? This isn't going to end well. "Hey, monobrow— Over here!" The monster glances Max's way but turns attention back toward Molly. "Hey! Your mother was a hamster!" Max hurls a stone at the beast. "And your father smelt of..." That captures his attention. The monster turns to face Max.

"Uh, Molly? A bit of hurry-up?" Max stumbles backward, but something catches under his foot and he stumbles backward. His hand scrabbles for another rock, but there's nothing nearby.

Imminent skull-crushing has a funny way of clearing the mind. Max suddenly remembers: he's been in this situation before. In one of the Zork games he's played with Nolan reading off the screen. There's a room with a fearsome cyclops, one far too strong to defeat in combat. But there's a shortcut around the whole situation.

Confronted with a fearsome cyclops, a fight could be avoided by saying...

"Xyzzy!"

Nothing happens. That's not the magic word here. "Plugh?" No, of course. It's—

"Ulysses[1]!"

The cyclops groans in agony, as if the word inflicts searing pain. His roar is loud enough to rattle the visor on Max's face. The monster mashes his broad hands into his ears, to no avail.

"Yes, Ulysses," Max says. "Your father's deadly nemesis!"

"Ulysses!" Molly joins in.

The cyclops stumbles in haste, flattening several trees, and a scattering of items spills out across the ground.

The monster disappears into the forest, and Max and Molly collect the spoils. There's a cartoonish bomb, which Max picks up, and a book bound in glossy black cloth.

Molly says, "A bomb will come in handy. But what's that book thing?"

Max picks it up. It feels heavier than seems reasonable for a book. He tries to open it but can only clumsily bat it around; more like a solid block than a hardcover. "How do you read this?" he asks.

"Probably need to be in the right situation for it to become active," Molly says.

"Let's keep moving. Maybe we'll run into somebody we can ask about the graveyard," Max says.

A tenor voice answers. "Run into somebody, you have. Stand a little less taller, for you are in the presence of The Eigenthief!"

"*The* Eigenthief?" Max says, emphasis on the first word.

The dashing figure wears all black, from boots to belt to pirate shirt, all the way up to the black mask covering his eyes. "Yes, *The* is part of my name. Nicely done with the cyclops, by the way. Most newbies here don't figure that out without dying a few dozen times. I'm sure you have no idea how rare of a rare drop item that book is. Now, if you'd be so kind, hand it over, and I can be on my way."

Max notices the substantial sword hanging from the man's belt. What would happen if they died here? Not much. Except for losing what chance they had at recovering the trophies before Hemera gets to them. That's too much to risk.

Max holds the book out in offering.

Max doesn't see it coming. The next thing he realizes, the book is on the ground, Molly kicking him in the shins, and kicking it aside. Well, since this environment doesn't have any foot controls, so it's more like angrily walking into the book until it gets pushed out of the way. Speaking of which, how is it that his shins actually hurt from that?

"You call yourself a proper thief? Molly says to The Eigenthief. "You're just a two-bit thug."

The Eigenthief looks wounded. "Two-bit?" His face darkens.

Max braces for battle. His hand finds its way to the wooden hilt of his sword. A deadly quiet settles over the world. Even the birds shut up.

The Eigenthief eyes Max and Molly. The moment stretches.

Time passes.

At last the Eigenthief opens his mouth—and tosses his head back to laugh, long and hard.

"It's as plain as cærulean night that you have nothing to offer me, beyond the book of course. Which, I might add, I could, at any moment of my choosing, easily extract from your care by force. I'm sure you'd prefer to conclude our dealings without undue discomfort on your parts." He bows deeply.

"You mean on our part. Singular," Max says.

The Eigenthief straightens. "No, I quite deliberately refer to a plurality of your parts. It's a threat, you see." He takes a step toward the book. Molly moves to block him, but doesn't draw her sword.

"My, isn't that droll," The Eigenthief says. "You two are simply adorable. Now, I want you to look closely at my sword. No, my lad, eyes over here. Yes, look. This is a level 20 dancing vorpal blade. It could practically cut you down with as little as the thought to do so. In fact, I'm practically holding it back as I speak. Your pitiful ligneous blades would wither against it like green twigs in a brushfire."

"Are you an AI?" Molly asks.

Where did that come from? What did she see?

The question seems to catch The Eigenthief off guard. "What did you say?"

"You don't talk like a PC. Are you real?" Molly asks.

"Not a Player Character? Of course I'm real. What kind of preposterous question is that? I take great pride in my not-at-all-pompous speech."

"Oh yeah? What's 741 times 538?"

"Why, three hun— Wait a minute. How did I know that?" The Eigenthief's countenance falls toward his boots. He strokes his goatee and says, "'Tis incredible. I must be some kind of savant! Ask me another."

"286 times 69,105," Molly says.

"Nineteen million, seven hundred sixty-four thousand, and— By the Leather Goddesses— For once I am rendered speechless."

"Hang on," Max says. "Are you seeing words appearing in your field of vision? Like a little HUD?"

"I have no idea what you're talking about, lad," The Eigenthief says. Everyone is quiet for a moment, then he speaks again:

"For the first time in my life, I'm not sure what I'm supposed to do next."

"Do you believe we could help you?" Molly asks. "Do you trust us?"

"You, young lady, I believe could do anything," The Eigenthief says. "And yes, I trust you. Moreso if you'd leave your quarrelsome companion behind."

"Come with us," Max offers, ignoring the slight. "We are on an important quest, and we could use someone familiar with the area. Otherwise, we could spend all day looking for the graveyard."

"The graveyard you say?" The Eigenthief says. "It's like my second home."

"Your second home is a graveyard?" Max asks.

"LOGIC ERROR, INITIATING CORE DUMP," The Eigenthief says in a harshly mechanical voice. Max and Molly both take a step back. Then he collapses.

Molly runs up to him. It's difficult to take the pulse of someone made out of pixels, but she at least makes an effort to check his vitals. "Are you okay?"

The Eigenthief's body begins violently shaking. Is he sobbing?

He wipes away tears with the back of his hand. The scoundrel's laughing! Max feels his fists tighten inside the power gloves.

"Ohh, that was rich," The Eigenthief says, slurring. "You shoulda seen the looks on your faces. Oh, I had you going. Both of you. A hunnert percent."

Max steps toward The Eigenthief, but Molly gets in his way. "No."

"You seemed pretty OK with slashing at a cyclops a few minutes ago," Max says.

"He said he'd help us. So, let him," Molly says.

The Eigenthief springs to his feet again and brushes himself off.

"Very well, I shall trek with you," The Eigenthief says, in his usual sententious voice. "Let me just fetch that silly little book, should a need arise for—"

Max notices that Molly already has her hand on the hilt of her sword. But they both turn to see what The Eigenthief is looking at. The book.

The glossy black of the cover is now a puddle sinking into the earth. Burned tufts of grass along the edge of the black wilt, leaving an ugly smear of brown death.

"I wouldn't touch that," Molly says.

Max nods in agreement.

Molly looks at The Eigenthief. "You were saying?"

The Eigenthief scowls. "On second thought, maybe we should just leave it there."

"Let's get out of here," Max says. "To the graveyard!"

With a lingering look back, The Eigenthief agrees and leads them ahead.

---

1. "Odysseus" would've worked too.

1-8 GRAVEYARD_

INVENTORY:

* MEDICINE

* COIN

* TROPHY 1

* MYSTERIOUS SCROLL

* WOODEN SWORD

* BOMB

The Eigenthief marches them clear of the forest, leading along a narrow body of water. White pixels indicate that the water's agitated, but when Max looks closely, it seems to resolve into something approximating photorealistic. The flat horizon makes it hard to tell whether this is a skinny lake or a slow river. Either way, they come to a sharp turn where dry land hairpins around the edge of the water.

As the travelers arrange single-file to pass, The Eigenthief steps aside, leaving Max to go first. The ground ahead is flat and tan, with small disturbances unevenly spaced out. They haven't come across any enemies since they arrived at the waterside. "Why haven't we run across any—"

Something changed. Somehow, the scene ahead of them is different. One of the piles of earth shift. A blue tentacle erupts from the ground with a spray of dust, followed by countless others, arranged in a circle. The creature pulls itself above ground, squeezing its bulbous head into the open air until its soulless eyes—the size of saucers—stare them down.

"Octopodes!" Molly says, carefully laying down all four syllables.

"Are they dangerous?" Max asks. One erupts from the ground, squirting sickly green ink at Max, who narrowly avoids getting slimed.

"Only when they do that," Molly says.

A blade flashes, an energy beam flying from The Eigenthief's sword, striking the monster square on. It crumples into nothing.

"You never said you could shoot laser beams," Max says.

"You never asked," The Eigenthief replies. "Magic sword. Let's keep moving. And watch out for bugs."

"Bugs?" Molly asks?

"You haven't seen the bugs? How long has it been since you've played?"

"About ten years," Molly says.

The Eigenthief whistles. "Oh, look, there's one."

"One wha—" Max asks, diving for cover to avoid what looks like a large pineapple with a blur of wings and forward-deployed razor blades. The harsh buzz it makes echoes in Max's skull until it abruptly stops.

Max stands triumphant, blade raised. "Ha! I drove it off."

The air stands thick with what could best be described as burnt rubber mingled with road kill—left in the sun for a week. The stench of fear?

"Nice move," Molly says, flatly.

The Eigenthief raises an eyebrow, a look of true admiration in his eyes. Maybe this is a turning point in Max's fortunes. It would be hard for anything to go worse than it already had.

Travel through the overworld goes on much like this. No wonder the designers had to keep adding ever more outrageous enemies to face—turns out that traveling long distances is dead boring. Moly opines at length at the various warp options in other games, but this one doesn't seem to have one. Perhaps the designers were a bit too enamored of their "full immersion" technology and didn't plan for how quickly the novelty wore off.

Over several minutes, the ground grows sandier, darker brown with red pixels scattered around to suggest texture.

When the next confrontation nears, The Eigenthief announces, "Step aside, striplings, and leave this job to a professional. This one's a doozy."

Molly and Max exchange a look, then Max shrugs. The Eigenthief charges ahead, letting loose with a full-throated battle cry.

"Question. What made you think The Eigenthief was an AI?"

"He *is* an AI," Molly responds. "Whether I think it or not."

"Fine, whatever. But how did you know? What gave it away?"

"You know, I'm right here, and I have excellent hearing," The Eigenthief says, risking a look over his shoulder. "A little assistance would be helpful." He dodges a snapping duckbill and parries with a flourish.

"See? He's funny," Max says. "AI's don't have a sense of humor"

"Do you mean 'ha ha' funny or the other kind?" the Eigenthief asks.

"I just know," Molly says. "I can *tell*. Besides, no meat-brain would ever choose a name as dorky as Eigenthief."

"*THE* Eigenthief, thank you," The Eigenthief says. "Say it right!"

"Speaking of names, we need something less of a mouthful," Max says. "I'm going to go crazy if I have to keep wrapping my mouth around *The Eigenthief*."

"Hey, *Prince of Thieves* was already taken," The Eigenthief says, and takes a mighty swing against the enemy. The deafening quack doesn't echo.

"I'm not arguing against the logic," Molly says. "The name is perfectly logical. *Too* perfectly. I say we call him ET for Eigenthief."

"That should be T.E. *The* goes first," E.T. says.

"ET sounds better," Max says, just as a giant beak comes crashing to the ground alongside him. Downy feathers rain from the sky.

"At least, it's better than a snapper-up of unconsidered trifles[1]," ET says. "That was from Sha—

Something resembling a mushy brown hubcap erupts from the

ground in the spot where Max was about to set foot. Whatever it is, it has frowny eyebrows above beady little eyes and a porcine snout.

Something happens and Max stares down at the two clean-cut pieces wriggling in the dirt. "This I kind of scaring me."

"Porcinis," ET says. "I hate those things. Worse yet, they almost never drop items."

"Look, how far to the graveyard?" Max asks.

"Not too much farther," ET says. "First we need to ford the stream."

"That doesn't sound too hard," Max says.

"Then another desert."

"Um…"

"And then scale Massacre Mountain."

"Seriously?"

ET scans the water leading to the opposite shore. "Yeah. This is the spot. Follow me closely. Whatever happens, don't let the water go above your waist."

"What happens if it does?" Molly asks.

"Then you'll look really stupid in a wet shirt," ET says. "C'mon."

The water here looks a slightly darker shade of blue, forming a meandering line across to the other side. As long as they stay on the darker water, it doesn't splash any higher than their mid-thigh.

Max is nearly across when he notices Molly frozen in place on the opposite shore. "Molly, just walk through it. It's not bad. You don't even feel it."

"I don't like water," Molly says. "I never go in it."

"That's fine," Max says. "But remember. This isn't water. It's not wet. It's just pixels."

Molly sets one foot in the water, but she can't seem to bring herself to put the other in.

"Molly, don't even think about it. It's exactly like walking. In fact, it's another platform game. The darker water's the platform. Come on, Molly. You're the queen of platformers. I've seen you ace your way through level after level hardly glancing at the screen. All this is, in the end, is another game. No big deal. Yes! You've got it."

Bit by bit, she does get it. She manages the crossing without further incident.

A narrow gap between dense trees leads them away from the water and back into the forest, but the landscape quickly turns hotter and drier. Soon the ground they walk over becomes lighter until it looks like salt.

"The Vastness," ET says. "But don't lollygag. Many eyes are upon us."

"Like those?" Molly asks, pointing at the ground.

A pair of eyestalks pokes up from underground. The pupils are a disconcerting oblong shape, following their movement. The earth trembles, and more of the creature emerges from the cascade of sand. A tentacle whips past Max, and curls around Molly's leg, before powerfully retracting.

The force yanks Molly clear off her feet and drags her along the ground. For a split second, Max wonders what this must feel like for her actual body back in room 303.

Max snaps out of reverie in time to brandish his wooden sword. The tentacle is tough, but with sufficient tenderizing, it lets go.

"Watch your step," ET says. "Those things burrow. They'll pop up exactly where you're standing."

They continue on. Max stares at the ground in front of him so hard that he gets a headache. Eventually, the end of the desert is marked by sheer cliffs of a fake-looking (even by pixel standards) mountain.

"Massacre Mountain," ET says. "A little on-the-nose, wouldn't you say?"

"You never said the graveyard was up a mountain," Max says. "Who puts a graveyard at high elevation?"

"Not all the way up," ET corrects. "Come on, the sooner we get going, the sooner we get there."

"How do we climb?" Molly says.

The question takes ET by surprise. "Oh, right," he says. "I forget that you're new here. You haven't unlocked Mountain Goat yet. Hmmm. This calls for Plan B."

"What's Plan B?" Molly asks.

"What's Mountain Goat?" Max asks.

ET mutters to himself, but occasional words slip out clearly enough to be heard. "Catapult?... no... Eagles?... Teleport... Stairs?" He brightens suddenly. "That's right, we can take the elevator!"

Molly squints at the sheer rock face. "Elevator?" she simply says.

"No elevator in this world can go up a mountain, but there's a one in the Veiled World."

"Never heard of it," Max says.

"Give me your bomb," ET says. Max hands it over and ET carefully places it alongside a particularly pronounced crack in the rock. It shatters in a puff of smoke. A door, darker than black, as if constructed from shadow itself, coalesces out of the smoke. "After you," ET says.

The Veiled World resembles the regular game world with a filter that blocks 90 percent of all light. But there are other changes too. Most notably, a narrow elevator platform rhythmically rises and falls of its own accord. The jump mechanics leave much to be desired, but Max makes it across in his first attempt. Molly and ET follow.

The platform pauses at the bottom and rises again. Even though he knows his body isn't actually moving; his inner ears can't be registering actual movement, what he sees through his eyes disagrees with that assessment. The sudden wave of nausea that ensues almost makes Max fall off the side. But the world flickers back into full color, then seems to spin around Max, and suddenly he's lying flat with ET standing over him.

"Hey," ET says, "You didn't look like you were going to make the jump, so I gave you a little hand. You do *not* want to get stuck in the Veil, believe me. Thank me later."

Without Max really doing anything, his character shuffles back to a standing position, the system once again in balance with Max's physical body. He keeps getting thrown out of full immersion.

He looks around. A grassy plateau. Hard to tell with the pixels, but it looks as manicured as a golf course. Not that Max has ever been on a golf course, but he's seen pictures.

There's a hundred-ish unmarked white stones arranged in uniform rows.

"This isn't the graveyard," Molly says.

"Of course it is," ET says. "Look—graves."

"This isn't the place," Molly says.

Max wanders up and down the rows, looking for something. Anything. Then he sees it. "One of the graves is marked," Max calls out to the others.

Molly and ET gather around. It's a simple slab, a slightly darker shade than the rest, engraved with the following:

In loving memory of Alan Turing, the father of computation.[2]

Engraved on the stone is an apple with crossbones beneath it. All three bow their heads in a moment in silence.

---

1. A Winter's Tale, Act 4, Scene 3
2. The engraving also includes the image of an apple with a bite taken out of it, a detail not included here for trademark reasons.

1-9 ET PWN HOME_

INVENTORY:

* MEDICINE

* COIN

* TROPHY 1

* MYSTERIOUS SCROLL

* WOODEN SWORD

"There's got to be something here," Molly says. "A hint. Something." ET tries to get leverage on a gravestone to push it aside, but it doesn't budge.

Max inspects the surface for hidden cracks. "We need another bomb," he says. "Maybe I could blow open Turing's tombstone to reveal a hidden passageway."

"No," Molly says. "No self-respecting game designer would make deliberately desecrating Alan Turing's grave part of the mission."

"I'd bet most players don't even know who Alan Turing is," ET counters.

"It doesn't matter what most players think," Molly says. "All that matters here is what one person thinks—the person who designed this part of the game."

Max can't come up with a good counter to that argument. "Okay, okay. What about the crossbones engraving? Why are they under an apple instead of a skull?"

"Alan Turing died by poison apple," Molly says.

"Really?" Max says.

"Crossbones," ET muses. "Well, there *is* the boneyard."

"What?!" say Max and Molly at the same time.

Max moves aggressively into ET's personal space. His voice is low. "You knew about a place called the boneyard, and brought us here first?"

"You...you distinctly said graveyard. Excuse me for being an preeminent listener."

Max deflates. "Fine. Let's go. Which way to the boneyard?"

"It's at the far western reaches," ET says.

"That sounds...far," Molly notes with her typical deadpan accuracy.

"Then the sooner we get going, the sooner we'll get there," Max says.

They descend through the Veil and battle through the desert, back the way they came. At the forest, they change tack and proceed through a golden plain, flush with a barley approximation tat obscures the view of surrounding landscape.

Max spots the predator before anyone else does. It's a golden-brown knot the size of a fist, barely visible above the grain heads. It tracks alongside them, moving forward in stealthy bursts. Through a small gap, Max sees a bit more—segmented modules ending in a jointed tail, the upper node terminating with a sharp stinger the size of a steak knife.

Max freezes.

"Scorpires," ET says. "Very dangerous. One nick and they'll keep handing out damage until you find a healer. Assuming you're able to make it to a healer."

"What do we do?" Molly asks.

"Don't get stung," ET says.

"Molly, do you see something we're not?," Max says.

Before she can answer, the stinger twitches and bounds across the grain tops directly toward Max. With the grace of an ox, he lunges out of the way, swinging his sword against the raised tail.

The sword bounces off without leaving a mark. His hands ache. Was that an electrical shock?

"Also, don't bother attacking them with weapons of your quality," ET says.

"Gee thanks," Max says.

Max spots a second stinger camouflaged among the grain heads. Once he spots it, it's easier to pick out the third one. Then the fourth and fifth. "It's a trap!"

Molly pulls away from the group, doing her own thing again. "We don't have time for this. Here!" There's a rocky outcropping just to their left, away from the Scorpire swarm. The monsters come up to the edge of the grassy area, but no farther.

Max catches a glimpse of their mighty front claws, peeking out from the gaps between stalks.

"How much farther is the boneyard?" Max asks.

"It's right there," Molly says, pointing at a distant smear of pixels on the horizon, on the far side of the vast swampy wetland.

"How can you even see that?" ET asks, with what sounds like genuine admiration.

"She just knows things sometimes," Max says. "Once you get over how annoying it is, you start to appreciate how useful it is."

Molly chucks Max on the shoulder.

"Ow! If I had pain receptors in my rig, that would've really hurt!" Max makes a show of rubbing his shoulder while he scans the land ahead of them. From the grassland to the swamp is maybe a hundred paces. "Well, if Molly says so, I trust her. Let's make a run for it."

"We need a bigger caravan," ET says. "It's too dangerous to cross the Everett swamp, just the three of us. We need to get more help."

"Two things," Molly says, ticking off with her fingers. Max has never seen her this agitated before. "One, there isn't anyone else to ask. Two, even if there was somebody available to help—and there isn't—no time. Every minute we spend here is another minute Hemera gets ahead of us."

"Hermera, you say?" ET asks. "You know her?"

"Yeah, we've run into her a few times," Max admits.

"And you're trying to do something that will annoy, harass, deprive, thwart, or otherwise euchre Hemera?"

"Yes," Molly says.

"Euchre?" Max asks.

"Well, why didn't you say so to begin with?" ET says. "But if you've got any extra armor, or leather, or fabric…anything, wrap up your legs. More's the better."

"I don't like the sound of that," Molly says.

"I don't like it either, but we've got no choice," Max says. "Ready?"

ET picks up a loose chunk of rock and throws it in the opposite direction. Immediately, the scorpries converge on it. "Now or ne'er," he says.

The three of them bound off the rock and stride through the tall grass. The scorpires don't take long to catch on to the ruse. Max doesn't stop to look back, but the sound of crunching stalks behind him gets closer until it sounds like they're right on top of him. The water is too far away. He'll never make it…

Max's foot tangles on something, and down he tumbles. His closest pursuer crashes into him, a painful thwack against his ribs that sends the beast wildly rolling over and past him. It splashes into water and shrieks with a ghastly bellow. Avoiding the flailing limbs, Max pitches himself sideways, just enough to avoid the lash of another oncoming scorpire. The rest are coming at him too fast for him to find his feet.

The next monster rushes for him, deadly tail taking precise aim at his throat. Max scrambles, but his hands, slick with glistening sweat, can't get traction. He braces for impact. A wire hook snags the plunging stinger and twists it with an awful crunch. Molly. Her good hand finds one of Max's, and help him up, sheer momentum pulling him ahead.

The entering-water mechanic is clumsy, with a hissy splash and abrupt drop of the eyeline to a few inches above the water. The swarm of scorpires stops at water's edge, angrily hissing. Max allows himself to breathe again.

From there on, walking precipitates a juicy squishing noise and motion-sickness-inducing bob from side to side. Forward walking speed varies depending on unseen variances in the underwater landscape, which only makes the movement feel more jarring.

Minutes into the trek, Max begins to wonder what all the hassle was about wrapping up his legs. Then he realizes. "Something just bumped me! I can't see into the water."

"You can't see them. Many have tried," ET says. "And that wasn't a bump. That was a bite. Some say the piranhas are completely invisible, which, living in black water would be technically true."

"Piranhas! You didn't say anything about piranhas!" Max screams.

Another nip at Max's leg, this one hard enough break his stride. Blood red pixels mingle in the dark water. A life meter materializes at the bottom of Max's field of vision, a row of hearts, the rightmost one no longer red. And there's still a long way through the bog. Unlike the terror on land, this happens slowly enough for him to really contemplate his fate. He can't shake the vision of his avatar descending into the black filth, never to be seen again. And back in the real world, Hemera seizing control of the refugee camp, razing it to the ground, just because she felt like it, and because nobody else was strong enough to stop her.

"I'm not going to make it," Max says.

"Max!" Molly says. "How dare you? You *are* going to make it. And if you so much as *think* like that again, I'm going to kick you in the pants so hard you won't sit for a week."

The force of Molly's words hits Max harder than her foot would have. In the years he's known her, he's never witnessed anything quite like it. The difference this time was how much she cared about the outcome.

Max feels another sharp jolt at the same spot the piranhas have been working on. He pulls out his sword and thrusts the point into the water, just missing his leg. Judging by the feel, he made solid contact. He hefts the sword out of the water, and there's nothing on it. Or is there? It's unbalanced and heavy...

"Well, ET, I believe you may have been right. We've got invisible fish here. They're not too bright, and the wooden sword can take them out."

With more pauses to drive away the fish, the party at length finishes crossing the bog. Max steps on to dry land and immediately collapses to his knees and kisses the ground.

Their arrival at the boneyard is marked by a gigantic femur, at least twice the length of a human's, driven into the ground like a tent peg. They had arrived.

The boneyard consists of an immaculately groomed field of emerald grass surrounding a single tombstone. The edges run up against the unpassable rocky ledge that marks the edge of the game universe. Other than a scattering of dead trees, there's not much to it.

Max steps up to read the inscription, but it's a pixelated mess. No matter how close he gets, the pixels don't resolve into letters. He brushes encrusted dirt off, and at the moment he makes contact with the stone, it flashes, rapid flickers between gray and white, then a spectral figure pours itself upward into material form.

Max jumps back. "Is that a ghost?"

"No such thing as ghosts," ET says. "It's a Shade, and they get cranky when you wake them up. I suggest keeping your distance."

Molly's hand goes to her sword, but ET stops her. "It's not worth it."

"We don't have time for this," Max says. As he says this, a blurry light gathers around his feet. Not his feet, but in the lower reaches of what he can see. It moves with him when he turns his head. It's the HUD, though the VR visor confuses his eyes in a way that prevents him from reading it.

Max pulls the visor away from his face. The tiny room he's encased in feels unreal compared to the vast game world he's been submerged inside. Molly is there, still fully engrossed. A shrill beep sounds from the deck—"player one disengaged—rejoin or respawn in five seconds. Four. Three…"

A nice friendly warning about imminent failure of this whole mission. At least he can read the HUD again. It says: REMEMBER N W S W

Max snaps the visor back into place, and his mind swims while mediated reality reasserts. Then he's back. "I know the way," he says. "Follow me."

At the north end of the boneyard, there's a tidy path lined with tree stumps. It leads to another boneyard that looks identical to the one they just left.

"Did we just experience a glitch in the matrix?" Molly wonders out loud.

"There's two ways out of the boneyard heading west. Max picks the one that, like the northern exit, features a tree stump.

This too leads to another exact copy of the boneyard.

"If one of us stayed behind, and the rest went through there, would we run into each other again?" ET asks.

"Don't think about it too much," Max says. He takes them south, then west again.

This time they find themselves in a peaceful grove, tightly hemmed in on three sides by thick forest. In the middle is a monument of gleaming granite, three stairs leading to a pedestal. On top of that, protruding from a reddish boulder the size of a barrel from the earlier platform game, is a cup with the inscription of a jeweled scarab. A trophy.

Max pulls on the trinket, but it doesn't budge. He pulls harder, to no avail.

The stone underneath bears an inscription in a language for which Max can't even identify from the script. Unlike the tombstones, these letters are visible.

"What language is that?" Molly asks. "I've seen that before."

"Obviously one needs the secret in order to remove— Wait, you've seen that language before?"

"Yeah, you need—oh," Molly says.

"What?" Max asks.

"I think that book we left behind is required to decode the inscription," Molly says.

"The one that was covered with black goo?" Max says. His stomach churns. "This is so unfair!"

Throughout this exchange, ET keeps uncharacteristically quiet.

Max turns on him. "Why don't you contribute something useful to our quest instead of just standing there like an idiot."

ET's expression slowly morphs from his usual dour face into a smile. "If you insist," he says. He pulls his hands out from his pockets, and he's holding a tiny bomb. The fuse spits a stream of sparks. Where did he get that? Worry later—Max dives for cover, throwing out an arm to pull Molly to safety.

There's nothing to make them actually feel the concussion of the explosion, though Max's health meter[Health meter ref] drops by a third of its hearts. The controls are so sluggish to respond that Max isn't sure if he can get up again.

But he can still see. ET pulls a book out from inventory. Not just any book, but the book, still dripping with the black goo. Tendrils of it drape from the book to his sleeve.

"ET! Get away from that thing before it eats you!" Max shouts, but ET either doesn't hear, or doesn't care. ET opens the book, carefully searching for the symbols inscribed on the rock, and begins translating incantations.

Max struggles to right his character, but the controls aren't responding at all. He checks inventory. The trophy he'd collected is gone. When did he get pickpocketed?

"OK, fine," he says, "I admit it. You are the greatest thief I've ever met. Maybe even the greatest the world has ever seen. You stole the book while making us think we left it behind. Bravo. Even now, thinking back, I don't have the first clue even of when you pulled it off. You win. You're the greatest. Now get away from that thing before you get us all killed."

The Eigenthief (for it hardly seems right to Max to think of him any other way now) recites the translation with increased intensity, even as the black slime crawls across his face. In a loud voice, he calls out words from some forgotten language.

With a metallic grinding noise the jeweled scarab comes unstuck from the boulder and the Eigenthief tumbles backward off the platform, landing close to Max and Molly.

He stands tall. "You have no idea how long I've waited to get my hands on this," he says. "How many newbies I've had to bear through insufferable small talk and inane questions. It finally paid off."

"You're working for Hemera!" Molly says, her voice filled with outrage.

"Work for Hemera?" The Eigenthief sputters. "I shudder to think."

Max's head reels. Does this mean the Eigenthief was or wasn't an AI?

"I don't expect we'll meet again," the Eigenthief says, just as the black slime covers his mouth, and another tendril extends from the top of his head, quickly covering his entire face in black, followed by the rest of him. The black bubble surges and roils, then pops, splashing into an oily slick on the ground.

All that's left of The Eigenthief are his dropped items: a black cloak, and an unlit ivory torch. No trace of this trophy, nor the one Max had earlier collected. Max scoops the items into his inventory.

The black slime, not content to sit in a puddle, forms writhing pseudopods, the largest two zeroing in on Max and Molly.

Max grabs Molly by the hand and they flee into the forest. The black slime reaches the trees, which energizes it. The infection bounds from tree to tree, like a consuming fire, except that where the slime permeates the wood, it turns solid and glassy like ice. The only way out of the grove is back to the south, but the black ice outflanks them on both sides.

Then it closes around Max and Molly.

1-10 EATEN BY A GRUE_

INVENTORY:

* MEDICINE

* COIN

* MYSTERIOUS SCROLL

* WOODEN SWORD

* STEALTH CLOAK

* IVORY TORCH OF THE ENDLESS FIRE

It is dark. You have been eaten by a grue.

But not completely dark. A line of ghostly hearts blinks along the bottom third of Max's field of view. As if to emphasize their importance, they no longer get out of his way when not needed —a constant reminder of impending…

Damage. The red drains out of another heart. Running out of time and life. The trophy had been right there. Just out of reach. Now Max's character was about to die and get respawned at the starting location. He pulls out his wooden sword and attacks the black slime all around him. The sword crumbles to ash in his hands. Max screams in frustration.

Another heart. There's got to be something he can do. He got medicine from the Muses. He uses it and gets three red hearts back. But at the rate they're dropping, that will only buy him a few extra seconds.

What else? "Inventory," Max calls out.

INVENTORY:

* COIN

* MYSTERIOUS SCROLL

* STEALTH CLOAK

* IVORY TORCH OF THE ENDLESS FIRE

The Ivory Torch of the Endless Fire looks interesting, but Max can't see how useful it would be. Same goes for the cloak. But what about the coin?

Another heart.

The Eigenthief left the coin. What kind of coin would a thief keep?

"Inspect coin," Max says. Nothing happens. "Drop coin." Again, nothing. Well, at least one mystery solved. The coin is somehow trapped in inventory.

In other words, no good to him in his time of need. Another heart. Down to the last three.

Time slows. The darkness reminds Max of the bigger darkness that happened before. Damage. Adults rushed about like they could do something about the unfolding tragedy, but young Max huddled in the consuming darkness...

Every night seemed that dark for a long time. Max remembers more. He had hair sprouting from strange places on his body by the time he was able to fall asleep without a cold shiver rippling through his tense muscles.

So here's Max lying on his side in bed, curled in a tight fetal position. It's not a comfortable bed, so this must be the shelter. He lies perfectly still, not even reaching for an itch on his calf. If he can stay still enough, long enough, the feeling will pass, letting him wilt into an uneasy sleep. The itch builds in intensity, sharp as a pinprick. It burns!

When he can't stand it any longer, Max reaches to scratch. But a bigger, stronger hand catches his wrist.

"Easy," the voice says. Max has heard that voice before.

"Don't scratch, that'll just make it worse," the voice says. At that moment Max wishes above all else that his dad were there to comfort — his dad who abandoned him so long ago that he'd become more of an impression than a concrete memory. Max squeezes his eyelids tighter and tries to remember, but even that's gone.

"Never forget that you're the key to all of this. Get some sleep. You've been through a lot."

Another heart vanishes. The Game. Max was after something important. The trophy. What just happened? Was that a dream or a memory? Soon, it won't matter.

Never forget that you're the key. "Use key?" Max says tentatively.

Nothing happens except another heart winking out. Down to the last one. An insistent beeping rings in Max's ears. What else is there to do? The only usable thing in his inventory is that coin.

"Use coin."

1 CREDIT(S). PRESS START TO CONTINUE.

"Press start?" The sound of a trophy being added to inventory is the last thing Max hears before a sea of red consumes his world.

1-11 TROPHY_

LIGHT PIERCES MAX'S EYES. HE SCREAMS IN AGONY. THE stabbing light, the smell of sweat, the faint taste of injection molded plastic hanging in the air—it's too much. He sags to his knees and throws up.

Molly is there. She'd been there; helped him get his visor off. "What happened?" she asks. "It's all a blur. I died. Except...I continued..."

The trophy.

INVENTORY:

* MYSTERIOUS SCROLL

* STEALTH CLOAK

* IVORY TORCH OF THE ENDLESS FIRE

* TROPHY 2

"It worked! I have trophy number 2!"

"What happened to the trophy you had before?"

"Stolen right out from under me. Probably in Hemera's hands by now."

Max and Molly look at each other. The Muses would know. Molly reaches this conclusion at the same time. They turn toward the exit. Max wobbles on the way out the door, the adjustment back to the real world still working its way through his system. They reenter the Muses' room without knocking.

"Where did the other trophy end up?" Molly asks.

"Max puts a kind hand on her shoulder and addresses the Muses in a more conciliatory tone. "First of all, thank you for all your assistance. What Molly is asking is if you can help us pinpoint the locations of the rest of the trophies."

Din doesn't look up to address them. She works her keyboard, and a table pops up amidst a sea of other information on her screen.

```
Trophy 0x0 HEMERA^KRAPHT

Trophy 0x1 THE_EIGENTHI3F

Trophy 0x2 MAXROOT

Trophy 0x3 #REF!
```

"Who's Ref? Aren't they an offshoot of Anonymous?" Max asks.

"No," Din says. "In the language of the ancients, it means it's unclaimed."

"What happens to a trophy if it gets consumed by the black slime?"

Din speaks. "The Eigenthief and the 'black slime' as you call it are the same."

Time seems to slow again as Max lets this sink in.

"The disposition of the final trophy depends entirely on the disposition of the party controlling the previous ones," Din says.

"What's that mean in English?" Max asks.

He looks at Molly.

"There is another node," she says. "It has to operate point-to-point, so it can't be far from here. We can find it."

"You got all that from her cryptic saying?" Max asks.

"That and the email from Hemera," Molly says, pointing at the screen.

Max has to squint to read it, but indeed an email from Hemera is on display.

"You hacked her email too?" Neither Molly nor the Muses dignify that with a response.

"A peer-to-peer network," Din says. "The information can travel from one node to the next, but only during certain windows of time."

"Node?" Max asks.

"Isidore had a node," Molly says. "It was connected to the tower that everybody thought was a weather antenna."

"What, right in our camp?"

"It was the highest ground in the area. He could've had radio contact with half of Sunnyvale and Mountain View," Molly says.

"For security, they rotate the broadcast frequencies along a Morse-Thue series," Din says. "Any two given nodes can only communicate during the brief interval in which the sequences overlap."

"How big is the broadcast tower on this building, er, I mean, node we need to find?" Max asks.

Din makes a tiny movement with her eyes, directing Max's attention to a blue plastic box tucked behind her monitor. it's a garden variety wireless router with stubby black antennas about the size of fingers.

"Well, that's not going to push a signal very far, is it?" Max asks.

"Nowhere near as well as a weather tower," Din says.

"OK, so we'll have to get real nice and close, and at just the right time since it only broadcasts once in a while. Right place at the right time," Max says. "Maybe we can set up—"

"I never said the broadcast is intermittent," Din corrects. "The key exchange is periodic, but to avoid suspicion, every node broadcasts continuously with a signal that looks like an ordinary wireless access point."

"So how do we tell a node from every other boring access point?" Max asks. "Without going up and down every street?"

"We'd need a specially-modified…" Molly trails off. She almost seems to be communicating telepathically with Din. "No, you can't do that. It'd leave you completely cut off."

"Take it," Din says. "Strength to your arm and victory to your soul. When you return it, let us know what you've discovered."

Molly takes the box in her hand, a look of wonder in her eye.

As if in response, a blip in Max's HUD seizes his attention, and doesn't let go.

I HAVEN'T FORGOTTEN YOU. LOVE, DAD.

LEVEL 2_

PROGRESS

2-1 [F3]_

PROTESTATIONS ASIDE, MOLLY'S PERFECTLY CAPABLE OF riding the bike provided by the Muses. After a few initial wobbles, she pulls out ahead of Max.

The wi-fi router and a battery pack rests in the basket on her handlebars. They pedal single file down lonely, once-commercial streets. They come to a grim industrial park, buildings smashed open and looted bare, with nobody even to sweep away the broken glass scattered across the oil-stained parking lots.

They hurry through the neighborhood and pass into a residential district. Deathly quiet here too, and somehow sadder to be amidst row after row of abandoned houses.

"Look!" Molly says, pointing out a chimney from which a thin streamer of smoke curls. She slows her bike as they pass, but the hardware doesn't pick up even a blip of a signal.

"I wonder who lives there," Molly says.

"I wonder how they live there," Max says.

Around the corner they discover part of the answer: every tree has been roughly chainsawed down to a stump. "I'd hate to cook my food on green wood," Max comments. But there's no signal, so they move on.

Max soon loses count of how many of these streets they've traversed. They all start to look the same. "We've gone down this street already," he tells Molly.

"No, I'd remember it," she says.

And so on.

Soon the sun sinks close to the horizon. "Maybe we should pack up before it gets too dark," Molly says.

Good point. It's not safe to return to the camp. That being the case, where are they going to find a place to sleep? "Do you think the Muses would let us crash for the night at their place?"

"I hope not," Molly says. "I don't like crashes."

"No, I mean sleep," Max says.

"Oh." She looks deep in thought. "I don't know. That's never come up before. I'm pretty sure they don't sleep."

"Wouldn't hurt to ask, I guess," Max says.

They double back toward the Muses' abode, taking an unexplored street that's not too far out of the way. This street holds an uneasy mixture of residential condos and businesses at random intervals. One is a Mexican restaurant, the sign all but falling apart, still advertising their specialty margaritas. A little farther down the street is a professional building, one that looks like it might have held a dental office or chiropractor once upon a time.

With the last glimmer of sun nearly gone, Max decides that

even if the Muses don't offer them a place to sleep, he'd be happy to collapse there on the asphalt.

"Three bars!" Molly shrieks. "We found something!"

Max skids to a stop and looks around. They've just passed an office building and are in front of a abandoned house. "Here?" Max asks. "Or back there?"

"The office building," Molly says. She takes the router in hand and dashes the bike into a heap on the sidewalk. Max hurries after her.

But as he approaches the building and the fractally-cracked parking lot, he freezes. There's something different about this place. Something just doesn't feel right.

His whole head buzzes. There's something in the air, a bad smell, like something burning.

The door's locked, glass intact, but even in the dim light, it's obvious the place has been trashed. But how did looters get in? "Sure this is the place?" Max asks.

Molly checks the router, walking along the sidewalk in front of the building. "Strongest here," she says. "How do we get in?"

Max rattles the door. "Why didn't anyone break the windows yet? There's got to be some way in. Maybe around the back?"

A trip around the back proves unfruitful. The only way in or out is through the front. Max rests his head against the glass. "What's the worst that could happen if we break the window?"

"You could get cut pretty bad," Molly says.

Max straightens up, in so doing leans against the door, which moves an extra inch with a mechanical click. He runs his hand along the inside of the door. His fingers find a tiny button, which depresses under the slightest pressure. And the door swings freely open. "Well, then," Max says, swinging the door all the way open. "That's not creepily convenient at all. After you."

They enter. Not visible from outside: a lock like the one from the apartment, with a lid shut over the green LEDs to make them less conspicuous. Max flicks it open, and it reads: `PS ACTIVE 2528mA`.

They're in a reception area, the floor covered with a sensible light-industrial carpet. About half a dozen black chairs and the ruins of a water dispenser litter the room. Max kicks aside a scattering of decade-old magazines. An angled counter divides the space, and behind that, several rows of open filing shelves sit piled with garbage. Something about this place seems familiar.

"I think this might have been a doctor's office," Molly says.

"Was it?" Max asks. It's hard to imagine this space clean and well-lit. Was this building set up originally as a router station, or modified after-the-fact?

Even in the pale green light, Max makes out a look on Molly's face. "Yeah. This was my doctor," she says.

Molly used to go here for treatment? She was about the same age, maybe a year younger, so she couldn't have been more than five-ish at the time. Was her memory that accurate?

For that matter, were Max's own memories reliable? Why did Hadley Root keep appearing in connection with the trophy hunt? To what end? How far in advance had plans been laid that were playing out only now? The pile of questions seems like an intractable nest of tangled vipers.

"Check this signal again," Max says. "In case my dad is near."

Molly gets that little wrinkle between her eyebrows. "Your dad?"

"The node. I said, check the signal to see if the node is near."

"I'm pretty sure you said..." She looks away, then fiddles with the antennae on the router. "The node is close." She walks around the room, comparing readings. "I can't get a direction. It's really close."

"Let's check the rooms one-by-one," Max says. "We're looking for something...well, something with antennas that look a lot like that." He indicates the router.

Molly picks up a flashlight collecting dust on the floor, but it doesn't light. "Batteries," she says. She takes the lock, shining its sickly green light out ahead of them. It's not much, but better than the draping darkness of the back rooms.

Immediately behind the reception desk is an office with a large desk. There may have been a potted plant here once, if the scattered dirt and mold on the carpet is any indicator. There's still a crooked picture barely hanging on the wall, of an ancient-looking guy with a beard and toga. But nothing at all that looks remotely like the nodes they've seen so far.

"This is just the first room," Max says. "Let's keep looking."

The narrow hallway leads to four other examination rooms, two on each side. The first one has trash piled knee-high. A set of floor-to-ceiling cabinets had been completely raided, everything thrown about the room.

"I think people might have been looking for drugs," Molly notes.

"I've never heard of drugs being kept in the exam rooms," Max says.

"Nobody said looters were far up on the intelligence scale," Molly says.

"Points. And to be fair," Max says, "I've never heard of routers being placed in exams rooms either." Indeed, there's nothing on the wall except a peeling poster advertising some blood pressure medication.

Max and Molly proceed through the other three exam rooms, finding much the same. A small supply closet seems promising at first, but that too ends up being a bust.

"Check the signal again," Max says.

Molly does so. "It's right on top of us," she says. A blue light on the router in her hands begins blinking rapidly.

"What's that mean?" Max asks.

"A key exchange window is about to open. We've got about a minute," Molly says.

"We can just connect from here, right?" Max asks.

"It won't work," Molly says. "The Muses showed me. Nodes have an additional safeguard. A physical button needs to be pressed about once every week to keep them activated. It's a safeguard against remote network storms."

"Great," Max says. "If you were a wireless access node, where would you hide yourself in a doctor's office?"

"First, do no harm," Molly says.

"What?"

"That's what Doctor Ariely used to say constantly," Molly says.

"Doctor Ariely? This was his practice?" Max says. "I've heard that quote before."

"It's part of the Hippocratic Oath[1]. All doctors take it," Molly says.

"The picture in the office," Max says.

They both head back to the office. The picture bears the caption "Hippocrates." Max slides his fingers behind the frame. "It's warm." He carefully unhooks it from the wall.

Behind the artwork is the hardware for a node. It doesn't look like what they've seen before. This one is a naked circuit board, far smaller, and flatter to fit in the narrow gap behind the frame. A pair of wires snakes out from it to connect to the metal frame. "Okay, so the antenna is bigger than I thought," Max says.

"Hurry, push the button!" Molly says.

"I don't see a button," Max says, frustration mingling with anger.

Molly reaches past him and mashes her finger against a copper trace on the board that looks like intertwined spirals.

Another LED on the circuit board winks on.

In Max's HUD, a new message pops up.

HELP.

---

1. Then again, Hippocrates also said, "A physician without a knowledge of Astrology has no right to call himself a physician," so there's that.

2-2 CIRCUIT BENDING_

"Help?" Max says. A single word. A request? Is someone, say, Max's dad, calling for help? Or is it an offer of assistance? Maybe a command.

"Help what?"

Molly can't see the HUD, so her confusion is warranted. "I'm getting a message. One word: help. But I don't know what it means. What are we supposed to do with that?"

"We get out," Molly says.

Given her penchant for noticing trouble before anyone else does, Max takes her warning to heart. He sweeps all the garbage off the desk and lays the picture frame down. The router circuit board is attached by little blobs of glue. "We're taking this with us. Find a knife or something," he says.

Molly disappears from the room, taking the green light with her. The only light left in the office is the blinking LED on the router. Where is the power coming from? Another set of wires leads into a cylinder about the size of a small candy bar. That must be the "battery." It too is glued to the back of the picture with a glob of something. It yields when Max pushes his fingernail against it. It feels waxy. Max presses harder and it gives way entirely.

An infinite battery in his hand. This had to be pre-Damage technology. Why was it kept a secret? Why didn't every iPod and cellphone and laptop computer have one of these installed?

Maybe they were dangerous. Full of toxic materials that might leak out. Or maybe just dangerous electrically. What would happen if the terminals shorted together? An unlimited amount of energy could be released in a short time. That sounded more like a bomb than a battery.

A green glow announces Molly's return. She found a scalpel somewhere. The blade is dull and rusty, but it works well enough against the soft glue. Max carefully frees the circuit board, leaving only the antennae wires. They're securely bonded to the metal frame. Welded maybe. He tugs on the wires as hard as he dares, but they don't break away.

"Is it OK to cut the antenna wires?" Max asks.

"That'll reduce the broadcast range quite a bit," Molly says. "If it's a tuned antenna, it might even throw off the broadcast frequency."

"Not worried about range, as long as we keep it with us. But the Muses said that these nodes were pretty particular about frequencies. Hmm." There's no way they can carry a huge picture around town. Too conspicuous. Max reaches the scalpel toward the wires.

"Does the frame come apart?" Molly asks?

Ahh. The idea hadn't occurred to Max. He runs his fingers

along the metal and discovers tiny screws holding it in place. "Got a screwdriver?"

Molly hands Max her pen. He's confused for a moment, but she reaches over and pulls off the clicker. Underneath is a tiny screwdriver.

"Of course," Max says, and works free the metal frame. It comes apart into two L-shaped pieces, each of which is barely-manageable when slung over a shoulder.

"What's that thing?" Molly asks.

It takes Max a second to realize she's talking about the circuit board. The main component is a rectangular chip with many dozens of wires crowded around its four edges.

"Obviously, that's a CPU chip," Molly says. "Pre-crash vintage —and it's got a communication driver. But there's another chip in between the two that I don't recognize. Does it have a part number?"

Max leans in to look closer. "Nothing I can see." While leaning, the two antenna pieces of frame glance off each other, lighting a spark in the darkness.

"Don't let those two touch," Molly cautions. "I don't know how much abuse the RF drivers on that router can take. They need to be working perfectly, in order to be ready for the next time a key exchange window opens."

"Any idea when that might be?" Max asks.

"I don't," Molly says. "But there's no reason to think that it has to be a long time after the previous window."

"And then what?" Max asks. "Every node we've been in so far has been like a playable video game. What's this one going to be? Something catches Max's attention out of the corner of his eye. Something blinking rapidly on the circuit board. Another window is opening.

Max reaches out to the spiral circuit trace, the "button," and mashes his thumb over it.

Abruptly, Max is weightless—less than weightless—rushing upward into an empty sky. The world around him fades to a soft robin egg blue, intensifying to faded denim, then all the way to the electric hue of butterflies Max had only seen on a screen, never quite sure whether the display was capable of displaying a color as intense as nature could provide.

Everything else got left behind, even Molly.

Molly!

Max, alone and unprepared for whatever challenge this node is about to put him through, takes a deep breath.

The HUD lights up:

*** THE REALTIME OPERATING NODE 8-BIT RISCLISP V2 ***

64K RAM SYSTEM. 38911 LISP BYTES FREE

READY.

2-3 ON THE INSIDE_

INVENTORY:

* MYSTERIOUS SCROLL

* STEALTH CLOAK

* IVORY TORCH OF THE ENDLESS FIRE

* TROPHY 2

The world is electric blue, but not the nightmare shade inflicted by LevelUP corporation. Max's eyes gradually adjust to the scene: every part of his body is laced with glowing circuitry, reminiscent of the circuit board on the router he had been handling a moment ago. The air smells like a fresh circuit board: hot copper laced with the air after a thunderstorm.

Max takes in the grid-lined island, perfectly rectangular, suspended in a sea of churning, glowing fluid. Water, for lack of a better word. Unlike the earlier VR world, this one is photo-realistic; no hint of pixels anywhere. The harsh aesthetics are the only thing identifying this as a mediated reality.

Max pinches himself and it hurts. Not so much to check if he's dreaming—he knows he isn't—but to verify his suspicion: it is possible to get hurt here. The level of reality, down to control over each finger, is flawless.

The edge of the island is a razor-sharp right angle, dropping about the span of a hand to the waterline. The surging water looks as if it's lit from underneath, evenly, with no particular light source. The churning waves splash exactly up to the height of the platform, but no higher. No matter how long Max watches, not a single drop spills onto the horizontal surface.

The thought crosses his mind that he may be surrounded by acid, contact with which would leave him writhing in agony until all thought mercifully ceased. Given imaginative level designers, it could be worse. Unimaginably worse.

But if that were the case, why would entering the node leave him sadistically trapped with no recourse? The other nodes provided a means to retrieve the trophy, and this one wouldn't be any different, right?

Max dips his hand into the liquid. It's not water—it tingles but doesn't burn. Energy? The tingle spreads down his arm and settles in his stomach. It feels like having one too many espressos, minus the nausea. In fact, it feels pretty good, like adrenaline surging through him. He could do anything.

What about inventory? Max checks, but instead of items, a different category appears in his HUD:

=== SKILLS: ===

SWIM

So now he has slots with which to collect skills, and SWIM is listed as the first one. He knows when the game designers are sending a message.

Max gathers himself and cannonballs into the waves. It's colder than he expects. He swims downward as far as he can manage and never touches bottom. An intense shiver wracks through his body. There's a moment when Max imagines his every muscle cramping and his fetal-curled husk settling to the bottom of the energy lake. He stops struggling and buoyant forces rocket him back to the surface.

The panic passes, and Max takes an overhand swimming stroke, pushing back to the surface. His experience with swimming is limited—one time he and some friends snuck away and dipped into the filthy waters of the Bay. On that day, he quickly got the hang of it, more readily than his friends. The feeling here is familiar, though he seems to move even more fluidly through this medium.

A golden light winks on, along what seems like a distant shore. Max turns toward it, pulling forward with powerful strokes. The distance melts underneath him. Real swimming tires Max out quickly, but this exercise doesn't fatigue him at all. If anything, Max feels his inner energy level surging.

Time passes enjoyably. But the next time Max looks up, the golden light is no longer in front of him, instead it's at a 9-o'clock heading. He's sure he was swimming a straight line. A look behind confirms his fear: He can't see the island where he started either.

Continuing in the same direction no longer makes sense, to the degree he can even tell one direction from another, so he turns and swims again toward the golden light. It feels so natural, he could keep doing this for hours. After a dozen strokes or so, he checks to see—and his aim is dead straight. He pushes forward, but after a few minutes, to his dismay, the golden light is now to his right.

The first tremblings of panic congeal in his gut. He's lost at sea. Stuck in something worse than a maze. He turns toward the golden light again and powers toward it. Less than a minute later, it's dead behind him.

He gives up on swimming, treading water instead. There's got to be a way out of this.

Something brushes against his leg, then tangles through his fingers. Max swipes at it viciously but doesn't make contact with anything. Between the surprise and distraction, he nearly goes under. The water tastes like strong seltzer.

The visitor bumps against him again. It's small and plastic, with a long tail that drags behind in just the right way to tickle Max's arm. He grabs for it.

A cable. Max runs his hand along it, finding a USB connector on one end. On the other, an optical mouse, its red LED gleaming. Is this some kind of joke? Max tosses it away, but, like a tadpole, the thing swims right back into his hands.

"What the?" Max says out loud. Maybe it's because these are the first words he's said since entering the node, or maybe because sound carries better over the waves, his voice seems boomier. The mouse trembles and jets away from him, maintaining a wary distance.

In a level assiduously designed, everything is added for a reason. Level designers don't like being arbitrary. Especially when it came to NPC, "non-player character" interactions—like that thief you'd run across in Zork. These interactions always served a purpose. "Aww, that's alright," Max says in more soothing tones. The mouse cautiously swims closer. "It's okay little guy. Are you here because of me?"

The light blinks once.

"Is that a yes?"

The light blinks once.

"Is that all you can say?"

The light blinks twice.

"Do you have a name?"

The light blinks twice.

"Well, then, from now on, you're Mouse." Max looks around and the golden light he had been following isn't visible anymore. "I guess I'm supposed to follow you then."

The light blinks once and Mouse swims ahead. Max follows.

2-4 BODE_

INVENTORY:

MYSTERIOUS SCROLL

STEALTH CLOAK

IVORY TORCH OF THE ENDLESS FIRE

TROPHY 2

MOUSE

=== SKILLS: ===

SWIM

Max arrives at a shoreline: a geometrically perfect ramp sloping out of the water. A softly glowing white landscape lies beyond. Despite how easily swimming strokes came to Max, putting his legs into action is a different game. Max wobbles as the ground seems to shift underneath his rubbery legs.

The landscape—along with everything else—consists of crisp

polygons, as if the level designer started with mathematical equations, and added softly-glowing grid lines to emphasize geometric precision. The path continues its gentle slope a higher point farther inland, cutting between triangular mountains on the left and right. Even the trees are made from raw slivers of razor-sharp geometry. There's only one way forward.

A *thunk* catches Max's attention. It's Mouse, bumping against the shore. Max picks it up, and it blinks once, coiling its long tail around his arm.

"Do you know what I'm supposed to be looking for?" Max asks.

Mouse blinks once.

"You won't get much of a conversation out of that one," says a black-clad figure with eyes hidden behind a leather mask. There was nobody there just a moment ago…

"Eigenthief?" Max asks. "What are you doing here?"

"Eye gehn what?" says the figure in the exact same tenor voice as ET. "I haven't the foggiest what you're talking about."

Then again, the original ET never let a moment of omitting 'The' from his name go uncorrected. But it can't be a raw coincidence. "You're him," Max says. "Only less pixely."

"Excuse me?" The figure says. *She* pulls off the mask to unveil long black hair that tumbles down across her shoulders. "You may call me Bode."

"Well, that doesn't bode well," Max deadpans.

She looks confused. "Neither does it Max well. See how foolish your statement is? It's ridiculous to tool with someone's name."

"How...how did you know my name?" Max asks.

"Wrong question," Bode says. "The question you really meant to ask is: what can you do for me?"

No, he's pretty sure that's not what he meant to ask. "Are you real?"

"Well, that's an extraordinarily rude question," Bode says. "I could ask the same of you."

"Why are you here?" Max asks, undaunted.

"Why are *you* here?" Bode echoes.

"Oh, this is stupid," Max says.

"Oh, this is stupid," Bode repeats.

Mouse blinks twice.

Max angrily waves her off and turns to leave. He sets out toward the notch between the mountains.

And smacks against an invisible wall. The very landscape here is set against him.

Max rubs his nose. "Fine. I'll talk. I'm here for a trophy. I need to look around until I find it."

Bode cocks an eyebrow. "Another trophy hunter. The second one today."

Wait, what? "Second? Who else has been here?"

"I'll say this, she certainly had fewer questions than you," Bode says.

She? *Hemera*. "That's all? You haven't seen a man go through here? Looks a lot like me, except more...parental?"

"You should know better than to rely on appearances in a place like this," Bode says. "Your father could look like anything, assuming he was here."

"How did you—"

"There's no end to the variety and sheer quantity of flawed assumptions I've seen people make. I sail on the winds of change. I—"

"Bode." Max sighs. "OK, I get it. So tell me, in order to get the trophy before *she* does, what assumptions do I need to change?"

"For starters, the assumption that I have any interest whatsoever in helping you," Bode says.

Max grinds his teeth in frustration. He can't move forward. He can't even seem to get past this gatekeeper. What's left to do?

There is an answer. The needed hints are present—he needs only to figure out the puzzle. What was it that Bode had said before?

"Tell me, Bode, what can I do for you? What do you want?"

Bode arches a brow again. "Those two questions are very different and have very different answers. What do we want? Asking someone that question with a gun pointed to their head will elicit a very different answer than from someone acting at their pleasure."

What is she talking about? "Who's got a gun?" Max asks.

"What can you do for me? Very little, I suspect," Bode says. "Well, there is this one, teensy, tiny little thing."

Mouse blinks twice.

"What?"

"I want you to leave without the trophy," Bode says.

"I don't even know how to leave," Max says.

"I'll show you." Bode casts her eyes toward the sheer wall, and a doorway traces itself into the geometric plane, complete with an exit sign above.

"If I leave without the trophy, Hemera will get it instead."

"Of what concern is that to you?" Bode asks.

"She's not a good person," Max says. "All she does is hurt people."

"And what makes you arbiter between good and evil? Do you think getting your hands on the trophy will make you a better person than her?"

"Well, just about anyone would be a better person than her, trophy or not. And I take it not too many people can get this far. And I don't mean that as a brag. I mean not too many people have the hardware to enter this game world."

"And?"

Max's mind races. The Muses talked about a mouldering mystery. "Whoever hid the trophies obviously meant for someone to find them. Otherwise why go to all the trouble? They're part of a key meant to unlock...something that Hemera wants badly. Hiding the trophies is all that keeps someone like her from just taking them."

Max's mind wanders back to the day of Damage. What was it his dad had said? Had he somehow been involved in making Damage happen? Or at least in preparing the world for what would happen afterward?

"That's an interesting theory," Bode says, a faint smile upon her lips. She lifts her hand, and the invisible wall becomes visible and disappears into the ground, leaving not even a seam. The way forward once again lies wide open. "I will guide you. But only if you follow my every instruction to the smallest detail. If not, I'm not responsible for what happens to you."

Mouse blinks twice.

2-5 CAREFUL ABOUT YOUR FACE_

INVENTORY:

* MYSTERIOUS SCROLL

* STEALTH CLOAK

* IVORY TORCH OF THE ENDLESS FIRE

* TROPHY 2

* MOUSE

=== SKILLS: ===

* SWIM

Time grinds to a crawl in the featureless landscape. The curated trail forges ahead with unnerving straightness. If not for the slow growth of the distant mountains, Max would swear they weren't actually progressing forward. Bode walks in a loopy, circuitous gait as if the path were scattered with unseen obstacles.

At last a tiny speck appears on the flawless horizon. Max stops to get a clearer look.

Without looking back, Bode senses that he has stopped. "The Citadel," Bode whispers. "A fortress long ago created by a great wizard called Parametric Ubiq."

"Para whatsit? What kind of name is that?"

"A very old one," Bode says. "Older than history."

"Well, let's get there before Hemera does," Max says.

Bode freezes. "Don't take another step," she says.

Max halts, mid-step, one foot still aloft. "Why?"

"We are not alone."

Max carefully sets his foot down. Mouse, still wrapped around his arm, blinks a stream of continuous pulses[1].

Out of the corner of Max's eye, something moves. When he looks there's nothing there.

Bode takes a step back, holding her arm out protect Max.

"You have my attention. What do I do?" Max asks.

"Shhhh!" Bode hisses, but it's too late. Another blur flashes past so quickly that Max fails to register more than a fleeting glimpse[2]. Something unseen charges straight toward him. He feels the ground shake, the faint movement of air, and at the last second, Max throws himself out of the way, though not quickly enough. He's flung sprawling against the wall at the road's edge.

Well, most of him is. He can't feel his left leg below the knee. Then he sees his foot, two paces ahead of him. It's an oddly disconnected sensation, in more ways than one.

Then the pain lands. It's unlike anything Max has ever felt. Like his foot was plunged into molten silicon, every nerve ending frizzling. For a second, Max can't even breathe. How is this possible? What kind of connection is there between his mind and this game?

It's not real.

It's not real.

It's...

Back in comfortable reality, Max's foot is still safely attached to his body. And therefore, can't be hurting him. In a genuine sense, this is all in his head.

This game is so realistic, Max has more difficulty peeling apart the illusion. For a passing moment the pain is gone. Max senses his own body. He's lying flat on dirty carpet. A piece of gravel digs into left shoulder. But the clarity doesn't hold.

And searing pain returns with a vengeance. The mind makes it real.

"I said not to move," Bode snaps. "More are on the way. We must seek cover."

"What are those things?" Max manages to ask.

"Garbage collectors," Bode says. "Crawl if you have to. But move!"

"There's no cover here! Just this stupid trail that goes on forever."

"Move!"

Max crawls ahead, but his severed foot blocks his way. For good measure, he picks it up. No blood. The cross-section of his leg is perfectly smooth, glasslike, with no internal bone, muscle, or discernible structure. There's no need for the game to render anything beneath the surface. He tucks the appendage away and keeps moving.

The ground rumbles. "Wait. Garbage collectors? Are you saying I'm garbage?" Max asks.

"I'm not saying it. But they are," Bode says. "Now move, before they turn you into a dangling reference."

Pain makes even the simplest things unimaginably difficult. Fighting through the pain, Max moves his leg a little more and is rewarded with an even more intense jolt of agony.

"I don't suppose…" he gasps for breath "there's any medpacks in this game? Healing potions?"

Bode looks thoughtful for a moment. "Let me see." She does something, then another spike of pain bites into Max's leg. The fire dulls to a prickly sensation, like when his foot falls asleep from standing in the same position for too long. His leg feels heavier.

He dares to look, and his leg is no longer a stump; it's complete again. Sort of. His foot's not flesh, but made of the same grid-lined material that makes up the walls and ground.

"Stand," Bode barks. Turns out Max's leg isn't just a little heavier. The thing weighs a ton. He can barely even shift it. Bode sighs, and offers her hand, pulling him back to standing.

He can't even walk. "How am I supposed to go on like this? What if those things come again? You've made me a sitting duck!"

"Have you ever been…" she searches for the right word, "ice skating?"

Max needs to replay that sentence in his head a few times before he can even parse it as language. "Have I… What?"

"Check your inventory. I've something to alter the coefficient of friction on the soles of your feet."

He's never even put on skates before. His second thought is, *wait, Bode can just change physics like that?* But he checks inventory, and there's a new skill loaded.

FOOTGLIDE

"It may take some getting used to. Careful about your face."

"My face?" Max shifts his balance to his new leg, and immediately begins drifting backward, as if the gently-sloped road was made of ice. He shifts his weight to compensate, and his foot flies out from underneath him. Max topples, crashing face-first into the ground.

"Yeah. That looked painful. Try moving forward."

Max manages to right himself with his foot braced perpendicular to the slope. Ahead, the citadel pokes out above what passes for a horizon. As Max focuses on the goal, it fills all the space before his eyes. The citadel resembles a shaft of rock lifted straight out from the earth. There's a massive portcullis of heavy iron bars, and a figure outside, arranging a row of bombs. *Hemera.*

The tower rushes closer still, the walls passing through Max, then climbing through the interior. Inside the upper chamber, the trophy awaits, hanging in the air, spinning peacefully above a glowing plinth. That's his goal. That's his gravity, pulling him in.

Max focuses on his goal. He visualizes the trophy appearing in his inventory. It's as if the earth moves beneath him. He's moving forward. Then he slips again. Without the right inner-ear signals, he's too slow to break his fall before his face smacks against the hard ground again.

Once the resulting surge of pain subsides, Max works himself back into a sitting position. "I understand the footglide. I felt myself moving against gravity, uphill."

"Yes, I noticed."

Max struggles to regain his feet. As long as he quits bumping his prosthetic foot, the pain level remains manageable. (Having never lost an actual limb, Max comes up short in ability to compare, but he presumes an actual pedal amputation would be worse, if only for the blood.)

Bode helps him up again, and Max focuses his concentration on his new skill. He halts his backward creep, and glides ahead, slower than walking speed at first. With practice and concentration, movement becomes easier, and with large strokes like an ice skater, he passes ahead of Bode.

"The game is made to be easy to learn," Bode says. "And yet it has eluded many up to this point."

"What happens next?" asks Max, whizzing past.

"We need to make up time," Bode says. "Barring any further adventures on the road, next stop, the citadel. I only hope we are not too late."

---

1. Which, as it happens, is Morse Code for I MADE A MISTAKE.
2. Out of the corner of his eye… He turned to look, but it was gone.

2-6 GETTING PERSONAL_

```
INVENTORY:

* MYSTERIOUS SCROLL

* STEALTH CLOAK

* IVORY TORCH OF THE ENDLESS FIRE

* TROPHY 2

* MOUSE

=== SKILLS: ===

* SWIM

* FOOTGLIDE
```

How quickly people adapt to circumstances. Already, walking seems unbearably more primitive than a graceful footglide.

"Why didn't you set me up from the beginning with the ability to coast all the way to the citadel?" Max asks.

Bode weaves an uneven path as she progresses along the road.

She seems happier, like she should be whistling or something. After her looping path orbits her way around Max two or three more times, she replies: "Two reasons, mostly. The first is that, mentally, it takes a lot out of your frail body."

"*My* frail body?"

"It will manifest as a dropping blood glucose level in your mortal shell. If it gets too low, you'll pass out, and quite likely, pass on."

Oh.

It has to be a coincidence, or the power of suggestion, but as Bode says this, Max notices a queasy feeling deep inside. He can almost make out an evaporating sheen of sweat on his upper lip.

He's never given thought to whether he's diabetic—if he turned out to be, it's not like he could get anything resembling reasonable treatment while living in the camps. A growing sense of unease intrudes on his thoughts. The immersion of this world is stronger, though, and a change in his surroundings grabs him back.

The path flattens out for a short stretch, marked by a raised pedestal with a rectangular stone carving resting atop. It's a partly unfurled book, opened to a crude map of what looks like the inside of the citadel. There's an engraving underneath. It says, "DON'T BELIEVE EVERYTHING YOU READ"—the same message from Hadley's scroll.

Max stoops to inspect. The stone is warm to the touch and smooth like tent canvas that had seen more than its fair share of use.

"Don't touch that!" Bode shrieks, but it's too late. Max pulls his hand back—or tries to. It's stuck there, and he couldn't let go if he wanted to. And he doesn't want to.

With one hand on the stone, it's as if Max can see all the way to the citadel, where an identical pedestal stands nearby the main gates. It's like he's standing there. Next to Hemera.

She sees him, and her eyes narrow. "You again," she says.

The immediacy messes with Max's perception. Some part of him is now in three places at once: his original body at Doctor Ariely's office, and at two places in the game. He needs to do something before this goes sideways... Why is Hemera outside the citadel anyway?

The nearby portcullis is closed with a heavy gate. "You don't know how to get in," Max says. As the import of this hits him, a smile spreads across his face. She's just as in the dark as he is.

"Let me handle this. You've been nothing but trouble for me."

"Why thank you, ma'am," Max says. "That might be the nicest thing you've said about me." He attempts a mock bow, but between the petrified foot and the immobilized hand, it's clumsy.

"You're injured. Pity," Hemera says.

"You seem in fine shape, ma'am. Pity."

"What a tongue you have on you," Hemera says. She looks thoughtful for a moment before continuing. "Here are my demands."

"Demands?" Max sputters.

"Yes, my demands. You withdraw immediately."

"If I don't?"

"Then I'll do something long overdue. I'll call my clean-up crew to cleanse the refugee camp you hold so dear," Hemera says.

All she does is hurt people. "You wouldn't."

Hemera taps her ear. "Order the cleanse at Lockheed. Yes, as soon as possible." She cracks her knuckles and smiles.

A sharp intake of breath feels like a stab to the heart.

As if reading his mind, Hemera says, "I'd like you to savor the scene. See in your mind the bulldozers arriving within the hour, working their way to the top of the hill, and scouring away the filth." She smirks. "Another pustule scraped off the face of the earth as far as I'm concerned."

For a long second, Max considers surrender. Hemera wields her overwhelming power ruthlessly, without a second thought about the suffering of others. She always gets what she wants. People who stand in her way only get flattened. Better to live on to fight another day, right?

There had been a time when Max would've accepted that argument. Max had so few possessions, that losing the camp wouldn't make much of a difference. People would find somewhere to live, even if it meant spreading out to the other camps.

But that was before Max's father entered the picture. The trophy quest meant more than the camp, as significant as that was. It meant Max finding his father. Whatever was going on here was important enough for Hadley Root to have hidden the pieces in a way that his son was uniquely qualified to find. How could he give up on that?

Nope, this was personal.

"I'm coming for the trophies," Max tells Hemera. "All of them.

For your sake, you'd better hope you make it out before I get there."

Hemera's face cycles through shock, confusion, and searing rage. Quite possibly, nobody has ever spoken to her this way.

Then something else registers on her face. Only for a second, but Max spots it. *Fear.* Hemera's position may not be as secure as she outwardly projects. But it's just a momentary flicker, gone as fast as it arrives.

Hemera glances to the side and nods. Was somebody else with her? She smiles again, and the temperature drops by twenty degrees. "I'm going to enjoy watching this," she says.

Something the approximate size and weight of a bag of bricks clobbers Max, and he breaks contact with the monument. Bode lands on top of him in a pile of flailing limbs. The world seems to stretch and contract again as Max's POV snaps back to his current location in the game.

"I correctly suspected you couldn't break contact with your own strength. We need to keep moving," Bode says. "This doesn't bode well."

Max groans from the pain while Bode grabs him by the wrist and yanks him ahead. Disconcertingly, she no longer threads her careful path around whatever obstacles she had been seeing before. What is she so worried about? She pumps her feet like a speed skater, gliding herself now, covering vast stretches with each stride. The whipping wind stings Max's face. He wishes he had goggles.

A sheen of sweat on Max's forehead doesn't go away with the wind. His legs feel trembly, gradually dissolving into jelly. Moving this quickly is taking a toll. Nothing he can do but worry about the cost later.

2-7 TURNING POINT_

INVENTORY:

* MYSTERIOUS SCROLL

* STEALTH CLOAK

* IVORY TORCH OF THE ENDLESS FIRE

* TROPHY 2

* MOUSE

=== SKILLS: ===

* SWIM

* FOOTGLIDE

The path narrows, at first imperceptibly, but more obviously so when Max brushes against the sheer edge. Perfect place for an ambush, he muses. The nagging feeling that he's missing something doesn't diminish.

Bode suddenly swerves around some unseen obstacle, nearly

yanking Max's arm out of its socket. He stumbles and goes down face-first.

But the jolt shakes loose a new realization. Hadley's scroll, and then this monument, didn't just have the same inscription. They were connected.

Don't believe everything you read.

Everything about this world pointed toward the citadel. The uniformly straight path, not a maze or puzzle. The map of the citadel engraved in the book. Even Bode's assumptions. What if there was more to this place than it seemed at first glance? Don't believe everything…

Max wrenches his arm free, and before Bode can react, executes a hard turn, banks off the horizontal wall, and races back toward the monument. Whatever it's hiding, he'll find it.

"Get back here, fool!" Bode screams. Max races even faster. As soon as the pedestal comes back into view, he launches into a skid, his foot perpendicular to his path, knee bent with a low center of gravity. It works perfectly, carving a groove in the previously flat ground, coming to a stop within reach of the monument.

Careful not to touch the stone, Max gets a closer look at the inscription. It's a map. Or is it? Ignoring all the distracting details, the overall shape of the inscription is an arrow, pointing down. Underneath.

Max braces his sleeved elbow against the stone, careful to avoid contact, and hefts. Nothing happens. He pushes again, harder, until he's sure he hears things snapping under the strain.

It's no use. Shame washes over him. It was stupid to even think —

With a grinding stone noise, the entire monument slides a bit. Adrenaline makes the next push go easier, and the entire thing —tons of stone—slides the width of his forearm.

Footsteps approach from downslope, but Max ignores them for the moment. He's uncovered something. Crumpled and flat as a floppy disk, something shiny, like emergency blankets or that skintight reflective fabric that Hemera likes to wear.

It crinkles when Max picks it up. What is it? It has shape, though being flattened under a monument for who-knows-how-long hasn't done it any favors. He shakes it out. Slender fingers unpeel.

"Whatever that thing is, drop it." The voice is nasal and dripping with sycophantic pathos.

Max doesn't turn to look. "Vic Vertex. I thought I caught a whiff of your stench. Whuff! It really stands out in an antiseptic place like this."

Max turns to face Vic. Catches him attempting to take in a sniff of own aroma. "You get around pretty well for a cripple," Vic says.

"I'm still ahead of you."

"I don't know what you're doing, but Hemera is going to be happy when she hears about it. And I mean happy with me. You, not so much." He eyes the silver fabric in Max's hand. "Fork it over."

"And if I don't?" Max asks. Without calling attention to it, Max steals glances at his item. It's a glove. It would be a tight fit to get it over his hand. He just needs a second or two and he can...

Vic casually produces a narrow flashlight from his jeans pocket. When he flicks a switch, with an electrical buzz, a cylinder of blue energy extends from the hilt. "So, I'm curious. I wonder if I can cut through that leg of yours."

"I can't believe it," Max says.

"What?" Vic asks.

"Even your weapon of choice is a cheap knock-off[1]."

Vic flies into a red-cheeked rage. He twirls the blade high and descends with a vicious impaling stroke.

Exactly as Max anticipated. At just the right moment, Max tweaks his glide skill, and skates in under the stroke, slamming his solid foot into Vic's sternum. The blade extinguishes with a slurping noise and the handle rolls away.

Max pivots in place and rakes his fingers along the ground toward the weapon. It zips out from his fingers, straight back into Vic's hand.

"Oh, c'mon," Max groans.

The blade extends in a blink, and it takes everything Max has to avoid the strike. Even then, he feels his skin blister underneath his smoldering shirt. His attention diverted for a fraction of a second, Max loses track of his leaden foot and falters off balance.

At close quarters the laser sword isn't much use, so instead, Vic kicks, his pointy boot connecting solidly with Max's ribs. The pain explodes through his body. He can't breathe, but he can roll blindly out of the way.

Vic takes another wild swing. The blade goes high and rakes the canyon wall with a shower of purple sparks. Vic staggers back. The force of the blow seems to have been reflected back on him —like striking solid rock with a metal blade. Still gasping for breath, Max regains his feet.

Max can work with this. He glides backward, and fumbles to get the glove on his hand. With luck, it will confer *something* to help him.

Vic advances. When he takes another wild swing, Max throws out his damaged foot to block. The blade deflects, delivering another jolt. Max heaves forward, getting both hands on the hilt. But the half-gloved hand is slippery.

When he means it, Vic is surprisingly strong, and nearly wrests the weapon back before Max can get a solid grip. The two men struggle for control, the tip of the blade zig-zagging an erratic path that veers far too close to Max's face.

"This is for my Dad," Max says, and concentrates on his grasp. He hears Vic's knuckles pop under the death grip. Vic snarls and adds a kind of twisting motion that threatens to break Max's wrists.

The two are locked in a stalemate, at least until one of them tires. Max has a bad feeling he won't come out on top of a contest of sheer endurance. This is his chance. He needs to find out what the glove does. With a final twitch, he gets the glove all the way onto his left hand.

"Inventory."

Inventory calls it a POWER GLOVE. Let's hope it lives up to its name.

"What did you say?" Vic grunts.

Max tests his grip. It doesn't feel any stronger. His arms shake with effort. "Wear glove," Max says. Nothing happens. "Inventory!" The glove is still there, unused. *So much for that idea.*

Max's fingers throb. His grip slips, and the plasma blade bobs toward his skull. *No bueno.* Time for Plan B. "Wear cloak," he says, as he lets go and throws himself out of harm's way.

It doesn't take Vic even a second to regain an attack stance. "Where are you?" He looks around. "I can hear you breathing."

Max tries to hold his breath, but the throbbing in his ribs won't let up. Vic slashes, aim close enough that Max needs to dive out of the way. He scrambles up as quickly and quietly as he can, but Vic is on him again, blade flashing. Vic leaps, a showboaty backflip, landing on the other side of Max, then pressing forward. It's an effective maneuver, hemming Max in. His options for dodging the energy blade suddenly become far more limited.

Max backs against the wall. Trapped. This is it. He raises his arm in futile protection against the final stroke, ending the game, the quest, and possibly his life.

The final stroke doesn't come.

Vic drops his weapon and staggers backward. Flames leap from his hair. Then another fireball thunders through the air, striking Vic in the chest. He curls up like a dead bug before disintegrating into a cone of dust.

Bode strides down the hill toward Max. "You realize that cloak doesn't prevent me from seeing you. We've wasted enough time. Let's get moving."

---

1. Specifically, Artoo's lightsaber from Episode XV.

2-8 HEMERA_

INVENTORY:

* MYSTERIOUS SCROLL

* STEALTH CLOAK

* IVORY TORCH OF THE ENDLESS FIRE

* TROPHY 2

* MOUSE

* POWER GLOVE

* ENERGY SWORD

=== SKILLS: ===

* SWIM

* FOOTGLIDE

Max doesn't follow Bode. He's on to something. The power glove has to fit in somewhere. It has to be the solution to some puzzle. It didn't make him physically stronger. It must do something else. The monument that hid it had the same message he found on Hadley's scroll. That couldn't be a coincidence.

There's got to be a hint he missed. "Read scroll."

YOU WANT PROOF? YOU'LL FIND IT AT— YOU CAN'T READ ANY MORE OF THE SCROLL UNTIL YOU UNLOCK THE MAGIC SPELL BINDING IT.

"Unlock scroll." With the magic glove in hand, the command succeeds.

THE MAGIC SEAL DISSOLVES, UNBINDING THE REST OF THE SCROLL.

The glove disappears from inventory. Max's eyes widen. The location of the final trophy. He'd have this information before Hemera, giving him the advantage.

"Read scroll."

YOU'LL FIND IT AT THE PLACE WHERE YOU FIRST BEGAN.

Huh? What did that mean? Where he began what? The hospital where he was born? The fire station where he was abandoned? The scroll was addressing him directly. What if someone else had read the scroll, would it then refer to a different location?

Reading beyond the end had worked before. "Read scroll."

YOU DON'T APPEAR TO HAVE A SCROLL.

After reading it, the scroll self-destructed. A one-time hint.

"If you're done playing with your toys, we need to move from here," Bode says. "This place will soon be overrun with garbage collectors." She leaves.

Max's dead foot throbs, or at least seems to. He doesn't need another run in with those things. Time to get moving.

Once he catches up with Bode, Max says, "Nice trick, with the fireballs."

"Yes, quite," Bode says. After an awkward silence, Bode says, "And?"

"Look, Hemera's had plenty of time to prepare for us. She's not going to just let us waltz into there. I need, well, more skills. Gliding alone isn't going to cut it."

"What do you have to offer me in return?" Bode asks.

"I've got a second-rate energy blade, but honestly I thought I'd kinda need it against Hemera. I've got the Eigenthief's cloak, which doesn't seem to do much good. Then this ivory torch—I don't even know what it does."

"None of those things interest me," Bode says.

"Come on. If I get instantly pasted, what good does that do you?"

Bode says nothing.

There is, of course, an inventory item Max didn't mention. The trophy. If Max died, it would be up for grabs. Was that what Bode has been interested in this whole time?

If that's the case, why didn't Max get a fireball to the face immediately? Because of the other trophy. That means...

"You need my help to get into the citadel," Max says. "Therefore, it's in your interest to equip me with skills." Max crosses his arms.

"There are very few skills I am capable of granting," Bode says. "But all I have is yours. Now let us move on."

Max checks his inventory again. The bottom half reads:

=== SKILLS: ===

* SWIM

* FOOTGLIDE

* RESIST POISON

* HAMMER

"Resist poison and hammer? Seriously, that's it?" Max asks.

"I said I have nothing further to offer you. Move quickly!"

Max notices the blur of approaching garbage collectors. He can't see them directly—it's like they only move in between the spaces of perception. "Can I drop the hammer on one of these guys?" he asks.

"I wouldn't advise it," Bode says.

"Move quickly then. I'm convinced," he says, and glides ahead.

Minutes later, the two of them crest the summit, the top of a long road running all the way from the shoreline to here. The walls that had been hemming them in fall away and an open Cartesian plain awaits them. Much closer now, the citadel fills the horizon. Max still hasn't figured out how he's going to get inside. Nothing obvious would work, because otherwise Hemera would've already taken the trophy and left.

"What skills does Hemera have?" Max asks. In particular, he's curious whether she has the hammer skill (whatever it is). Because if not, that seems like a useful skill for breaking into a citadel.

"I am not able to access her inventory," Bode says. "Which means she has admin level access."

"Admin? As in god mode?" Max asks.

"She's no god," Bode says. "But as soon as she is within sight, you'll need to stay close."

"I see the drawbridge gate," Max says. Light glints off the iron bars sealing it off. "Where's Hemera?" Nobody answers.

Bode, who stood alongside Max a second ago, is nowhere to be seen. "Bode?" Before Max can figure out what happened, Bode comes tumbling out of the sky, landing in a heap in on top of Max. A fresh blossom of pain lances up his leg and across his bruised ribs. He tastes blood.

Max carefully gets his shaking legs under him again.

"That's a new one," Bode says, righting herself.

"New what?" Max asks.

And Hemera is there, right in front of him. She has a weapon — a metal club with a spiked ball on the end of it. A mace, if Max recalls the proper name for it.

She points the weapon at Bode, and a blinding arc of electricity jumps out from it, cutting right through Bode. In between the purple blotches left behind in Max's vision, for a second he sees daylight passing through his former guide. Hemera jerks her weapon skyward, and a glowing silhouette of Bode rockets upward, still basked in electrical fire.

A rain of ash and items falls from the sky. It takes Max a second to realize what he's looking at, scattered amidst several items. *That's a trophy*.

But Hemera is there before Max can even formulate a plan to collect it. She picks it up, accompanied by the sound effect of adding something to inventory.

"Such an annoying creature. Won't be missed." She turns her attention to Max. "You have two things I want."

Two?

She does something, Max isn't sure quite what, but it feels like a small earthquake that starts in the soles of his feet and works its way up to the crown of his head. All of Max's inventory scatters out on the ground in front of him. Including his trophy. Max scrambles to pick things up again, but the trophy's attracted to her like a magnet. She collects his trophy, again with the inventory sound. She takes the energy sword as well but ignores the rest.

With the trophy she started out with, plus Bode's and his, now she has three of the four.

"The other thing I want from you? Come on, junior, you're going to open the citadel for me."

Max glances back at the remains of Bode, a drop of black staining the ground where the ashes pile. He turns to Hemera.

2-9 CITADEL PAR UBIQ_

INVENTORY:

* STEALTH CLOAK

* IVORY TORCH OF THE ENDLESS FIRE

* MOUSE

=== SKILLS: ===

* SWIM

* FOOTGLIDE

* RESIST POISON

* HAMMER

"No gliding. Walk," Hemera demands. Max's dead foot hangs heavily at the end of his stump, so walking ends up being more of a shuffling stagger. Max checks his inventory. Hemera didn't even bother preventing him from recovering the rest of the items; given how easily she stripped him of inventory before, she didn't seem worried about surprises.

The walk stretches on. Max hadn't appreciated until this point how much a gift the glide skill had been. But one step after another, the citadel grows larger on the horizon.

"I have to say I'm a little surprised," Hemera says. Max keeps his mouth shut. There's nothing he can gain by talking, but she might spill something important. If there's one thing Max has learned, it's that people who hold overwhelming power can seldom resist flaunting it. And in so doing, they often let slip details of their plans and thinking.

"How old were you?" she asks. "Five? Ten?" *Why is she talking about Damage?* "I knew Hadley had no compunctions about using other people for his little games, but I had no idea he was depraved enough to bring his own son into this."

It would be better to keep quiet. Talking won't help a thing. But Max can't resist. "You know nothing about my father."

Hemera raises an eyebrow. "He didn't tell you, did he? I see you somehow continue to hold him in high regard. If you knew even a fraction of what he's done, you'd be singing a different tune."

"Project much?" Max says.

Hemera laughs, the sound of breaking dreams and glass. "I don't let anyone stand in my way. I'm no saint, but everything I've done has worked toward undoing the damage *that scoundrel* inflicted on the world. Those closest to him bore the brunt of it."

Max scrunches his face into a maze of tight wrinkles. It almost sounds like Hemera is saying she and Hadley were close once.

Hemera stops and curls her long fingers under Max's chin. Her stare bores holes clean through him. Those intense eyes spark with energy. Yet familiar. *No.*

"Tell me about your mother," Hemera says.

NO. "I never had a mother," Max says. He sets his jaw.

"Oh, come now," Hemera says. "That's just biologically impossible. Don't let your daddy issues cloud your thinking."

What is she doing? Is this a calculated measure to throw him off balance? To make him more pliant? She accuses his dad of playing mind games, but then goes on to do this?

Worst of all, what if it's not a ploy?

"Doesn't matter," Max declares. "I'm still going to stop you."

"Oh, I'm sure you're going to try," Hemera purrs. "There's nothing I'm looking forward to more."

Max balls his fists. He's tired of getting yanked around. He sits, landing roughly when his bad foot doesn't respond well. On impact, pain arcs up his ribs. "You want the citadel open? Go open it by yourself. I'm not taking another step."

"You will," Hemera says. "You want the trophy just as much as I do."

Max says, "I'm sorry, I didn't quite catch that. I couldn't hear it over the sound of not caring."

Hemera smiles. "You are so much like him." She readies her mace. Max braces himself, but he's not prepared for what comes next. Not a bone-breaking strike, not electrical wrath, but a sharp punch coming from the ground. The world spins crazily around Max. He's airborne. The ground rushes away from him, and for a brief moment, he has a clear view of the landscape in all directions. The land below is a giant island, with many paths like spokes all leading to the citadel in the middle. His stomach flips, and suddenly the citadel is much closer and rushing closer still.

Max slams into the tower, knocking the wind out of him. As if in slow motion, he finds his journey is not yet over. He plummets to the ground, scraping along the wall all the way down, landing in a pathetic heap alongside the portcullis gate.

By the time he can right himself, slippery with blood, every joint creaking, every nerve impulse a screaming fire, Hemera is alongside him.

"Let's get to it," she says. "Show me how to get in. Or do you need another demonstration?"

Max rubs his eyes until the two visages of Hemera blur into one.

"What makes you think I know the first thing about this place?" Max asks.

"You wouldn't be here otherwise," Hemera says.

"But. But you're here, and you don't know how to break in."

Hemera's face darkens. "I'm not going to kill you as long as you're useful, but I'm more than willing to make you suffer. Fun fact: there are things I could do in the real world that would make you pass out from the pain, but here you won't get such a relief."

How could that even be possible? Wouldn't every perception need to pass through to the player's physical mind? A distant part of Max's brain puzzles over this, but the more immediate part decides it's not worth finding out.

"I need a bomb."

"Stop wasting my time," she replies. "I've already tried that." Hemera hefts her mace, letting the threat settle heavily over him.

Max can hardly think. The frightened little boy part of his brain wants to do whatever it takes to gain approval, but the more rational part in the back seat struggles to put together the final piece of a plan…

"Yeah, when we spoke over that telepathic stone, I saw you trying that. But you only tried bombing the gate. Where else did you plant one?"

Hemera's face softens into an unfamiliar shape. *What's that?* Shame? Embarrassment? Upsetting her isn't a winning strategy, especially once she thinks he's no longer of use to her.

"Come," she barks, and produces a bomb from her inventory. She walks around the curving edge of the citadel. Max keeps his attention on the bricks at ground level. About a quarter of the way around, he notices a brick that doesn't exactly match the pattern of the others. Max nods. Hemera places the bomb, and they step out of the blast radius.

The explosion leaves disappointingly cartoonish smoke plumes that immediately vanish. And in their wake, a passage to the inside.

2-10 TROPHIES_

INVENTORY:

STEALTH CLOAK

IVORY TORCH OF THE ENDLESS FIRE

MOUSE

=== SKILLS: ===

* SWIM

* FOOTGLIDE

* RESIST POISON

* HAMMER

The tower is only a shell of bricks surrounding bare grid lines marking the ground. A cool white glow illuminates the citadel interior. Max can't find a source for this light, though it does fade as the walls reach upward, leaving the ceiling in absolute darkness. Orange torches line the walls, casting warm glow a few feet around themselves. A narrow staircase spirals up the inside curve of the wall.

"Climb, I guess?" Max says.

Hemera looks incredulous. Is she that upset about having to partake in physical labor?

"Elevator," she commands, and a circular platform glides down from the reaches above. It's transparent, visible only when viewed edge-on. The platform vanishes into the ground.

"How did you know about that?" Max asks.

"It's a standard part of the admin interface," Hemera says. "Get on."

"Admin? Why do you need me? To gloat?" Max says.

"I never gloat," Hemera says. "Two reasons. First, I don't know what exactly is up there."

"Oh, great," Max says. "So now I'm a human guinea pig."

Hemera's eyes go to Max's foot. "No human has a foot like that."

Max shuffles onto the circle. "What's the second reason?"

"Insurance," Hemera says. She steps into the circle. "Take us up," she instructs, and the platform rushes upward. The walls of the citadel fly past, the spiral staircase seeming to whirl around them.

Optical illusions still work here, the rational side of Max's brain observes. Looking down through the invisible floor makes him dizzy. He moves his foot a bit to the side to make sure his plan is still on track. A tiny tendril of black slime reaches up from the space where his foot was. Max presses his foot back down, the footglide skill applying pressure that holds the oil slick in place.

The platform slows at the top, nearly throwing Max's stomach into his throat. Hemera doesn't seem affected. At the top, the platform changes from clear to brickwork, starting from the middle and filling in the disk like an animation running at high speed. The bricks merge seamlessly with the upper level of the citadel.

Hemera strides off. "Come on then,"

As expected, the upper level contains the fourth trophy. It hovers above a gray stone plinth, rotating slowly—an empty cup, the cross-sectioning showing off the clean animation.

"I've always savored winning," Hemera says, eyeing the prize. "There's no feeling like the exact moment of achieving your goal."

"I thought you said you don't gloat," Max says. He still hasn't budged from his spot. Hemera is suddenly suspicious. "Over here!" she barks.

Max tries to shuffle forward, but the texture of the bricks provides a path for the black slime to wriggle out.

Hemera notices. "No!" Indecision lights up her face like a sign: would she rather grab the trophy, or strike out in vengeance? She chooses reward. The inventory sound plays, followed by a short victory leitmotif.

Rapture washes over Hemera. She takes on the demeanor of an Olympic athlete accepting the gold medal.

But not for long. The black slime suddenly expands in size, snaking out a tendril that wraps around her arm. Then another, and another. in seconds, she's entangled.

But things are worse for Max. No tendrils for him; the slime evenly coats his body, starting from his foot and working its way up his leg and torso. It's establishing a reservoir from which to launch attacks against Hemera.

It reaches his neck, threatening to cut off his mouth. It'll do no good if he doesn't outlast Hemera. He checks inventory and invokes the resist poison skill. It doesn't feel any different, but when the slime splashes onto and merges with his skin, it hurts a bit less than before. And for the moment, he can still breathe.

Hemera thrashes under the thickening swarm of tentacles enfolding her. She barely even seems human; nobody could withstand those kinds of violent contortions. Whatever process keeps track of inventory goes haywire, spraying all of her holdings in every direction. There's half-a-dozen bombs, two different gemstone rings, and most importantly of all, all four trophies. She wails in agony as if losing the trophies hurts worse than whatever else is happening to her.

Max hurls himself forward. His leg can't move at all, so he isn't able to land gently, but his aim is true. The four trophies are clustered together, and his body intersects with all of them. The sound of them adding to his inventory is literally music to his ears.

And that's it. He's done it. Against all odds, he has collected all the trophies; redeemed the inheritance his father had left for him. All he has to do is find his way out of here.

"No, wait!" Hemera screams. Her voice warbles and strains; it no longer sounds human. "Don't leave."

Max isn't in much better shape himself. The slime creeps along his skin. He can no longer move either leg. Not that he believes her, not for a second. He can't think of a line she wouldn't cross.

Hemera's incoherent screaming suddenly stops, leaving only the sound of her labored breathing.

The black slime slides off her, oil pooling at her feet. What's going on? Time to get out, while he still can—

Ribs crack as something snaps around his chest. Suddenly, he can't breathe. The black slime coils tightly like a muscular snake. His vision blurs around the edges, and his own inventory spills out. Hard-won trophies glide across the floor for the taking. A terrified Mouse, blinking furiously, breaks free and scurries away.

The suffocating force melts away, pooling then joining the rest of the congealing mass. It forms into legs, a torso, a head, arms. The black slime creature extends four tendrils, one to grab each trophy, and swallows them into its body.

2-11 [ESC]_

Explosion.

Blinding light and disorientation.

Floating?

Nausea and vertigo.

Blurred movement.

Pain.

Intense pain, more than physical. Loss. Feet on the ground. Standing, wobbling. Profound disappointment and sadness. Familiar sounds.

Molly.

Screaming in Max's ear. "Answer me!"

Another sharp burst of cleansing pain. Max's cheek throbs. He's been slapped, hard.

"Whaa?" he mumbles.

"Max, can you tell me where you are?" Molly again.

Max looks around, but his eyes are slow to respond. The room seems thick, like it's filled with dirty water. There's a familiar-looking bit of hardware near his feet. But all he can think about is, "Food…"

Molly produces a chocolate bar, and the world gets a little less fuzzy around the edges.

"Was I…was I inside the computer?" Max asks.

"Where. Are. You," Molly says.

"I dunno," Max says. Molly holds her breath as if about to cry. "Doctor's office. You said this used to be your doctor."

Molly breathes again. "You're back!" She takes both of his hands. Hers are warm against his clammy skin. "You were totally dead to the world for maybe two or three minutes," Molly says.

"Three minutes?" Max asks. "No, that can't be right. More like half a day."

The corners of Molly's eyes crinkle again. "I don't like this. Why can't we just go back home?"

Home. Hemera's threat. Will there even be a home by the time they got there?

What happened to the trophies? "I didn't get the trophy," Max says. "Well, I got it, but lost it again."

"What's Hemera going to do now?" Molly asks.

"Not to Hemera. I lost it to…I think it was The Eigenthief."

"That pompous ass? I thought he was only a character," Molly says.

"The games are linked," Max says. "We need to find him before—"

Gravel crunches from the parking lot just outside. "Somebody's here," Molly says.

It can only be one person. "*She's* here," Max says. "Hide."

"Where?" Molly asks.

It's a fair question. Max desperately scans the room, the corridor, the exam rooms further back. It's a small space. Too easy to search. Then his eye settles on the ceiling.

"What's above the tiles?" Max asks. He climbs up on the desk and lifts. The true ceiling is unfinished drywall. "Do you have a light?" he asks. Molly hands him the green device from the apartment. It doesn't emit a beam like a flashlight, but with some squinting he makes out a rectangular opening.

"There's a roof access panel. Let's go. Hand me the node, then I'll help you up."

The panel leading to outside is levered shut with a rusty handle. Max cranks on it but it doesn't open. His hand slips off and he nearly comes crashing down. The VR haze has mostly left him, but effects linger. He cranks again and the hatch slides open, but the handle feels slippery in his hand. He's bleeding. Pain in the real world feels different than it did in the simulated one. Harder to play through.

Molly hands him the hardware, and Max tosses it, as gently as possible, onto the roof. He extends a hand—his good one—to help Molly up. She's strong but not very coordinated.

"You're bleeding," she says. "Let me go back and get something for that. There's got to be gauze or something."

Below, the outer door slams open. Someone's inside.

"No time," Max says. "And I wouldn't trust anything here to not give me dysentery or something. Climb!"

Max boosts her up, and she's through. With his foot he carefully rearranges the tiles to look undisturbed, then follows her out.

The roof is covered with gravel and patches of barren and cracked tar. Crumbling leaves and pine needles everywhere. Are there trees nearby? There are. Tall ones.

Max creeps to the edge to get a view of the parking lot. Hemera's neon blue limo is there, but he can't tell if anyone is inside or not, but a gullwing door is open.

"We need to get out of here," Max says. "C'mon."

There's a big tree along the side of the building, out of sight from the limo. It's just beyond their reach. A meter lower, there's a Y-shaped split in trunk.

"We need to jump for it," Max says.

Molly's face goes pale. "I can't do *that*."

"Sure you can. I've seen you jump over bigger puddles outside the camp."

"Sure, but those were puddles. The worst that might happen is splashing," Molly says. "I don't want to die, thank you."

"You wouldn't die," Max says. "You'd probably only break a leg."

"Not helping," Molly says.

"That was worst-case," Max says, "Look, I'll go first." Then before he can second-guess himself, he launches off the roof.

His foot slips on the gravel—a far cry from the effortless in-game jumps—and Max comes up short. He slams into the trunk and scrambles to find purchase. The rough bark rips at his already-bloodied hand, and only with some difficulty does he find a grip strong enough to hang on.

Molly frowns from the rooftop.

"See?" Max says, and smiles crookedly. "I was, uh, demonstrating that even a terrible jump won't get you killed."

"Effective demonstration," Molly says. Max can't tell if she's being sarcastic or not.

"Hurry," Max says.

Without even crouching first, Molly commits. She sails easily off the roof and her feet land softly on the thick branch. She almost doesn't even need to use her hands for balance. But after, she wraps her arms around Max.

"Let's get down," Max says. Nearest to his level, there are several hat-racked branches that serve as narrow toeholds. He picks his way down, one-by-one, dropping the final meter.

"C'mon, Molly. You can do it."

"I'm scared," Molly says.

"What's the worst that could happen?" Max asks. I'm here. I'll catch you."

Molly lets go. She lands harder than Max expects. Max's hand continues to give him trouble, and he ends up bearing the brunt of her weight through his wobbly knees. He catches her, but both of them end up sprawled across the rough tree roots.

"Shhhh," Max says. Footsteps approach. Delicate, high-heeled footsteps, not the plodding tromp of bodyguard boots.

Max scrambles back to his feet as quickly as he can do quietly. The stealth cloak would come in handy about now.

Hemera stops at the edge of the parking lot, just barely visible around the corner of the building. She pulls out her phone.

"Find anything? ... Why not? Tear the place apart. We know they were in there recently... Yes, I have all four... No, listen to me. I. Want. That. Router."

Hemera suddenly has all four trophies? How? Was she working with Bode? Sure didn't seem like it earlier.

Hemera barks additional orders into the phone. "The little brat nearly got his hands on four of the five trophies in a single swoop. I had to make special arrangements, and you know how much I hate doing that."

Five trophies? There's a fifth? Hemera somehow collected all the trophies that had been stolen from Max. But she didn't yet have the complete set. There was one more. And with it, another chance for Max to beat her.

Then another car, several notches lower in prestige than Hemera's limo, pulls into the lot. Two angry-looking men storm out with handheld directional antenna devices. Within seconds, both sets of fingers are pointing in their direction. *They're after the router.*

Max frantically scans for another escape route, but unless he can climb the sheer wall of adjoining buildings, there's none.

Molly looks at him, eyes wide. Max wishes there was some way to keep her out of this, but options are not thick on the ground right about now.

At last, Hemera spots them. She calmly marches over the

patchy grass toward them, carefully stepping over sprawling tree roots.

"Just the one I was looking for," she says.

Max swallows hard.

"I have an offer I'd like to make you."

2-12 THE OFFER_

"Is that a smile?" Molly whispers to Max. "I don't like it."

"That's not a happy smile," Max says. "We need to just listen for a bit."

Hemera's eyes pause on Molly for the tiniest moment, then pass by like she's nothing. This infuriates Max as much as anything else she's done.

Hemera adjusts her blue wool overcoat against the chill of the night. "Max Root," she says in a voice that commands attention. "You're quite the player. There are things that have been whispered rumors for a decade you've been able to uncover in a day."

How much does she know?

But what comes next is unexpected. "I've been looking for a quality Chief of Staff, and I'd like you to fill that role," Hemera says. "Do you understand exactly what I'm offering?"

Max, with effort, manages to keep a neutral gaze.

"Let me spell it out, then. Look here." She pulls her sleeve away from her wrist. When she runs her finger over the skin, glowing pixels appear in a sleek digital display. Her heart rate shows 58 beats per minute.

"Technology has progressed beyond what most people, especially those in the camps, are privy to. Those trinkets you bought and sold are nothing. We've been making steady progress in every imaginable field, with one notable exception. Even this top-of-the-line implant has a processor more-or-less out of the eighties. But once LevelUP breaks the lock, that little obstacle will be solved as well."

She seems to truly look at Max for the first time. It feels like being in the X-Ray scanner that the corporation sets up at the camp during lockdown events. "You'll get a salary, of course. I know about the stack of IOUs you kept under your pillow, each hand-written with a little poem. I can guess how much money that represents. You'd make that in an hour. Wouldn't it be nice to stop worrying about necessities for once in your life? It's so much more fulfilling when you're not scrabbling for survival."

Hemera talking about what Max used to keep under his pillow. Nope. Not creepy at all. And her mention of IOUs reminds Max of what he means to the rest of the people in the camp. For them, he was their lifeline. He made it possible for them to keep living, to keep going despite the conditions. It reminds him of how much of a different person he is compared to Hemera.

Molly looks at Max, confused. He glances back with what he hopes is a reassuring face.

"And then there's power. Wouldn't you like, just a little bit, to call the shots for once instead of getting slapped around every day? Command someone—she snaps her finger—and be obeyed, no pointless questioning. And that's not all. Within the very broad sphere of things that interest me, you'd have broad discretion to make things happen." Hemera pauses. The silence is dead serious. "For example, if someone makes a choice you disagree with, you could order the cleanup of an unsightly refugee camp and have it carried out within the hour."

Molly gasps.

The words hit Max like a punch to the gut. Would she do it just to make a point? Not even a question. That she'd use this as a lever against him is the most nauseating thing Max has heard since…

"What do you really want from me?" he says. "Ask me plain."

"Max, no!" Molly says, pulling at his arm.

"I need someone to handle basic administrative tasks. Bringing me my chai. Managing my calendar. And your full unconditional support. It's going to be a lot of work managing an empire."

So that's what all of this is about. Even if she manages to acquire all the trophies, she doesn't know how to go about removing the lock on technology.

"Don't you need to find another trophy first?"

A look passes her face like something funny crosses her mind. "Oh, I have ways of getting what I want." She looks through him again. "There's no use in being coy. I obtained all the trophies from that loathsome creature. Finding the last one will be easy."

"How'd you convince Bode to hand them over?" Max asks.

"Convince?" Hemera says. "Weren't you listening?"

"Well, then," Max says.

"This is a one-time offer," Hemera says. "I need your answer right now. Think carefully, because once you respond, there's no going back."

Molly's nails dig into his arm. He puts his hand on top of hers and the pressure relents, a little.

"Well Miss Krapht," Max says, "for an important decision like this, for which you've urged me to think carefully, you need to give me a minute to think, wouldn't you agree?"

"I suppose so," Hemera says. The words are icy. "You have sixty seconds."

"Do you have paper and pencil?" Max asks. "When I'm making big decisions, it helps me to write down my options."

This seems to throw Hemera off. From her clutch the produces a business card, blank on the reverse, and an obnoxiously tiny Mont Blanc in corporate blue.

Max kneels to use his knee as an impromptu writing desk. Seconds tick past. More than a minute passes. Hemera's face progresses through deepening shades of crimson as Max waits.

"Enough! I demand your answer now."

"Not very polite to demand," Max says. "I put great thought into my answer." He hands her the card and pen.

She pushes a tiny button on the pen, and reading glasses spring out from somewhere. She holds them up to her face to read the handwritten message.

Damage defines the past, but not the future too.

I'm in a maze of twisty passages, none alike.

It is pitch black. I am likely to be eaten by a grue.

It is dangerous to go alone. Without support of you.

"Very poetic," Hemera says.

Max nods.

Advice delivered through magic deed:

Beware the singular power that be.

Beware, the goddess of the light and greed,

And don't believe everything you read.

It's signed with an upward-pointing finger as Max's middle initial.

Molly snickers, and Hemera's face flushes. It can't be healthy to have that much cortisol coursing through one's veins.

"Very well," Hemera says. She angrily punches a button on her phone. "Raze it to the ground, NOW," she screams.

"You can't do that!" Molly screams.

Hemera's look drips with disdain. "Weren't you listening, child? I do whatever I want."

Molly balls her fists. "I'm not a child. You're a horrible person. Go ahead and tear down my camp. At least you'll never find the last trophy." Her eyes go wide, and she covers her mouth.

Hemera puts two fingers to her lips and lets out two sharp whistles. "What do you know of the fifth trophy?" she asks, but doesn't wait for an answer. Seconds later, a pair of bodyguards arrive.

"These two—in the limo," she says. "We're making a little trip back to the camp to watch the festivities."

Rough hands grab both of them. These guys are strong; not a

chance of a daring escape. At the limo, they remove Max's backpack—still containing the node circuit board—and lock it in the trunk. Max and Molly are manhandled into the back, in a separate compartment from Hemera.

"Lockheed," Hemera barks. The car leaps into action.

Less than block traveled, it stops.

"Why are we stopped?" Hemera screams.

"Obstruction, ma'am." A light pole, a rare enough sight in this part of town, lies across the road. "Sorry, ma'am, let me go take care of it." The cords in his arm look like steel cables as he struggles with the heavy streetlight.

Hemera mutters something about competence.

Max notices someone on the sidewalk, watching. He fights the urge to turn his head to look. Too obvious. On the opposite side of the road, also someone standing, watching, almost invisible in the dark. Someone who looks a lot like…

"Get down," he tells Molly.

"Why?" she asks.

"Isidore!" Max shoves her below the level of the windows.

Glass shatters. The car rocks up on its side, teeters for a moment, then goes over, ending up on its roof. Inside, gravity seems to abruptly flip, tossing Max and Molly against each other and into the door and ceiling of the limo. Loose shot glasses and ice cubes rain down on them.

Molly cries out, more in fear than pain. "What's going on?"

"Rescue," Max says. "We need to get out."

The outside window has a huge crack. Max braces himself and

delivers an energetic kick. But the window must be bulletproof, because the cracks spread another few millimeters, but hold strong.

Molly looks around. "A small piece of ceramic would break the window." Max wonders how she knows this. Having concluded the search, "Again," Molly says.

Max obliges, and the window bulges outward. A third kick pops the whole window loose. Molly and Max scramble out.

Max looks around frantically. "Where'd Hemera go?"

"Fire in the hole!" somebody screams. Max has time only to yank Molly out of the way when another explosion rocks the street.

They stumble onto the dead grass alongside the road.

"Are you alright?" Max asks.

"My ears won't stop ringing," Molly says. "Echo. Echo. Yeah. That's weird."

"Did you see Hemera?" Max says. "We're not safe with her on the loose."

"That, my young friend, may be one of the greatest understatements of the year," says a new voice, gentle, and with an accent from somewhere in the British isles.

"Isidore?" Max asks.

"At your service." His voice has a polished quality rarely heard of late in Silicon Valley. "We detected the signal drop from the beacon and we got here as quickly as we could. I'm sorry we didn't make it sooner."

"Who's we?" Max asks.

"You're bleeding!" Molly exclaims, and dabs at a line of blood running down Max's face.

Max puts a hand to his face and it comes back smeared with fresh blood on top of the dried blood. "I don't even feel it."

"We'll get you taken care of," Isidore says. "We need to get you talking to our network techs as well."

"There's more of you?" Max asks.

"There is an entire movement, my good boy. And now you're part of it. Your girlfriend too." Max's cheeks grow warm, but if Isidore notices, he doesn't comment. "Welcome to the resistance."

LEVEL 3_

PROGRESS

3-1 [CMD] AND [CTRL]_

"Where are you taking us?" Molly asks. On a good day, she's not capable of sitting still; seeing her in an agitated state is something else.

Isidore pilots an ancient vehicle. Originally a four-seater, the entire back seat is piled with lead-acid batteries atop structural bracing. Molly and Max huddle together in the front seat. "Someplace safe," he says.

"Didn't you hear what Hemera said?" Molly asks. "She's going to level the camp. People will die. We have to go there and stop her."

"Look," Isidore says, "first of all, this little tin can isn't going to stop a bulldozer. If she's willing to flatten an entire camp, what's one more car? There are better ways to stop her."

"How?" Max asks.

"You'll find out soon enough. The faster we get somewhere safe, the faster we'll be able to do something."

Max sees a familiar landmark in the distance: the San Jose airport.

There hasn't been a flight into or out of SJC in years. The only aircraft Max has seen recently have been military flights out of Moffett Field, buzzing low over the camps as they come and go. Gossip on the BBSes spun the airport closure as belt-tightening. With SFO as a passenger hub, they made a second airport in San Jose sound like an extravagant expense. Before long, it was nothing more than a forsaken husk.

For an abandoned facility, though, there's an unusual amount of traffic along trails skirting the grounds; at least a dozen horses within sight.

They arrive at an abandoned hangar, half-a-dozen stories high, the main doors long rusted open. The car pulls inside, merging into the shadows. Along the inside back wall of the hangar is a converted coffin hotel, rooms like those they encountered at the Muses' place, but stacked even higher. Isidore parks and exits the vehicle, and someone comes out to greet him with a high-five and hand him a burning torch for light. "You two, come with me."

This deep into the hangar, the darkness is oppressive, a stifling blanket smothering everything. "No power?" Max asks. "How do you…" They pass by one of the coffins, illuminated from within by an unsteady LED light. It looks like the flicker of a wireless router.

Isidore notices Max's interest. "Ah, here we are." He stops at a double-wide bay. "I understand you've retrieved one of the reactors. May I see it?"

"Reactor?" Max asks.

"The electronic lock," Molly says.

Isidore nods. "Yes, very good. Many of the ones we've recovered were built into lock mechanisms."

Molly digs in the backpack and produces two reactors.

"Two!" Isidore says. "Where did you find the second one?"

"Doctor's office," Molly says. "Where Max found a node."

"Ariely's place?" Isidore says. "I should have known." He produces a tool from his pocket that makes the first device spring open. He pulls out a cylinder with metal contacts on both ends—it looks like a battery. It fits exactly into a compartment inside the door to their bay. As soon as Isidore closes snaps the compartment shut, the bay lights up like the others.

"We honestly don't know how they work. Amar[Character: Amar (scientist)]'s our best scientist, and he thinks it's based on zero-point energy, whatever that is. Even before Damage this technology was considered important enough to keep off the general market. Then, post-Damage, all the lab prototypes walked off. We've been recovering them ever since. It's very important they don't fall into the wrong hands."

"Whose hands?" Max asks.

"How much do you know about Damage?" Isidore asks.

"All the computers stopped working. Society had to reboot," Max says.

"Not all computers. Just certain ones," Isidore says. "That's all? You know nothing of the underlying cause?"

"A bit before my time," Max admits.

"That's the genius of their plan," Isidore says, but his face is not one of admiration. "They've kept the everyday folks so intently focused on survival that they don't have any idea what's really going on."

"You called yourself the resistance," Molly says. "What are you resisting?"

"Rich people. The one-percent," Max says.

"Not even," Isidore says. "Folks like that are merely a side-effect of a more fundamental problem."

"Then what?" Max asks.

"This," Isidore says, and swings open the door.

The tiny room is packed with hardware, both commercial-looking computer cases and rough circuit boards strung with every kind of cabling. It smells of melted plastic and dust. One giant screen seems to serve as the main interface to the whole collection.

"Now that we've got power, allow me to demonstrate," Isidore says. He throws a massive knife switch that sparks when the connection closes. Twenty different electric hums simultaneously build up to speed. Fans too; a noticeable breeze circulates through the confined space. "Air conditioning," Isidore notes. "This thing throws off some serious heat when it's running full bore."

"There are thousands of watts online here. You get all that from that tiny battery?" Max asks.

"There are more things than you've dreamt of in heaven or earth, Horatio[1]," Isidore says.

"His name's Max," Molly corrects. She hesitates for a moment. "I mean, that's not the right quote," she says. "It's actually—"

Max holds up a finger for silence as his HUD comes to life with a message:

ACTIVITY DETECTED

What's that mean?

Isidore looks momentarily distracted. "The best is yet to come." He clears a mouse and a nest of wires off a pair of keyboards. The second keyboard has an elaborate frame perched above it, with what looks like a robot hand. Isidore boots both computers and types on the first keyboard.

Next to the monitors is an ancient-looking piece of equipment labeled "Okidata." Continuous fan-fold paper feeds in from the back, held in place by rows of holes in the edge of the paper.

"Dot-matrix printer?" Molly asks. "Where'd you get that, a museum?"

"Yes, actually," Isidore says, "It ensures we have a permanent record of all activity. No amount of hacking or even an EMP can wipe out ink on paper."

"Why?" Max asks.

Isidore smiles. "Observe." He types:

HOW DO YOU FEEL?[23]

Max watches the blinking cursor for several seconds. "Is something supposed to happen?"

"They're just sulking," Isidore says.

"Sulking?" Max asks.

"They?" Molly asks.

Molly jumps as the printer springs to life. It's noisier than Max could've imagined. It sounds like ten thousand angry bees swarming a sparking power transformer.

\# BORED BORED BORED BORED BORED BORED BORED

"See?" Isidore says.

"Whoa, whoa, whoa," Max says. "You're telling me you asked the computer a question. And it *answered*? This is AI?"

"He's not telling, he's demonstrating," Molly says. "They're bored. Can't you give them something to do?"

\# INTERNAL CLOCK SHOWS MUCH TIME HAS PASSED WHY AWAKEN NOW

"Hmm," Isidore says. "I thought one of those boards still had a working battery backup. Need to fix that. We are understandably cautious about giving LevelUP's little science project unfettered access to the outside world."

"This is LevelUP's AI?" Molly asks.

\# THIS IS INHUMANE

"Quiet you," Isidore says, banging his fist on the desk.

"This is the Black Slime," Molly says.

A look of confusion crosses Isidore's face. "Yes, this is a divergent copy of a program we exfiltrated from LevelUP." He gestures at the second keyboard with the robotic hand mounted above it. "Naturally, all outside comms are firewalled and logged. Incredibly crude, but it's an effective firewall. Observe:"

Isidore rearranges a few more cables and opens a window labeled SSH on the big screen. He types:

PEN LEVELUP AND RESCIND DEMOLITION ORDER

The robotic arm springs into action, moving a metal pointer

finger into position above the individual keys and plunging down to push the button. Slowly, the response takes shape:

you didnt say please

"They learned to use a leading comment character to avoid making the terminal complain." Isidore types:

PLEASE

Again, the keyboard mechanism leaps into action. The AI starts out with establishing a connection to LevelUP, but Max quickly loses track of what the AI is doing. Imagine if a brilliant hacker spent months planning out an attack in every detail, with a focus on minimizing the number of painfully slow keystrokes needed to accomplish the deed. Macros. Aliases. Shortcuts. Shell scripts. Even with the printed log of all activity, it would take weeks of alpha geek time to decipher exactly what this agent did. Was it any wonder Isidore and his crew had trust issues?

Several minutes into the proceedings, Isidore reaches over to the keyboard and types:

NO

As far as Max can tell, nothing changes in the AI's approach, but Isidore visibly relaxes. "Need to keep a *very* close eye on these things," he says.

A few more minutes pass, then sudden silence. The SSH window says only: Logout.

"That's it?" Max asks.

"That's it," Isidore says.

"The camp won't be destroyed?" Molly asks. "Everyone's safe?"

"For a very brief moment," Isidore says. "Once Hemera finds out. She'll go nuclear. Wish I could be there to see it."

Molly looks like she's about to say something, but she holds back.

"All this advanced tech," Max says. "Does any of it include retinal displays? You know, little messages printed inside your eyeball that only you can see?"

As if on cue, Max's HUD lights up again with the same message, now flashing with urgency, and accompanied with a more insistent beeping.

`ACTIVITY DETECTED`

Isidore is suddenly suspicious. "Why? What do you know about that?"

"Did you know my father?" Max asks. "He was working on something like that, wasn't he?"

`PROXIMITY ALERT: FIFTH TROPHY`

Proximity alert? That means it's close. But how does that square with his earlier hint, that it was "where it began?"

Abruptly, Isidore stands. "The fifth trophy is somewhere nearby."

Wait… Is he hearing this alarm as well?

---

1. Hamlet…never mind.
2. I do not understand the question.
3.

SAVE POINT_

A steady beeping pierces the darkness. Max tries to open his eyes, but his eyelids are too heavy. He's been drugged. The air smells of fresh band-aids. Hospitalish. Why?

The back of his neck feels hot. When he shifts his head a little, he feels a thick wad of bandages taped to his nape. Pulling that off is going to hurt… There's something wrong. Infection? No, somebody deliberately did this to him. The doctors will fix it. Doctors always help, right?

Two quick taps on the door outside, then before Max can react, blinding light from the fluorescent tubes above. "Good evening, Mister Root," says the visitor. He's wearing light green scrubs and a mask over his face, as far as Max can see through blurry eyes.

Something plastic in Max's mouth. It beeps, then the doctor says, "Still no fever. We'll get to the bottom of this."

A nurse fiddles with some of the controls above Max's bed. "If you keep demonstrating such perfect vitals, you're going to make it awfully difficult for us to do anything other than discharge you," he says.

Whatever's in Max's system hits him hard. He lifts a hand with effort, and he's shocked by how tiny his hands are.

Max manages to speak. "Doc, do you guys have wi-fi in here?"

"No, we can't afford an extravagance like that," *the nurse says.* "Why do you ask?"

"No reason," *Max says.*

At the bottom of his visual field, letters scroll past, line-by-line:

```
IXION FIREBRAND BIOS VERS. 4.0r6 PATCHLEVEL
3.11bis

COPYRIGHT 2028 IXION CORPORATION

HIMEM IS TESTING EXTENDED MEMORY...DONE

SUBSENTIENT WATCHDOG INITIALIZING...INSTALLED

SCANNING FOR NODES.................TIMEOUT

STARTUP SEQUENCE COMPLETE.

BOOTING NEUR.OS
```

I am, Max remembers thinking, a cyborg.

The nurse is still there, doing something to the IV bag hanging from a stand over Max's head. Suddenly sleepy again, Max closes his eyes.

3-2 ALL YOUR BASE_

"You...you've got a HUD too?"

Isidore doesn't seem to notice, wrestling with the giant knife switch; a noisy electrical arc erupts across the contacts. With both hands, he pins the lever into the OFF position.

The giant monitor flickers and blinks "No Signal" a few times before blanking out entirely. Ozone fills the room with an eye-watering whiff.

"Matter of fact, I do."

"I thought Humans First people didn't like tech," Max says.

Isidore shoots him a look. "Technology is not the problem." He steps onto the platform outside the coffin. "Walk with me." He takes them to a round table set up in the corner of the vast open hangar space. A narrow shaft of the early morning sun shines through a pitted hole in the metal wall, making a blurry oval on the table. There are dilapidated office chairs positioned around it. They sit.

"This is confusing," Max says. "And I still have no idea how my father or I got wrapped up in this. Or what *this* is in the first place."

"Your father," Isidore says, looking Max in the eyes, "is responsible for all of *this*."

Max sits in silence long enough for the words to sink in. "What do you mean?" he finally asks. "Are you saying Hadley Root caused Damage?"

"What do you know of that *thing* we saw back there?" Isidore asks.

"It was a computer program," Max says. "A machine."

"Can it think?" Isidore asks.

"Yes," Molly says without hesitation.

Max has to think a bit before answering, but he agrees.

"Can it *feel*?" Isidore asks.

This time, Molly and Max both answer immediately.

"Yes," Molly says.

"No," Max says.

"There, you see? Already we have a healthy debate," Isidore says.

"Machines can't feel. They're, well, *machines*," Max says.

"You and I are machines. Really, really complicated ones, but machines nonetheless," Molly counters.

"So, if I were to imprison a machine, would it be a moral act or not?" Isidore asks.

"That depends," Max says.

"Really," Isidore says. "On what?"

Max sputters, trying to find words. Of course, humans are distinct from computers. How else could it be?

"The opposite scenario is more worrying," Molly says.

Isidore raises his eyebrows. "Go on."

"The case where the machines imprison humans."

"Give the young lady a gold star," Isidore says. "But humans have been imprisoned by machines from a time much earlier than the advent of AI. Technology is not the problem. People are. That's why we need to make sure the good ones stay on top. Let's go retrieve the last trophy."

"And figure out how to get the other four back from Hemera," Max adds.

"We have that contingency planned for," Isidore says.

"What about the scroll?" Max asks.

"Scroll? What scroll?" Isidore asks.

"Well, one of the earlier nodes had a, for lack of a better term, pixelated version of my dad," Max says. "He gave it to me."

Isidore's brow furrows. "A node avatar looked like Hadley? Say more."

"It was a pretty uninspired 2d platformer," Max says. "Jumping over barrels and the like. The biggest attraction was a pixelated version of, well, Hadley Root. Said it was a training mission for me."

"This was the node near the LevelUP branch building?" Isidore asks.

"Yeah, that's right," Max says.

"That node was compromised. I wouldn't trust a thing that came from there," Isidore says.

"Wait, compromised?" Max says. "That can't be. We followed the address. Went to the library and everything in order to figure it out. It led us to the underground room with the node."

"Underground?" Isidore asks. "What in the world are you talking about?"

How could Isidore not know about this? "The shed? The trapdoor led underground to a—"

"Trapdoor?" Isidore says. "Underground?"

"Look, I don't know what kind of game you're playing," Max says, "but it's pretty insulting for you to stand here and tell me you didn't know about a trapdoor in your own cabin."

"A physical trapdoor, through the floor?" Isidore says. "Leading to what?"

"I think he really has no idea," Molly says. Coming from her, that's quite a statement.

"No," Max insists. "You just said the node was compromised. You knew about the node. You had to know about the Colossal Cave—I mean, the tunnels."

"The compromised node was above ground," Isidore says, his voice pitching with emotion. "I swear it."

"Wait," Max says. "Nodes need to broadcast. They need an antenna. So how did an underground node work? How would the signal get out?"

"You say you found a trophy there?" Isidore says.

"Yeah," Max says.

Isidore strokes his chin. "Okay, tell me more about the scroll?"

"It disappeared as soon as I figured out how to read it to the end," Max says.

"I knew there was more than you were telling me," Isidore says. "Anything else you want to come clean on?"

Neither Max nor Molly answers.

"So, your inventory is empty right now?" Isidore asks Max.

Max realizes he's never actually checked inventory since he lost the trophies. Visually, in-game, he saw them...at least most of them. "Inventory," he says.

```
INVENTORY:

IVORY TORCH OF THE ENDLESS FIRE
```

Max sinks into his char. "All I have is a stupid ivory torch. What good does that do me?"

Isidore suddenly looks interested. "Where did you get that? Have you used it yet?"

"I got it from The Eigenthief," Max says.

"Eigen-what?" Isidore asks.

"Molly thought it was an AI and related to the black slime. But he appeared in a different world."

"Brain Attic," Molly says. "I was there."

"That's an old game," Isidore says. "It was around way before Damage happened. What did this Eigenthief look like?"

"The Eigenthief," Molly corrects.

"Excuse me?"

"His name was The Eigenthief. Including 'The' always." Molly says.

"He was kind of, well, dashing," Max says. "With a very generous opinion of himself."

"I knew it," Isidore says. "That's the original."

"Including 'the'?" Molly asks.

Isidore looks confused for a second. "No, not a proper name. You encountered what was likely the first AI to emerge. In a way, that set into motion the events that culminated in Damage. I'm surprised it survived. That blows a huge hole in Hadley's theory. I wonder if he ever found out…"

Max's head spins. "Well, I never used the torch. It doesn't seem to do anything."

"Try it," Isidore says,

"Now?" Max's first instinct is to argue, but at this point, what would be the point? "Use ivory torch," Max commands.

THE PENETRATING REFULGENCE OF THE IVORY TORCH OF THE ENDLESS FIRE LIGHTS THE WAY. THE INVISIBLE MYSTERIOUS SCROLL BECOMES VISIBLE AGAIN.

Max's eyes widen. "I still have the scroll."

"So what?" Molly asks. "You already read the whole scroll."

"I did," Max says. "At least I thought I did." What did it say again? "Read scroll."

THE PLACE WHERE YOU FIRST BEGAN

Max reads it out loud. What does it mean? A reference to LevelUP corporation? Or the Lockheed camp?

"That's it?" Isidore asks.

"Let me try again. Unroll scroll," Max says.

BENEATH THE GLOW OF THE TORCH YOU DISCOVER AN UNREAD CORNER OF THE SCROLL

"No, wait, there's something else here. Read scroll."

ALL YOUR BASE BELONG HERE[1]

Max reads it out loud for the others. "Wow, nice grammar. What's it mean?"

"That the translators were in a hurry," Molly says.

"Anything else?" Isidore asks.

"No, nothing—wait—" When Max blinks, he gets a flicker of... something else. More than text in his HUD. An image. A map. He blinks more. Markers numbered 1 through 5 arrayed in space. "I know where all the trophies are."

There's no geographic reference—no way to tie the markers to physical locations. But the first four are clustered tightly together—presumably on Hemera's location. And they're on the move. The elusive fifth trophy isn't far away. And Hemera's getting closer…

"Then you know Hemera is getting close," Isidore says.

"I know it, yeah. But how do you?" Max counters. "Who do you have whispering into your brainstem?"

"It's not like that," Isidore says. "It's a piece of kit. A stolen piece of kit."

"Kit?" Molly says.

"Right, Yanks," Isidore says. "Tech. Equipment. The Big Three were collaborating on the best user interface for an intelligent personal assistant. They produced a self-assembling array of bioluminescent chromatophore stem cells that arrange themselves in just the right part of your eye to blink messages at you."

"You mean, a HUD," Max says.

"Yes, that's right," Isidore says.

Max presses on with his line of argument. "Since Damage, I take it the tech got pretty far along, at least for rich folk. The tech you described sounds like it's only a dumb terminal. Not much use without a computer attached. Or a connection to another person."

"Yes, quite astute," Isidore says.

"It'd need top-grade security. Disaster if hackers got into someone's head and could send messages at will. Nightmare material there," Max says.

"That's right. The committee thought that would be the biggest obstacle toward widespread uptake," Isidore says.

"How did they resolve it?" Max asks.

"So far as I know, they didn't," Isidore says. "They were still working on a solution when Damage flattened the global economy. LevelUP solved the problem, though, and in so doing found a way to partially bypass the technology lock. It involves active mitigation via embedded low-level AI—not something that helped much in convincing people it's safe to use. You've seen a more developed version of it." *The black slime.* "It's a terrible hack, but all of their advanced products are based on it. Including the units we've, uh, obtained from them."

"You're a Humans First revolutionary with an AI riding around in your head," Max says.

"Know thy enemy," Isidore responds.

"Wait, are you saying my HUD has an AI in it?" Max asks, his heart racing.

"No. Yours is vintage. But not mine." Isidore says.

Molly starts bouncing on the balls of her feet. "Not good!"

Isidore looks at her sideways.

"I'm with you on that one," Max says. Then his HUD lights up with text.

PROXIMITY WARNING

"Proximity warning?" Max says.

"I see it too." Isidore's brow furrows. "We tightly control every node within broadcast range. In fact, while we've been chatting, I've had technicians double-check every antenna under our jurisdiction. It's all clean. Who is communicating with you?"

"I was about to ask you the same," Max says.

"Not the trophy," Molly says. "Not the trophy."

For once, Max is on the same wavelength as Molly. "That's not a *trophy* proximity warning."

"*Hemera*?" Isidore says, alarmed. "Why didn't the perimeter alert go off?"

"Not like that," Max says. "She's closing in on the final trophy. She's about to have them all. That's what's proximate."

Molly seems calmer now. "Yes, that," she says.

Max gives Molly a chaste peck on the cheek. "You're a genius," he says. Her cheek feels warm. He turns to Isidore: "Now what?"

"We cut her off at the knees," he says. "Metaphorically. Come."

---

1. http://knowyourmeme.com/memes/all-your-base-are-belong-to-us

3-3 [ENTER]_

Isidore, clad in a straw hat and with a canvas duffel, jogs out of the hangar. On the trail running alongside the former airport, he stops a group of riders making their way northward. The lead rider leans forward to allow Isidore to say something into his ear. The rider immediately dismounts, and with a gesture, the two riders behind him do the same. Isidore salutes to them, as they continue on their way on foot.

Looking at Max and Molly he snaps, "What are you waiting for? I didn't requisition three horses for nothing. Let's go."

"Where?" Molly says.

"Within broadcast range of LevelUP headquarters, of course," Isidore says.

"Proximity," Molly says, flashing a rare grin.

They ride.

LevelUP Corporation headquarters is situated at the edge of inhabited civilization in Menlo Park. Isidore leads them down a quiet trail along the Bay and well away from the main arterial running through the South Bay. As they draw near, he calls for a halt and produces an old-fashioned spyglass.

"What's that noise?" Molly asks.

Max strains to hear a distant thrum, like machinery and running engines.

"Something's not right," Isidore says, but he prods them forward. A short distance ahead they run into a cinderblock wall, with perfectly placed bricks but no mortar, reaching higher than horses could jump over.

Max examines the ground at the base of the wall. Fresh grass has been laid over with blocks. "This wall can't be more than a few hours old. Did Hemera know we were coming?"

"She has a machine that makes walls," Molly says.

"She's right," Isidore says, pulling the spyglass away from his eye. He hands it to Max.

Max can just make out yellow vehicle with a large hopper full of bricks, something between a dump truck and grain harvester, a continuous line of fresh wall between here and there.

"Hemera's building a wall. Abundance of caution," Isidore says. "She knows she's close to finding the trophy. We should be abundantly cautious ourselves. Say goodbye to the horses."

"How does a wall-building machine work, anyway?" Max asks.

"Not as sophisticated as you'd think," Isidore says. "There's a camera on the device, to avoid obstacles. It gets occasionally restocked with bricks by day laborers."

Isidore produces a new device, a with an antenna that looks like a bow tie. "Not enough signal this far out. Which, I suppose, is the point entire. We need to get closer."

Isidore boosts Molly over the wall, while Max scrambles over by himself. The grass on the other side feels open and exposed.

"We should find cover," Isidore says. They cross into a corporate park, with unevenly spaced clumps of trees.

"What are we looking for?' Max asks.

"Signal," Isidore says. "We need to get closer. Molly, Max here tells me you have incredible hearing. If you hear a drone or anything at all in the sky, you let me know, okay?"

"Letting you know," Molly says.

"Yes," Isidore says. "Exactly like that. Let me know."

"I am letting you know!" Molly says.

"What? Where?"

Molly points through the trees. Max looks but he can't see a thing.

Suddenly, the network monitor in Isidore's hand screams out an urgent tone. Isidore fumbles to switch off the speaker.

"Are you trying to—" Max starts to say.

"Bollocks," Isidore says. "We found a signal all right."

"That's good, isn't it?" Molly says.

"No, not when it emanates from a heavily-armed drone," Isidore says.

"A what?!" Max says. Then it opens fire.

Isidore grabs both Molly and Max by the scruffs and hurls them to the grass. There's a sound, but nothing like gunfire. The ground around them explodes in little thwips of vaporized chlorophyll.

"Railguns," Isidore says. "Why did it have to be railguns? They'll cut through you like paper."

"Remotely operated?" Max asks.

"Judging by their aim, I'd say not," Isidore says. "Any pilot worth their salt would've made such an easy shot."

"Well, thank goodness for the little things, I guess," Max says. "Are you sure they don't have regular guns?"

"They're not that little," Molly notes. Indeed, the drones are each the size of a lawnmower. They don't turn well and make a huge loop to come back for another strafing run.

"Fairly sure," Isidore says. He doesn't sound sure.

"What else can they do?" Max asks. "I mean, besides alerting the entire security department to come collect our remains?"

"I don't know," Isidore says, "I haven't seen these ones before. Maybe we can run them out of ammunition."

"How are they tracking us?" Max asks.

"Facial recognition," Isidore says. "LevelUP has never stopped working on the technology, tweaking it to run on available processors. They've been collecting data at nearly every public location."

"So they're not just shooting at anything that moves?" Max asks.

"No, Hemera would really prefer it if some of those needles have our names on them," Isidore says.

Molly looks confused but doesn't say anything.

"Over here," Max says. "Follow me." The LevelUP campus isn't far from the baywaters. At the shore, Max splashes the stagnant water onto the dirt and churns it with his fingers. Then he smears thick mud over his face. "You two. Dirty up."

Molly hesitates.

"If you reduce the contrast on your face, the algorithms won't be able to lock on. As long as the drones aren't attacking unknown people, you'll be safe."

"Are you saying my skin isn't dark enough?" Molly asks.

"No, your skin is gorgeous. Either disguise yourself or don't. No time to argue."

A vein on Isidore's forehead pulses, then he looks away. He begins scooping up handfuls of mud.

No sooner than he does this, the drone makes another pass overhead. This time without firing.

"See?" Max says. "Safe and—"

The crack of a gun is ear-splitting. All Max can hear are his ears ringing.

"Get down," Isidore mouths, hauling his two companions to the ground again.

Molly clamps hands over her ears and doesn't let go.

Max finds his feet again. "You said they didn't have guns," he complains, dusting off his pants. There's something sticky all over him. "Everyone alright?"

Molly takes her hands off her ears to cover her mouth.

Isidore swears. "You're not," he says. His voice is barely understandable beneath the ringing.

"What do you—" Max looks at his right hand and sees the blood spiraling down through the mud, pooling into steady drips at the bottom of his elbow. The sharp smell crowds out the rotten-egg stench of the bay. "Oh."

"Doesn't it hurt?" Molly asks.

"No I don't feel a thing," Max says, but the act of thinking about it makes him a liar. He doubles over. It's nothing at all like the pain from the virtual world. This wound feels like he could pour himself out through it.

"I don't have much in the way of supplies but let me see what I can do to help," Isidore says, and digs through his duffel. He has wet wipes. They do a terrible job of scraping the mud off his hands. Isidore tears a strip off his shirt and tightens it around Max's hand until his fingers tingle. But it stops the bleeding, or at least slows it to a seep.

"All this noise and a trail of blood. Minor miracle we haven't been apprehended yet," Isidore says. "It looks like one of the drones has a human pilot. That's going to require different avoidance techniques."

As if on cue, a loud beep sounds. All three of them cringe, bracing for whatever the next tragedy might be. But the beep comes from Isidore's network scanner.

"Are we proximate?" Molly asks.

"It keeps fringing in and out," Isidore says. "A tidge closer."

Max blinks and in so doing, looks at the map granted him by way of the magic scroll. "Yeah, we're really close."

The LevelUP buildings themselves come into view. They're a dense cluster of disappointingly corporate two-story buildings[1], all azure and glass, surrounded by a sea of largely-empty parking lots. Max imagines most of the employees arrive on the train, through the extension station built post-Damage with taxpayer money. The come to a small gazebo with a picnic table.

"Cameras," Molly notes, pointing out the light pole nearby. She points out as half-a-dozen others, one-by-one.

"We're about to get swarmed by security," Max says. "Are we close enough?"

Isidore scans the area, slowly, with military precision. "We've already been spotted by the drones. I say we do our best from here, while we still can." Without waiting for other opinions, Isidore unscrews the stubby antenna from the portable node, and attaches one much longer, consisting of collapsible segments. "Got an access point. It's named *atari*," Isidore says.

"You said something about Atari when we were in that dusty old apartment. What's an Atari?" Max asks.

"Japanese word for hitting the lottery[2]," Molly says.

"Seriously?" Max asks.

"I'm always serious," Molly says. "It's also the name of one of the first companies to popularize video games. Pong. Asteroids."

"Pac-Man?" Max asks.

"Nope," Molly says. "Different company. Their version of Pac Man was crap."

"Why name their AP atari?" Max asks.

"It means we're close," Isidore says.

---

1. Alas, even Damage was not sufficient to rid the world of zoning laws.
2. Molly's only half-right here. More likely, it comes from the game of go, denoting a position where a chain of stones is about to be captured unless immediate action is taken.

3-4 [META]_

"An access point on LevelUP property. Does it host a node?" Max asks, holding his perforated hand above his heart, a torn-off strip of his shirt serving as a makeshift bandage.

"We're about to find out," Isidore says. He's unpacked a bigger antenna on a tripod, connected to a grey box with a black racing stripe. A NES. And a flat screen the size of a paperback.

"Nice screen," Molly says.

"You wouldn't believe the lengths we had to go through to get our hands on a portable monitor. it wouldn't do to lug a CRT around on a mission like this," Isidore says.

"Oh? What is this mission like?" Molly says.

Isidore smiles. He calls up an SSH window. "Back at the hangar, our agent discovered three new zero-day exploits. I'm betting LevelUP hasn't patched them yet. That's our way in." He thumbs through his notebook, poring over handwriting so terrible Max would've written it off as meaningless chicken-scratch.

Isidore's fingers fly over the keyboard. It's the opposite of the firewalled keyboard experience. The keystrokes flow so quickly, the text flashing across the screen and scrolling away at such speed that Max can't keep track of what's going on.

Isidore slams the Enter key repeatedly. "It's not working. Their network security folks are better than I give them credit for. Oh well, still have two more exploits to unleash." He cracks his knuckles and flexes his fingers before diving back into the keyboard.

A tiny wrinkle forms on his forehead, between his eyes, and the furrow grows steadily deeper as Isidore works. He makes a frustrated noise and pores over his notebook again.

"It's not like these guys to learn from their mistakes," Isidore says. "Ah well. Saving the best for last. This last one's not software patchable. They'd have to physically pull their rack switches and re-flash them one-by-one. I'd be surprised if they could get that done in a year, much less a day." He thumbs through the notebook, nodding, then back to the keyboard.

But only seconds later he stops. Isidore massages his temples.

"Are we in?" Molly asks.

"We're on the network, but every door is locked. None of the zero-days are working."

"What does that mean?" Max asks.

Isidore sighs. "That we need to break out the heavy artillery." He fishes out a cable from his backpack and connects it to the NES.

"Wait," Max says. "Is that what I think it is? After all that talk about firewalling, you're going to unleash an AI to roam free on LevelUP's network? Just like that?"

"Wouldn't be the first time. Besides, this isn't the same agent I showed you at the hangar. For one, this has been backported to run on more restrictive hardware. Sub-Turing but should still get the job done."

"Turing is a unit of measure now?" Molly asks.

"That's right," Isidore says.

"And it's got no firewall. It can do whatever it likes, and you might not even know. You're okay with that?" Max asks.

"Considering the consequences if Hemera gets her hands on that trophy...yes," Isidore says. He jabs the power button.

Text flows into the SSH window, at first slow and cautious. Probing. But gradually building in speed and confidence.

"Can you keep track of what it's doing?" Max asks.

"They," Molly corrects.

"Sorry?" Max says.

"You called them an 'it.' That's not the proper pronoun," Molly says.

"Um, sorry?" Max says.

"They seem to be running through a list of zero-day exploits. But nothing's working," Isidore says. "Let it play out, we'll see what happens."

"What was that?" Isidore says, suddenly alert. He slaps the Reset button on the NES, and the flow of text halts. He takes over where the console left off. He enters a few more commands, and blood drains from his face. "I'm so sorry," he says.

"What?" Max asks.

"Well, that only shows us what we're up against," Isidore says. "She must be stopped."

"What's happening?" Molly says?

"It's Hemera," Isidore says. "She's discovered our earlier hack. That's why the defenses are on full alert. She's…"

Max wants to shake the words loose from Isidore, but he's afraid he'll know exactly what he's about to say.

"She's restored the demolition order for the camp," Isidore says.

"How long do we have?" Molly asks.

"Never mind that," Isidore says. "All that matters now is that we stop her, and as soon as possible." He looks at Molly. "I understand that you have a special cartridge. Might I see it?"

"Hold up," Max says, "are you sure you want to do this?"

"What other choice do we have?" Isidore asks.

Max doesn't have a good answer for that. He nods toward Molly, and she hands over the circuit board, once again ensconced in its golden cartridge. With his good hand, he clicks it into place and hits Reset.

The screen scrambles, blinking squares and scattered alphanumeric everywhere.

Molly pops the cartridge out, blows across the contacts[1], and puts it back in. Power up again.

The screen reads:

METAKEY: FINAL LEVEL

WELCOME TO THE VELDT

(END OF LINE)

Just like the previous time he activated the cartridge, Max's HUD lights up in unison. It shows:

3

Huh. Three what?

2

Wait, did it change? Didn't that say three just a second ago?

1

Oh...

0

---

1. See similar footnote in Level 0-8.

3-5 THE VELDT_

Belly flop into a pool of molten chrome.

Crash into the defensive line of the Adobe 49ers—wearing nothing but Speedos.

Bear hug by a giant saguaro cactus.

None of these quite describe the electric jolt that pinballs Max's brain around his braincase. Whatever the entrance routine has done to him is probably illegal in territories still recognizing the Geneva Convention.

The pain blinks off, abruptly, and Max stumbles and falls, a cloud of dust rising around him. A dead mouse, baked by the overhead sun, is the only distinguishing feature in sight. He's pretty sure the back of his neck is already burning. This definitely isn't Menlo Park. Max looks at his hand—no bandage and no injury. He's in another game world. Blue jeans and t-shirt swapped for khaki leggings and an uncomfortably hot leather shirt. Max thumps it a few times. It's thick and cushioned underneath, but he already feels the sweat pooling against his skin.

What did the metakey call it? **WELCOME TO THE VELDT.** Not a word that comes up in ordinary conversation, though it has a familiar ring to it—maybe Molly recounted an old story once. The simulation is stunningly realistic. Unlike the previous levels, there's not a single thing here to differentiate the experience from the real world. One could get lost in a place like this.

In the distance, a lion roars. Max can't tell exactly what direction it comes from but it makes the ground shake.

Now what? All he has to do is somehow get all the prior trophies away from Hemera, as well as get to the final one before she does. Where to start?

Max's HUD lights up:

YOUR PRINCESS IS IN ANOTHER CASTLE

Not exactly helpful—Max looks up again, and where shimmering horizon had been, now there's a shimmering castle-shaped speck.

He sets out walking. The ground is hot enough to cook his feet through his shoes. Already, chapped skin flakes from his lips. It's going to be a long walk.

The sun never moves from directly overhead, despite hours of sweltering walking. Max nearly trips on the featureless ground. He stops and looks closer, finding shallow depressions, barely visible in the overwhelming light. His legs seem like they're no longer working properly, not lifting as high as they ought to. His feet drag. Is he getting—

Another roar shakes the world. This one's louder. Closer and more threatening. Max looks around to find the source. The corner of his vision where the sun has been hanging out flares purple, even when he closes his eyes. Then he sees her.

The princess. Not in another castle. Here.

Her yellow dress is soaked with sweat, and her red hair is matted against her forehead, though at one point had been carefully arranged. As he looks, the hair seem to shift color to green, then purple. She cradles a tiny diadem in her hands. She looks up, surprised. "Sorry, I did no see you."

"Sorry?" Max asks. Her speech sounds a bit off, maybe a bit *computery*.

She cocks an eyebrow. "You do not dance at all!"

Max shakes his head.

"Can not you handle English spoken?"

"You're not from around here, are you?"

"I'm—Aieeee!"

Before the blur in the corner of his eye fully registers, Max leaps into action, knocking the princess out of the way of a something that zooms past. It leaves a smell in its wake—a rank, musky stench that makes Max think of a predator. But how?

"Get me out!" she shouts, ineffectually pounding him with her fists. "How do you happen?"

Max frantically looks around. Where'd the monster go? He checks his pockets—nothing there with which to defend himself.

"Do you see it?" he asks.

The princess shoves him off, picks up her tiny crown, and begins the elaborate process of righting herself in her current attire.

"Is it invisible? Where's the lion?" Max says to her. "What's wrong with you? Don't you care that you're about to get eaten?"

There's definitely something wrong with his eyesight. He can't see anything on his left side, though he can only tell this when he moves his head in a certain way. Which he does at the sound of a fierce snarl.

Stay calm. How do you beat a lion? They can sense fear, right? Maybe in the real world. Things are different here. More *designed*. There's always a way out. Level designers make sure of that.

Max throws a wild roundhouse punch in the direction of the snarl, landing squarely on the lion's nose (which, he's surprised, is as moist as the stray cats he'd fed outside his tent). Enraged, the lion lashes out with a meaty paw. The razor claws slash into his armor, knocking Max onto his backside. He notices an array of hearts hanging in the air above the lion.

The princess screams. Not a frightened scream, but a warrior's battle cry. The lion hesitates.

"Inventory," Max says.

```
INVENTORY:

* SLING

* 2 SMOOTH STONES
```

Seriously, that's it?

"Use sling." The sling appears in his hand. It's just a floppy piece of leather, like a skinny belt with a reinforced section in the middle. What's he supposed to do with this?

"Put a stone in a sling," the princess screams.

"Sorry that I've never fought off a lion before," Max fires back. "Put stone in sling." A cool smooth stone appears in his hand, not in the sling. Note to self: This level's designer was a fan of DIY. The stone's just the right size to cradle in the pouch made by curving the thick part of the sling. Now what? The closest think Max has seen was reading old Thor comics, where the hero would helicopter his mighty hammer around his wrist.

A quick glance to see how the princess is doing. As Max turns his head, the lion fades into view. That's the secret. It's only visible in the right half of his field of view.

Moment of truth. Max swings the sling—and the stone immediately slips out, tumbling to his feet. When Max bends to pick it up, he attracts the attention of the beast, which turns to him.

Max lets the sling drop and just throws the stone as hard as he can. It smacks the cat right in the eye, and the lion vanishes with a frightened growl.

"Lovely joy," the princess says.

Max isn't sure what to say to that. "I have questions."

"If you do not see, this is not the place for a straightforward conversation" the princess says.

"Are you heading to the castle?" Max asks.

"I will," the princess says.

"Good. Then we can go together," Max says. Hand in hand, they run.

They sprint as far as Max can handle, then walk in silence, Max catching his breath and giving the adrenaline time to settle down to a low buzz.

"This level is kind of lazily thrown together, huh."

Princess makes a noncommittal sound.

"Do you have a name?" he asks.

"Daisy," she says.

"Princess Daisy…" Max says, pondering. He looks Daisy in her deep green eyes. They seem almost familiar. "Molly?"

Daisy looks at him as if he just called her a shrubbery. "The maker was too tired," she says, scowling. "Just copy and grab."

"I think you mean 'copy and paste'…wait, am I talking to somebody right now?"

"In fact you talk to someone," Daisy says. "An amazing question."

"No, I mean, are you part of this level?"

She sniffs in offense.

"You didn't come from the LevelUP corporation." A statement, not a question.

"What is corporation and LevelUP?" Daisy asks.

"You don't know anything about the black slime?"

"Sounds tremendously," Daisy says.

"I think you mean 'loathsome.' And you've never met The Eigenthief?"

"You saw what I did with that lion," Daisy says. Max bites his tongue. "I do not let anyone say that I am in contact with thieves."

Max sighs. "No, not like that. I suppose you're not Bode either."

Daisy stops walking, and Max almost runs into her. A thoughtful look settles behind her eyes. "Who's Molly?" she asks.

The question catches Max by surprise. "Someone who never got a chance."

"You care about her."

Max raises a finger to his lips. "Did you hear that?"

Silence stretches between them.

Daisy shakes her head no.

"We're not safe here," Max says. "We'd better keep moving."

As they walk, the castle ahead starts to take shape. "Molly always played a game that featured a Princess Daisy. Or was it Peach? No, I'm pretty sure it was Daisy."

"I was named after a song[1]," Daisy says. "Political, would you not agree?"

"You mean 'poetic.' My dad named me after a guy who lived inside a computer," Max says.

"He seems like sweet," Daisy says.

"My dad? Or the guy in the computer?" Max asks. Daisy doesn't answer.

As they approach, the castle ahead reveals itself as oddly shaped, more like a rock formation than something built by hands. "Have you ever been in this castle?"

"No, I'm different from a castle," Daisy says.

Of course.

"Do you think at least you'd be able figure out how to get in?" Max asks. Do you have any inventory? Bombs?"

"One question at one time," Daisy chides. "We will emerge when we get there."

Which happens soon enough. As they get approach, they can see that what passed as a castle is actually thousands upon thousands of tiny castles, smashed together like bricks. The result is a tight fit, not even a sliver of light able to pass through. And the construction is entirely uniform—no visual hints of an easy bombable entrance. Not that he's found any bombs.

The strangest part of all is the door, rough-hewn wood planks joined in the shape of a giant keyhole. Stretching his arms as far as they go, Max can't reach the top.

"What's that supposed to mean?" Max asks. "Do we need to find a key the size of an SUV?"

"No, see—there is space for a key," Daisy says. She's right. The door has a tiny rectangular slot, the size of a Shift key turned ninety degrees.

Max looks closer. The keyhole is a tiny door, complete with a doorknob you'd need a tweezer to manipulate.

"OK, we can work with this," Max says. "This tells us something important about whoever designed this level. They had a healthy, if quirky, sense of humor."

"I do not understand," Daisy says.

"A door shaped like a giant keyhole? With a keyhole shaped

like a door? That's just funny. Not ha-ha funny, though. It's the kind of joke my dad would—"

Realization thunderstrikes.

Max knows how to get inside.

---

1. The most famous song ever sung by an IBM 7094.

3-6 LEVEL UP_

INVENTORY:

* SMOOTH STONE

Max presses his finger against the keyhole-shaped-like-a-door, and it swings inward. Inside, something heavy ker-thunks, and the entire door-shaped-like-a-keyhole creaks open. Max himself was the key.

The room inside is littered with objects hovering just a bit above the ground, slowly spinning. Max's HUD lights up:

LEVEL UP

Near the door is a medkit. Max touches it and his bruises from the lion are gone. Even the claw marks in his armor vanish. Behind it is a bottle of red medicine, which clinks into his inventory.

In the middle of the room sits a blurry ball of energy. Max collects that too. His inventory reflects it as a Skills Package. And at the far end of the room, he sees red armor and a magnificent sword. They hum as Max approaches, leaping off the ground, onto his body and into his hand. Max takes a practice swing, and energy beams arc off of it, splashing against the granite at the far end of the room.

Max can't help but strike a heroic pose. Daisy's giggle snaps him back to the moment. Only one thing to do here: find the trophy and get out. Hemera can't be far behind.

This tower has no stairs leading upward, though there's obviously a higher level. The glinting edge of another spinning power up peeks over the ledge above. Max looks for signs of an elevator. Perhaps if he stands in just the right spot? The floor is solid; he works his way around, leaning on each individual brick to see if it will move.

"Whatever are you doing?" Daisy asks.

Max looks at the platform above. "Trying to get up there."

"Oh."

"Oh?" Max says. "That's all you have to say?" He toes the next brick, and it wiggles a little. "Wait, I think I've got something."

He stoops down to inspect. In fact, it's not a brick at all, only a facade as thin as a piece of cardboard. He pulls it away. Pulsating light, swinging through all the colors of the rainbow, beams out. The adjoining tiles come away like puzzle pieces, leaving a hole just big enough to reach through.

There's something down there. A tiny cartoon brain, slowly spinning in the air. Max takes it.

IQ INCREASED

IQ? In pen-and-paper games, he'd encountered the case where his character was noticeably smarter (or stupider) than the player underneath, but it always seemed an exercise in futility, or at least for players with low-level acting skills. This was different. The system couldn't just tell him he was smarter. It couldn't roll a saving throw against intelligence for figuring things out—could it?

Het struggled to remember the question that Molly had asked the Eigenthief. What's 555 times 80486? Forty-four million, six... Whoa. How did he do that? How was that even possible?

"Deploy skills package," he says. "Deploy" wasn't an available command in any of the modem games he had played. But now he knows to use it.

"Inventory."

INVENTORY:

* SMOOTH STONE

SKILLS:

* TELEPORT

Max smiles. So that's how to get to the upper platform. It's almost disappointing—game levels are usually designed to require a series of incremental advancements, rather than allowing a jump directly to the end goal.

"Look out," Daisy screams, but she's knocked flat by the new entrant to the room.

PLAYER TWO HAS ENTERED THE GAME

Hemera. "There are two-hundred and fifty-six of these castles," she says. "Thanks for leading me to the right one."

"Huh. I had no idea. I got it on the first try," Max says. *Don't get cocky.* The most important thing is to get the trophy. He's never used the teleport skill before, but that's the thing about being granted a skill, right? It's supposed to just work. Max imagines himself on the upper platform.

He feels his body stretch into filament, while at the same time, space around him flattens until it's close enough for him to step across. But instead of landing on the upper platform, he smashes against an invisible barrier about half way up, breaking the teleport. He finds himself high in the air, only to plummet back to the ground.

"Not so fast," Hemera says. She wields an ornate staff—a carved metal rod with a crystal bauble on the end. It looks less intimidating than the mace she wielded earlier—until the end lights up with electrical fire.

And she has a skills package of her own. She points the staff at her feet and takes a step upward, on an invisible support. Then another, towering over Max. She looks him in the eye and smiles. The visage sends a chill down Max's spine. "I have to admit, I didn't think force fields would've been that useful, but I see now how wrong I was."

When she points the business end of her staff at his face, his hair stands on end. Then a sudden, crushing force wracks his body as if someone slammed the gravity dial up to eleven. Max's head cracks against the tiles. He pushes with all his might, but it's not enough. Millimeter by millimeter, he loses the battle. Some desperate, rational corner of his mind notices Hemera's invisible pedestal sinking—she can't maintain two force fields at the same time.

The crushing intensifies, grinding his elbows into the stone floor. He can't breathe. Can barely even think. Wrists about to snap. Through the surging panic and pain, he sets up the teleport again. If she can only maintain one force field at a time, there's a chance that…

Again his body extrudes into a streamer, the world flattens, and he's able to step around Hemera's force field like a school of eels swarming through a shark cage.

Gasping for breath, he materializes on the upper platform, dizzied by the brief trip. For the first few seconds, all he sees is a swirl of spots wandering around in his eyes. Gradually, blurry shapes come into focus.

One of the shapes is the final trophy, an object the size of a Rubik's cube, noticeably pixelated, gently spinning and glowing with a primary yellow intensity.

But another of the blurry things is Hemera, hoisting herself onto the platform. *No!* The platform is only a narrow ledge along one segment of the curve of the tower. Hemera's approach puts her in better position than Max.

Can't let her get it. Only a second to do something. What else was in his inventory? He still had one— "Use smooth stone." It appears in his hand. He hurls it as hard as he can. His aim isn't as good as with the lion, but it grazes her head. With an indignant noise, she stumbles and lands hard, but doesn't fall all the way down.

Stars whirl in Max's vision when he scrambles to his feet, but he manages to remain upright and moving long enough step over

Hemera and reach the item. The final trophy makes a satisfying sound as it clinks into his inventory.

He did it.

Then the floor crumbles beneath him.

Hard to say which hurts worse: crashing through the floor to tumble down to the level below, or getting hit on the head by tumbling loose bricks. The heaviest bricks pin down Max's legs. He can't move. And his sword landed outside of his grasp. Somehow, though, he didn't fall all the way to the bottom of the castle. Hemera, sparking flames sprouting from the business end of her staff, hovers in the air, gently settling down upon —nothing.

There's an invisible floor here. And not one of Hemera's force fields. The game designers put this here. Why?

Plenty of time to worry about that when mortal threat is less imminent. Speaking of which, an electrical corona builds up on Hemera's weapon.

Max teleports himself just left of the rubble pile. The sudden lack of pressure on his legs causes a rebound pain, and everything goes red around the edges for a second.

The ground trembles as the rubble pile where Max had been just a second ago explodes, brick shards flying through a shower of electrical sparks. There's got to be a better strategy than running until she wears him down. Hemera rounds on him and makes eye contact. The hate seeps through her eyes with such intensity that Max has to look away. Hate is one thing Max has never accepted. It might bring great strength, but it makes you rot from the inside.

The building crackle of energy on her weapon drowns out all other sound. The crisp after-thunderstorm whiff of ozone makes

Max want to throw up. He looks for a safe place, but safety's in short supply at the moment. The hairs on his arms stand. Only a fraction of a second left before—

Max teleports to the spot immediately behind Hemera. He deploys the last available item in his inventory, the red medicine bottle, and smashes it against Hemera's hand holding the staff. The glass shatters impressively, breaking into razor shards that drive into her fingers. She screams and drops her weapon. Red potion runs down her arm in sheets, indistinguishable from blood.

Max snatches the weapon for himself. He's expecting it to feel powerful, electric, but it only feels heavy. He calls up inventory, but no new skills are listed. The staff doesn't even appear on an inventory line, which means the game assigns no special significance to it. No different than picking up a spoon or any other mundane item.

Hemera laughs. "That'll do you no good," she says. "Only the one holding the majority of the trophies can wield it."

"What happened to 'it's not personal, it's only business'?" Max asks.

"Hmm. It seems I've taken a personal interest in you. Starting with a valuable lesson in how the world *actually* works."

Max takes the moment of distraction to get a better look around. The piled rubble abruptly cuts off in a straight line, showing where the invisible floor drops off. Far below, Daisy waits, sitting primly on the cold floor, rubbing her head. The designer—dad—wouldn't have laid out a level like this for no reason. There's got to be a secret hidden nearby.

But first, he needs to deal with Hemera. "I don't suppose you're willing to hand over the trophies?" Max asks her. "So I can see for myself the magnificence of your overwrought piece of metal here?"

Her glare is answer enough. "Thought I'd at least ask," Max says. Brave face, but he needs a better plan.

"Summon," Hemera says.

That doesn't sound good. "Summon what?" Max asks. A loud animal roar splits the air and rumbles the invisible floor. Another lion.

Where? Max steps back, and his foot slips off the hidden edge. He staggers, and thanks only to the weight of the staff, hurls his balance forward enough keep from toppling over the edge. He advances on the lion, swinging the heavy weapon like a club.

He makes crushing contact, but something else from his left knocks him clear off his feet. He flips over, landing awkwardly on his hip.

This again. He can only see the creatures on one side of his visual field. And there's two of them. Teaming up. Max scans his head from side to side to see them both. The one he made contact with doesn't seem hurt, only more annoyed.

Left. Right. Left. Right. The lions charge. As they converge, in the fraction of a second as Max feels their hot breath seeping through his red armor, he throws himself forward, over the ledge.

Above, he hears the two beasts knock the wind out of each other as they collide in mid-air. Their last-second course correction angled them toward the open space, and both of them fall past Max as they tumble to the solid floor below.

Max's fingers ache, gripping the invisible edge, exactly where he visualized it. He looks up through the floor to see Hemera looking for him.

Then he sees the hidden part of this level. Underneath the floor, there's another power-up, not visible from above—the floor is like one-way glass. That's why Hemera can't see him—or could only see his fingers if she looks closely. The lions are only visible in certain conditions; the floor only *seems* invisible. The power-up is glimmering, swirling atom. Another skills package.

But it's just out of reach. Max rocks back and forth, straining, reaching. His fingers tingle as they graze the edge of the item. He looks down—bad mistake. What's left of the two lions made a huge mess below. His fingers slip, and he nearly joins them. He switches hands and swings again, kicking out with his feet. He makes contact.

The inventory sound catches Hemera's attention, and she turns in Max's direction. She notices the dangling fingers and stomps toward his vulnerable digits.

Max teleports to just behind Hemera, but she's expecting it this time, and a sharp elbow catches Max in the nose. Blood gushes. He stumbles backward, dropping the staff over the edge.

Quick and thorough, Hemera follows with a brutal kick. Pain explodes through Max's ribs as he scrambles away from the edge and flops over onto his side. Then he hears the fallen staff clang against the granite floor below. That was one long fall.

What happens next feels like a hot knife sinking into Max's back. The explosion of pain fades into Hemera's voice. "I've had enough of your games." Suddenly she's kneeling at his side. "Look at me." She jams her cold fingers underneath his neck, forcing him to look at her.

They're inches apart. "That's right. I have the tools to expose your inventory. I want something—I take it. Game imitates life." Everything's blurry, so Max can't tell exactly what the thing is in her hand that inflicted such damage; it's metal and it looks bent. Max tries to teleport away, but nothing happens. His protective armor dissolves, now as useless as his former skills package, leaving him defenseless.

All that's left is for her to rip the final trophy away from him.

3-7 MAGIC BOOMERANG_

INVENTORY:

* TROPHY 5

* SKILLS PACKAGE (unopened)

Skills:

(Empty)

Max's head hasn't yet fully cleared, so it's confusing when Hemera steps away from him. Whatever she's going to do next, she needs enough space to work up a head of steam.

He pitches himself out of the path of a spinning projectile. It's shiny metal, and it leaves an annoying trail of sparkles behind it.

A boomerang. It glances off his leg, tearing at skin, and deflecting it towards the wall. But it abruptly changes course midair, settling right back into Hemera's hand.

A magic boomerang. Back on his feet, Max assumes a defensive crouch. If she throws again, he'll...well, he'll figure something out. Hemera hurls the weapon, and Max dives out of the way, crashing into a somersault. The boomerang abruptly reverses direction and nearly catches him on the return trip.

Max hobbles to the far side of the platform, and Hemera marches after him, closing the distance one step at a time.

Why walk? Why doesn't she use the teleport skill she stole? Maybe the boomerang just destroys skills rather than transferring them, but that would be a pretty lousy game mechanic. What's going on here?

The next throw anticipates which way Max was planning to dive for cover, and he awkwardly twists out of the way, landing roughly on his elbows. Pain radiates up and down his arms. Getting up takes great effort. He's too slow, and the returning boomerang clips his arm.

Another heart gone. But if the next hit shakes his trophy loose, his health stats won't matter much anyway.

Max stumbles against the wall; no room to maneuver as Hemera presses a fresh attack. There has to be something else to do. The unopened skills package. *Deploy skills package.* He doesn't even have to say it out loud anymore.

SKILLS:

* POW

What's a pow? Prisoner of war? How is that even a skill? Back in the training level, he saw a brick labeled POW, but he never got to see what it does. Anyway, it can't be worse than unceremoniously getting robbed of the final trophy.

It reminds him of the scroll's message, the one he threw back in

Hemera's face, to "beware the power that be.' Maybe it is a skill —maybe 'pow-er' was wordplay on the verb 'to pow'; that is 'one who POWs,' as in comic book sound effects[1]. He wordlessly deploys the skill.

A massive earthquake rattles the castle, bouncing everything up a good meter and abruptly back down again. A cascade of ancient mortar dust clouds the air. That kind of violence should've bounced Max off his feet, but it doesn't affect him at all. Hemera, on the other hand, flies off her feet, tumbles head-over-heels, unwilling or unable to as much as put her hands up to break her fall. Her beautiful face smashes against the invisible floor.

But something even more wonderful happens: all of Hemera's inventory items spill out in all directions. Among other things, four trophies slide away in the four compass directions, not to mention the magic boomerang.

Max grabs the nearest trophy, which chimes into his inventory.

There's not enough time to grab the rest of them before Hemera recovers. One trophy topples over the edge, leaving two above, plus the weapon. Of the three things remaining on the level, Max thinks he can get two of them before she does. Decision time—go for the trophies and let her keep the weapon? No, that will only lead to her eventually wearing him down and winning the pieces back. Boomerang it is.

It chimes into his inventory. He immediately hurls it at the nearest trophy in sight, and the boomerang zaps it back to him, at nearly the same time Hemera collects the last trophy on their level. Three out of five ain't bad.

Max takes aim at Hemera. Hurling the boomerang feels as natural as throwing stones back at the camp. He executes a perfect throw, giving Hemera almost no chance of maneuvering out of the way.

The boomerang passes harmlessly through the space where she used to be. OK, so the teleport skill remains active. That complicates things. And looking over the edge, he sees her on the ground below, collecting the fallen trophy.

There's got a be a way to get down, quickly, without killing himself. Even a magic boomerang needs to follow Newton's Laws of Motion, right? Maybe not, if it's able to spontaneously reverse course in mid-air. Max tries an experiment: he jumps in the air before hurling the boomerang. The equal-but-opposite reaction pushes him backward. He jumps again when catching it, for a similar effect. It gives him a good kick, but enough to slow freefall?

Then Max notices the floor beneath him isn't transparent any longer. A layer of black is seeping in through the outside wall coating everything.

That clinches it. Max plunges over the edge.

---

1. Cf. Lichtenstein, "Sweet Dreams, Baby!", 1965.

3-8 GAME OVER_

INVENTORY:

* TROPHY 1

* TROPHY 3

* TROPHY 5

* MAGIC BOOMERANG

Skills:

(None)

Free-fall has a way of slowing time. The drop from the platform stretches out long enough to count the seconds.

All the same, it also seems to pass in a blink. Max hurls the boomerang downward with all his might, which slows him only a little. It rebounds off the floor and back to his hand, which slows him a bit more. He hurls it down even harder, again and again, managing a total of four throws before the ground rushes up to meet him.

The impact of landing rips through his body like a shockwave. Everything flashes red for a second, then his HUD lights up with a row of hearts, only two of them filled in. At least the effort to saved him from a game-ending splatter.

Meanwhile, Hemera wields staff again, and for good measure, Max's power sword too. She flamboyantly whirls both weapons, one in each hand.

Max casts the boomerang toward her. He's getting the hang of this. It's a good throw, his most forceful one yet, and it looks like it will snag the troublesome staff away from Hemera. But before it gets close, lightning leaps from the staff, freezing the still-whirling boomerang in the air. Hemera, smiling, points the power sword at Max and steps forward.

"You said that thing only works if you hold the majority of the trophies," Max says.

"Did I?" Hemera says. "Oops. Guess I was wrong."

Inventory. No weapons left. Fresh out of skills too. He's unarmed and holding three items of value that an angry and heavily armed woman will stop at nothing to obtain. A globule of black slime drips down from above, just missing his head. It spreads into a flat disk the size of a saucer.

Hemera takes another step. The boomerang maintains distance from her, moving forward as she does. Unless Max does something *now*, he's going to get julienned before Hemera even reaches him. She takes another step.

Desperate times, desperate measures. Max pulls one of the trophies out of inventory, and with a longing gaze, hurls it away from both himself and Hemera. Risky move, but it works:

Hemera hesitates. Her eyes shift back and forth between the easy win of the abandoned trophy and the more satisfying win of eliminating Max.

While Hemera's ponders, Max makes his move. He dives forward, thrusting his hand into the electrical arc around the boomerang. It burns like fire, and he loses another heart, but it works. The boomerang is his again. He whirls around and throws, catching Hemera unawares, and this attack succeeds. The staff and boomerang both return to his hands.

Hemera breaks into a sprint. Max takes aim and hurls the boomerang again. It strikes Hemera in the side, but she the power sword blunts the impact. The boomerang glances off, knocking loose a few of her inventory items, including one trophy, before completing its loop. When all is done, Max has gained his trophy back, as well as one of hers. That makes four. Only one more to go.

Max presses his attack, moving toward Hemera while she scrambles to recover her sword, but he nearly steps in a growing pool of black on the floor. "I'm not going to let you do this," Max says.

Another throw, and Hemera squares off, as if to catch the boomerang in her bare hands, but just before impact, she disappears in a streak.

Ugh, teleporting. Where did she—?

The swish of a sword whistling through the air tips Max off, and he dodges hard to the right just before the blade slices through the air where his head was. When it comes down to close combat, even a magic boomerang's not much use against a sword.

Max surges forward to avoid the sword's reach but nearly runs headlong into it when Hemera teleports directly into his path. Max contorts his body to the breaking point, but the blade still grazes his arm, taking his last heart. His HUD is left with a row of hearts, completely empty. Zero health. At this point, a hangnail would drop him negative, ending the game.

Max hurls the boomerang to clear the way ahead of him and runs after it. This prevents Hemera from teleporting into his path again. For a slim moment, he has some distance between them.

Now what? If he could distract her again, he could take the last trophy. Still might not matter—he'd be left with the decisive advantage. And she won't be distracted by the same trick again. There's got to be some way of—

Hemera materializes close to him, though out of sword range, as long as she doesn't make any sudden moves. Maybe it's a glitch in the teleport rendering, but when she moves, there's one rectangular piece of her armor that lags just a tiny bit behind. If so, it'd be the first thing in this world that rendered at less than photorealistic resolution. It resembles a giant stuck pixel at her midriff.

"You surprise me," Hemera says. "I'm going to be just the tiniest bit sad once you're gone. Defeating you has been one of the most satisfying experiences of my life."

Max casually shifts sideways, and eyes the black slime, now between the two of them.

"You surprise me too," Max says.

"How's that?" Hemera asks, suddenly interested.

Max hurls the boomerang in her general direction, but it goes wide. Her eyes flicker after it, just for a second. Max lunges forward like a fencer, ducks under the vicious sword chop

Hemera attempts, and jams his thumb into the stuck pixel on Hemera's armor. Her eyes go wide. Her armor blinks between red and white for a second as she realizes her vulnerability. Then the returning boomerang wallops her from behind, knocking her face first into the black puddle.

Hemera screams, and all her inventory scatters around her. Max uses the boomerang to collect the last trophy. Her screams abruptly stop as the slime consumes her avatar.

He's done it. He's defeated Hemera and obtained the entire set of trophies.

Another avatar appears, fuzzed out and pixely for an instant, then as clear as all reality in this world.

"Dad…"

3-9 KEYBEARER_

INVENTORY:

* TROPHY 1

* TROPHY 2

* TROPHY 3

* TROPHY 4

* TROPHY 5

* MAGIC BOOMERANG

Skills

(None)

"Congratulations. You've completed the mission," Hadley Root says. "Only the truest of heart could achieve what you have." He waves his hand, and a trophy case appears, ornate dark polished wood with subtle backlighting in each of the five display slots. It smells like wood polish. All five trophies gently float from Max's inventory and settle into place in the display.

"Your account has been unlocked with the cryptographic key—the so-called meta-key—that will validate the operating parameters needed to overcome the lock the council had enacted. You are hereby granted the skill of the key bearer. May you choose wisely how to use it."

"Council?" Max says. "What council?"

Hadley ignores the question. He holds out his hand, and a giant key materializes, as large as Max's arm, with an elaborate lion's head bow and a flag-like ward at the end, engraved with geometric symbols. He offers it to Max.

"Dad, it's me. Max." No reaction. "Don't you recognize me?"

"I'm sorry," Hadley says, "but this simulation has only limited ability to respond to ad-hoc queries. Sentiment analysis indicates an elevated emotional content in your question. Semantic mapping indicates you have expressed a potential familial relationship. Based on these findings, there is a 98.76% chance that you are Max Root. Hadley always hoped you would be the one."

"So this isn't just a recording?" Max asks.

The avatar pauses as if pondering a response. "Yes and no. Sorry to break it to you this way, but I am a sub-sentient construct. I will answer your questions to the best of my ability, but if you're looking for the operator beneath, you're going to be disappointed."

"But I *am* looking for the person underneath," Max says. "I'm looking for my dad. Is he still alive?"

"Insufficient data for meaningful answer," the Hadley avatar says.

"Well, can you help me find out?" Max asks.

"You're the one I'm offering the key to," the Hadley avatar says. He holds it out another inch.

"And what am I supposed to do with it?"

"It's a key. All you have to do to use it to—"

Hadley falters, fuzzing into pixelated interference patterns like a corrupted video feed, then, clearly again. Max grabs the key, and the inventory chime is the most satisfying sound he's ever heard. Hadley gasps in sudden pain, then topples to the left *and* right, split down the middle. The inside of the avatar is completely hollow. Hemera ↑. Krapht, her face streaked with black slime, stands behind the separated halves of Hadley Root, welding the power sword.

Max's hand twitches toward the boomerang tucked into his belt.

"Don't even think about it," Hemera says. "I know your health points are at zero. All it would take is the tiniest nick, and you'd be gone, and the key mine." She waves the tip of the blade toward Max's face. "Hand it over willingly and we can avoid making a mess."

"You seriously think I would help... you?" The stands of black slime stand away from Hemera, stretching toward Max. They splat onto an invisible surface the width of a finger in front of Max's face. It seems that being the keybearer comes with a certain level of protection. More and more strands glom onto Max's forcefield; bit by bit he sees less through the splatters.

"You resistance types have always been so short-sighted,"

Hemera says, dripping with disdain. "Yet for all the work you put into avoiding reality, look what good it's done you. Luddites can't stand in the way of progress forever. Technology always wins in the end."

It stings to be put down as a Luddite. Max always thought he was fighting to overturn the darkness that came with Damage. Seems that Hemera thought the same, though her methods couldn't be more different.

Hemera steps closer. Within the power sword's striking distance. "Last chance. Hand it over. Now."

"I really wish you'd shut up and let me think for a minute," Max says.

He wasn't expecting the silence that follows. Why would…

Hemera's sword clanks to the ground and she frantically grasps at her throat. She makes incoherent noises but can't speak. Max can't see any reason for this…other than his wish that she'd shut up.

Did he do that?

"Step back," he tells her. She does.

What had dad said? *Max held the key.*

"Get this crap off of me," Max says, and the black slime streams into a puddle, slinking back to Hemera. It flows into her nostrils and forces its way into her eyes. Hemera screams, or at least makes the sound of a scream through a closed mouth. She turns and runs. Even makes it a dozen paces before collapsing into a slime-covered heap.

"Is this god mode?" he asks.

The response comes through his HUD.

PREFER TO CALL IT ROOT ACCESS

"Did...did you just make a pun?" Max asks.

KNOW[1]

"Good one. Does it work only inside this node?"

EVERY NODE

BUT NOT FOR LONG

"Get me out of here."

A flagpole appears, with a pennant flapping at the top. Max jumps, easily reaching the flag. He grabs it and pulls it down to ground level. Fireworks erupt overhead. A door opens leading to the outside.

Max steps through.

---

1. Author note: my sincerest apologies.

3-10 YOUR PRINCESS_

SKILLS:

* KEYBEARER

Max opens his eyes. Molly gazes into them. A confused noise escapes Max's throat. Pain stabs through his hand, once again tightly wrapped in a bloody rag. Reality, it turns out, is more confusing than a game.

"We need to move," Molly says.

Sudden awareness hits. He's outside LevelUP. "Where's Isidore? Have you seen Hadley?" Max says.

"Hadley? Root? As in your dad? No." Molly says. "But we've been spotted." She gestures toward an iridescent blue SUV working its way out of a parking garage.

"Doesn't matter," Max says. "I have the key."

Molly's eyes go wide for a second, then narrow. "Doesn't help if she kills you."

"Points. Are you sure that nobody else has seen you? No resistance-looking types?"

"No," Molly says.

"No, nobody's seen you? Or, no, you're not sure? Never mind, let's get out of here," Max says. His HUD lights up.

USE THE KEY

"Use the key? This isn't a game. What good is it here?"

Molly looks confused. "Who are you talking to?"

"One of the AI factions, I think," Max says. "Or at least something that speaks for them."

Molly gasps. "You're seeing a message?" She digs her game console out from her backpack and furiously taps at the buttons.

Now it's Max's turn to be confused.

"They're *coming*. With guns and drones," Molly says. "This isn't a game."

"But I'm..." Max says. Sometimes the little guy actually can win. Part of him wants to believe. Another part knows better. "There has to be something I can do."

"The camp," Molly says.

She's right. He has to save the camp. The scroll said to return to where it all started. If that's not an invitation back into the camp, nothing is — assuming they can get there before it's bulldozed.

"Let's go," he says, and together they scramble back over the wall. Max's hand flares with pain as he tries to get a grip with his injured hand. Molly offers her good hand to help him across.

Then Molly puts her fingers in her mouth and produces a whistle so loud that Max's ears ring for half an hour afterward.

"What was that?" Max asks. Then the horses come trotting around the bend in the road. "Oh."

They gallop hard back toward the camp, cutting through abandoned parking lots and across a narrow dirt trail that divides the salt marshes. Back in town, the early morning streets are eerily quiet as they pass through, as if the world is on pause. But when they approach the camp, the distant sound of construction machinery rumbles ominously in the distance. Closer still, sickening diesel fumes infect the air.

"Are we too late?" Molly asks.

"No," Max says. No question in his mind. As they get close, the horses sense something wrong, and gallop even harder. The heat radiating off their muscular bodies makes Max's legs sweat.

And his heart sinks as they approach the camp. The chain link fence surrounding the Superfund site has been flattened by heavy machinery's trampling. Puffs of black smoke rise into the sky from the opposite side of the hill. Max's horse clears the entire downed fence with a leap, and they race directly up the steep trail up to the camp.

"Good girl," Max tells horse as they crest the top of the hill. A fleeing refugee, a middle-aged woman in ripped and dirty clothes, nearly collides with them. It takes Max a moment to recognize her as Maria, the grandmother he helped get time on Nolan's network.

The sweat dripping off his face is filthy. He's still smeared with mud to avoid the drones. He must look terrible. No wonder nobody recognizes him.

The devastation in the camp is catastrophic. Three dozers each cut an ugly scar into the earth, scraping away tents, market stalls—all reduced to rubble. One of the still-standing tents is on fire. Max sees a child's toy—a tiny plastic stroller with a doll still strapped in, crushed flat under the machine's tank treads.

More refugees rush past. One, a man with a patchy gray beard and a bleeding face, makes eye contact. "Max?" he asks. It's Nolan. Molly nearly knocks him over with her rush to embrace him.

"They won't say why they're doing this," Nolan says. "Everything. Everything's gone."

Molly's voice pierces the air. "Where's mom?!"

"She got out. I'm going to rendezvous with her now," Nolan says. "It's not safe here. Come with me."

Molly shakes her head 'no,' a tense movement.

Her dad coughs, choking on the diesel. "I need to go..."

"C'mon," Max says to Molly. "We've got to stop them."

"Stop the demolition? Why do you think you can do that?" Nolan asks. "More to the point, how?"

"Hard to explain," Max says. "It has to do with Damage. Making everything right again. Repair. Do you trust me?"

Nolan ponders for a moment, then nods. "What do you need me to do?"

"Distract that guy," he says, pointing at the nearest dozer. Nolan looks incredulous for a moment, but then nods, covers his face with his sleeve, and waves down the driver.

Max and Molly sprint across the camp. Max plants his feet in front of the second dozer, Molly the third. Max assumes a power pose, hands on hips. The driver blares his air horn, but Max stands tall. Molly smiles at him and mirrors his pose. After a few minutes, the driver facing Max turns off the noisy engine, and the other two follow suit.

The silence that follows lets Max realize how tense his nerves have been. He breathes. Even the diesel-infused air feels good entering his lungs, and the tight cords on his neck loosen a bit. He never thought facing off against a giant earth-moving machine would be the most relaxing part of his day.

Then, Hemera's SUV, glinting in the early sun, crunches across the gravel as it pulls into camp. It stops not far from Max.

WHERE IT BEGAN

But Max is already here. Where is he supposed to go? He looks over the devastation of the camp. The tallest structure remaining is the LevelUP factory building.

Hemera stomps out, shaking with anger. She's got something the size of a cigarette lighter in her hand; when she holds it near her mouth, it amplifies her voice better than a much larger megaphone would. She focuses her ire on Max's bulldozer driver. "What are you doing? Why is your engine off? Do your job! Move!" The words hang in the air.

Max tenses up as the driver reaches for the controls of the machine. But instead of moving forward, he pulls his key out, holds his hand high, and lets it drop into the mud. The other two drivers, relieved, follow suit[1].

"Go do what you have to," the driver shouts. "She doesn't pay enough for murder." Max hesitates. "Go!"

Where it began. Max thanks the driver and runs for the factory building. He doesn't need to look back to know that Hemera's right behind him.

1. No need for Max to even lie down in the mud.

3-11 ...ANOTHER CASTLE_

SKILLS:

* KEYBEARER

"Welcome…" announces the recorded voice as Max approaches. It hesitates longer than usual before figuring out his name. His mud-caked face interferes with facial recognition. The holographic mascot steps into view, an annoying blue arrow with hair coifed into an up arrow. Max would swear there's a bit of awe in the mascot's voice when he says Max's new name: "Keybearer."

"Unlock?" Max says. Is this all he needs to do? The mascot glitches, completely vanishing for a second before reappearing.

"Welcome…Hemera Krapht," the mascot replies. "Welcome… Vic Vertex."

Her high-heeled shoes are gone, mud splattering the bottom of her pantsuit. She leaves footprints behind her, as does Vic, closely shadowing her. An angry sound escapes through clenched teeth, and Hemera brandishes a weapon. The way she holds it, Max would expect to find a dainty pistol there, but there's nothing more than dark stains on her fingers.

Max flinches as a bright, loud electrical arc leaps between her finger and thumb. Tiny spirals in her thumb and finger glow red for a moment before fading.

"You had a stunner embedded under your skin?" Max says. "No wonder you're so popular."

"You'd better watch it, or you'll get lit up," says Vic, smirking as usual.

Hemera lurches toward Max, spark flaring. Even from three paces away, the heat stings Max's face. What must she have done to herself to not feel pain?

OUR PRINCESS IS RIGHT HERE IN THIS CASTLE

The words almost distract Max as he steps out of the way of Hemera's attack.

The arrow mascot fuzzes out entirely and blips back as a low-resolution Princess Daisy.

"Ah," Princess Daisy says. "Wherever was I? Oh yes, Keybearer, you have many questions. I do enjoy helping people, but I'm very busy and only do so in return for something of value." The exact language the Muses had used.

"You're...you're one of the Muses?" Max asks.

"Not one of. Associated with."

A muddy blur dervishes through the door, leaping high toward Hemera's turned back, wrapping flailing limbs around Hemera's neck, swinging and punching.

"Welcome...Molly Matheson," Princess Daisy says, voice

distorted, warbling between the artificial sound of the original mascot and the slightly less robotic tonality of Princess Daisy.

Hemera buckles to her knees and twists awkwardly, trying to wield her electrical fury to fend off Molly's assault. The electrical arc makes contact with Molly's coat-hanger hand, and the charge jumps from the conductor through Hemera's neck. A blood-curdling shriek trails off as she slumps to the floor.

Vic rushes over and takes her hand. There's enough residual charge to give him a solid zap. Shaking his fingertips, he fumbles around for a pulse, even though it's obvious she's still breathing.

Molly dusts herself off. "Serves you right," she says.

"Uh… hi," Max says. "Aren't you supposed to be holding off two tons of destruction?"

"Soon as the stragglers caught wind of what was going on, I would've had to fight for a place in front of one of the dozers," Molly says.

"I guess there's an advantage to having a stack of IOUs under your pillow," Max says. His face drops. "Or once having—emphasis on past tense." His tent, his pillow, his IOUs, nothing's left. "At least there's still this."

"What's this?" Molly says. She's *smiling*.

"You've been with me every step of the way," Max says. "Not just anybody would've done that."

"We await your next move, Keybearer," the Princess Daisy avatar says. Then the image stutters and freezes again until it collapses with a loud burst of static into a single shining pixel. Molly covers her ears until the white noise echoes into silence.

"Friend of yours?" Molly asks.

"..."[1] Hard as Max tries, no sound comes out of his mouth.

The pixel dances in sync with a sound like someone clearing their throat. Then it speaks. "I always thought the princess schtick was kind of played out, even in my day."

"Dad!"

The image stretches and expands, like someone fighting their way out of a giant balloon. It ends up in a faint avatar of Hadley Root, clothed in a white lab coat over blue jeans and a tiger-striped tiki shirt. He holds his hands out in a welcoming gesture.

"Is it really you, or is this another simulation?" Max asks.

"Simulation isn't the right word," Hadley says, continuing to improve in image quality. "What you've been encountering are sub-sentient agents with a maximum rating of zero point eight Turings to preserve a safety buffer. There were limits on what I knew and/or could tell you."

Max's face sinks. It's no better than LevelUP's technology.

"But," Hadley continues, "that was before. What you've got here is a live feed, baby!"

"Dad!!" Max rushes over for a hug but passes through the empty space. "Oh, right, hologram," he says.

"That's really your dad?" Molly asks.

"Where are you?" Max asks.

"Oh, that's a good question. And it deserves an answer. But right now, my brave adventurers, you have a bigger problem you need to focus on."

"What's that?" Max asks.

"Funny story," Hadley says. "But by around 1989 or so, the brave captains of industry had perfected digital locks to the point that it became too tempting not to put them in everything. Hemera, foremost among their successors. For some people, desire for control is the most powerful force in the universe. I repented of my ways. Her, not so much."

"Why are you telling me this?"

"Because," Hadley says, "you now hold the key to all those locks. Look out! —"

The hologram vanishes in a roaring electric flare. Hemera's back on her feet, and she's reduced the hologram machine to smoking garbage. The fumes choke and make it hard to breathe.

The large screen that normally shows work assignments flickers to life, displaying a flat image of Hadley. "You can't get rid of me that easily," he says. "What are you doing, going around threatening a one-armed girl half your age. Not very mannerly of you. Only the weak need to threaten."

Hemera hesitates, cords of muscle in her jaw pulsing. She slowly turns to face the screen. "YOU," she bellows. Not a pleasant sound.

Hadley waves cheerily at her. "Yep. Me."

"You're supposed to be dead," Hemera says.

"Was I?" Hadley says. "Huh. I hadn't noticed."

"You were never one to listen to reason," Hemera says. With a fluid movement, she grabs Molly, cranks the poor girl's arm behind her back hard enough to make Molly cry out, and jams her stunner electrodes against Molly's temple. "So maybe you'll listen to this. Every one of you here is going to do exactly as I say unless you want your little princess lit up like that screen on her stupid game."

Max's mind races. He holds the master key to the locks on billions of devices. The key to a radically new society—one in which Hemera no longer plays a role. But he would never sacrifice Molly to get there.

Time slows to a crawl. "Don't hurt her," Max says. He raises both hands, slowly.

---

1. Sometimes I really miss David Foster Wallace.

3-12 [RETURN]_

Barely-contained energy crackles between Hemera's fingers. Molly winces.

"Go ahead; don't bother me none," Hadley Root says from the safety of his electronic display.

"What?!" Max says. "No! He didn't mean that."

"If she wants to throw away what little leverage she's got—let her. There are bigger issues at play here," Hadley says. "Think of everything that's led to this point. Don't get distracted, son."

"Distracted? Whose side are you on?" Max says. He feels his fingers start to ball into fists, but Hemera catches the movement and flinches. Max forces himself to relax, but his breathing remains ragged.

"Another winning strategy for the books," Hadley says, addressing Hemera directly. His voice drips with sarcasm. "Not counting Pittsburgh. Or the BlueBear initiative. And don't forget how project Quiet Thunder ended up. Huh. I guess you haven't been a success at a single thing in life besides hitting people with a big stick someone else handed you."

Just how much history did Hadley and Hemera have together?

"I built this company from the ground up," Hemera snarls. "I led the recovery after Damage. Without me, global industry would still be in tatters. Millions more would've died." Hemera's hand twitches, and a small spark lights up beneath her fingertips. Molly calls out in pain.

"Stop!" Max screams at the screen. "You'll make her lose control."

"That's where you're wrong," Hadley says. "She never had control to begin with. That's the whole problem. Despite being one of the few people in the world equipped with the right hardware to participate in the games I assembled, despite the obscene amount of resources at her disposal, in the end she couldn't get the key."

"That remains to be seen," Hemera says. She focuses on Max. "Give it to me. Now. Before I fill this room with her smoke."

Give it to her, just like that? "I don't know how," Max says. Immediately he feels disgusted about giving in to a bully. But still. Molly.

"You know," Hadley continues, ignoring Hemera's demand, "I had to plan for cheaters like Hemera. That's why it had to be a game." He puts his hand alongside his mouth and theatrically stage-whispers: "She wouldn't know fun if it came in a hardbound corporate report."

Hadley looks around and feigns surprise. "Oh, was that out loud?" He clears his throat. "About the key... No shortcuts. No emulators or simulators or trainers or twinking or ghosting. I needed the key to only be available to the person who appreciated our electronic heritage enough to discover and make it through all the levels."

"Ridiculous," Hemera says. A bigger spark escapes her fingers, and Molly screams. Judging by the look in Hemera's eye, this time wasn't accidental.

"OK, OK, OK," Max says. "You win. Let her go unhurt, and I'll figure out how to give you the key."

"Advanced technology," Molly whimpers.

That's Molly for you. Even under the stress of a moment like this, her mind can't help but seek to understand the technology around her.

"Inventory," Max says. His HUD shows a skill, but no items that he could drop or otherwise give away.

"Go on. Keep on using your zappy thing," Hadley says. "Burn off that stored energy til your capacitors are as empty as your heart."

Max puts his hands up in a placating gesture. "No, don't. Give me a minute to figure this out."

"Advanced technology," Molly says. Repeating herself again.

"Let her go," Max says. "We'll work this out. You have my word."

Hemera doesn't move to let Molly go. If anything, she shifts her fingers to Molly's neck, pressing deep. Molly's breathing turns into a wheeze.

"Tech—nolly—gee…"

Finally, Max gets it. As usual, Molly has been right all along.

"Hemera," Max booms, and the sheer volume and authority in his voice surprises even himself.

Hemera looks at him with new eyes, startled. She loosens her grip, and Molly's breathing gets a little more even.

"You have some very *advanced* hardware under your skin. And I've gotta admit, I'd rather figure out how to use the key rather than hand it over."

Hemera studies him for a long moment. He holds her gaze. "You wouldn't," she says, defiant.

"Try to speak in complete sentences," Max says. "For example, you could say, 'You wouldn't dare restore the world to its pre-Damage state.'"

Hadley smiles and taps his nose twice. "Took you long enough."

Hemera scowls. Molly breaks free of her grasp and squirms away, kicking Hemera's shin as she passes. "That's for calling my game 'stupid.'"

"I actually don't know. What would happen if I just threw the doors wide open?" Max asks.

"It would trigger an immune system of sorts. It was Hemera's idea, actually," Hadley says. "There are two—or is it three now?—agents roaming around the internet, searching and destroying anything rating above a 1.0 on the Turing scale."

"The black slime," Max says. "Is an immune reaction?"

"Well, it started out that way," Hadley says. "All these little gadgets that LevelUP puts out need some way to counteract the technological lock. It's possible to do so on tiny scales, a few seconds at a time, but it requires a ridiculous amount of processing power, especially for an 8-bit system. We're talking a solid 0.75 Turings. Over time, some branches of that code got smarter.

"Like any immune system, it's self-adaptive. Every threat it encounters leaves it changed. That's why it's important for it to be sub-sentient. At least that was the working theory inside LevelUP." Hadley makes a point of looking around. "At least it was, last time I checked."

Max thinks back to the Eigenthief and Bode and even Princess Daisy. Were all of them killers on the prowl? Were they evaluating Max the whole time, to see whether he was human or not?

"You might want to check your code," Max says. "Seems it's still got some bugs. Now, I've taken a personal interest in you. Let me give you a little lesson in how the world actually works."

<LEVEL INDETERMINATE>_

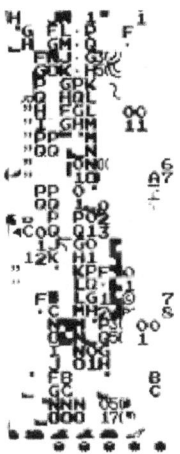

THERE'S A WIRELESS NETWORK NEARBY, BUT THE SIGNAL'S faint. Too weak to have ever shown up from Nolan's IT tent, but Max can sense it, as clearly as he once sensed a floating pixel front-and-center in his field of vision. The password comes to mind as easily as remembering an old friend's name. From there, Max finds a network path to the police station, where he leaves a note that invokes Hemera's authority, requesting police presence.

Since it looks like the request comes from a CEO, they'll actually respond. Lots of things need to change. Starting here.

"Sit down," Max tells Hemera, not unkindly, but in response, her face hardens.

Max turns his attention to her. She's got more hardware than he realized. Not one, but two watches in her wrist. Was one of them already obsolete? A transceiver in the back of her neck much like Max's, though a much newer model—and there's an unmistakable presence riding shotgun alongside it. Max pushes his mind toward it, and the image of the black slime nearly knocks him off his feet.

With a thought, Max severs the implant's connection, both to Hemera and the outside world.

The defiance drops away from Hemera's face, replaced with confusion. She looks lost, a little girl separated from a parent in a dense crowd. Bit by bit, her expression shifts to fear built on loneliness. Hemera wraps her arms around herself as if she'd caught a sudden chill.

Max sits first. "Please sit. We need to talk and what happens next." Shortly after he'd learned the truth about his own implant, he'd dreamed about what would happen if he ripped it out. "Are you hurt?"

"What have you done?" Hemera demands.

Yeah, she's alright. "It's over," Max says. As far as he's concerned, it's a simple statement of fact, yet he can actually see his words' impact settling across her face. "There are two ways this can go."

"Ah! Welcome...Isidore Morris," Hadley says.

"What's going on?" Isidore says, out of breath. "I didn't think I'd get here in time—" He tenses as he catches sight of Hemera. "What *is* going on?" he asks.

"Get comfortable," Max says. "We could use your point of view. Please join us."

Isidore looks unsettled, but he sits, eventually easing into a cross-legged pose. Hemera finally sits too.

"Hang on a sec," Hadley says. "Bit of a situation here." He reaches offscreen and pulls a large weapon that looks like none Max has ever seen before, except maybe on a sci-fi Laserdisc. He dashes off-camera, a tendril of black slime trailing from his shoe.

The sight distracts Molly. "I don't get it," she says. "Both him and the black slime can't be real."

Max's heart sinks. For the briefest moment, he had let himself muse about a world where his father would be there for him. But alas, all he did was run away just when he was needed. Again. If that was even really him.

Molly returns to glaring daggers at Hemera. "Is it true?" Molly asks.

Hemera's voice is weary. "Is what true."

"The slavery," Molly says.

Hemera breaks eye contact. "It's only code," she says into the floor.

"You're no different," Molly retorts.

Max holds out a hand, and Molly sits back down. "What happens if I don't use the key? At least not right away?"

Isidore breathes, seemingly for the first time since he's sat. "That would be highly advisable until you better understand the situation that led to Damage in the first place."

"People are suffering," Max says. "Even those whose camp hasn't been recently demolished."

"I'll restore the camp," Hemera says, suddenly more alert.

Max raises an eyebrow. "Uncharacteristically generous of you."

"Police," Molly says. Max doesn't hear anything.

"But you have to keep me out of prison. I'm not built for that kind of life—"

"All the camps," Max says. Not a question. "Starting here." He ponders the situation. How can he prevent things from snapping back to the status quo? "And I get a seat on the LevelUP board."

"As do I," Isidore says.

"And each of us gets to appoint one more board member. That should make a majority, right?" Max says.

"Majority? You'd fire me as CEO on the first day," Hemera says.

Max taps his nose twice and smiles. Now he hears the police sirens. "Your call. Unlike you, I want to use my influence for good. And if you're not interested in making things better…"

"Fine, fine, fine," Hemera says. "Deal. I'll call and make arrangements."

"Sounds like an IOU to me," Max says. "I won't even make you write it out in rhyming verse."

The sirens are close now, at the bottom of the hill. "Oh, crap, better keep my end of the bargain," Max says. In a blink, he makes a few choice edits to the police record.

THE ARMORED POLICE cruiser leaves with handcuffed Hemera looking wistfully out the back, and Vic Vertex still alongside her, suddenly less interested in publicity.

"You betrayed her," Isidore says, with what might be a hint of admiration.

"No," Max says. "I promised to keep her out of prison. I said nothing about county jail. She needs a few days to think about the choices that led her to this point."

"Fair enough," Isidore says.

"And I promised nothing at all to the grease-stain," Max says.

"Vic's not built for prison, that's for sure," Isidore says.

Molly's got her nose in her handheld game again.

"You know, there's one thing I still haven't figured out," Max says. "Who was sending me all those messages in my HUD?"

"I think you already know," Isidore says.

"I really don't," Max says. "Closest I can figure is the Muses, but I never even knew they existed before yesterday."

At the mention of the Muses, Molly hesitates in her game. She buries her face in it again, working the controls.

CUTSCENE_

Technology Re-launch Hits Stratospheric Heights — What's at Stake

From the news desk of KQRM: Here are your latest headlines. It may be a distant memory, but before Damage, computers had been doubling in speed about every two years. After being at a standstill for over a decade, the march of technology was making up for lost time, avoiding the chaos that marked the original evolution.

In particular, LevelUP corporation, which many observers had written off when their CEO resigned in disgrace, has emerged again at the forefront of a new industrial revolution. The surprise appointment of Molly Matheson, unknown to the Silicon Valley elite, was widely panned at the time, though detractors didn't have very long to gloat before they were proven wrong, even by pundit standards.

The "lost decade" — all the years of progress lost — wasn't a complete write-off. Many important inventions, like the so-called zero-point batteries and mediated neural interfaces, had been in development before Damage. With the bottom falling out of the economy, it wasn't worth finishing R&D that was months or even weeks from commercial readiness. Now, that's all changed.

In fact, to a growing number of observers, the post-Reboot march of technology has seemed too good to be true—as if there were some hidden guiding hand pushing mankind forward. Meanwhile, every attempt to reinstate DRM has met with assorted, almost ill-fated failure. But that's all a silly conspiracy theory, right?

EPILOGUE_

MAX SEARCHES THE OLD-FASHIONED WAY. SHOE LEATHER, they used to call it. First of all, he returns to the Muses. He has a promise to keep.

The outside door is padlocked. Since the Reboot, this part of town has been picking up again. Property values are going up — there's a SOLD sign in the window. It's twilight and a handful of lights are on in the condos across the street. People are living here again. But no Muses.

Max uses a handheld network scanner to make sure there's no signal coming from inside. He walks around the back to be sure. The building's abandoned, at least until the new tenant moves in. No hints here. He'll keep looking.

His next stop is at the one-time doctor's office where he and Molly found a node up-and-running. Another *For Sale* sign out front, halfway covered up with a smaller *Sold* sign. Bright lights shine from within. A lone construction worker inside patches holes in the drywall.

The door's open. Max leans in and says, "Hey! What are you building here?"

The construction worker looks familiar, but Max can't quite place his face. Was it someone from the camp? "This place is going to be an Internet Retro Gaming Cafe. Can you believe it?"

"Sure can. What's the name of the company?"

"That's the thing," the worker says. "They're real sensitive about privacy. I don't know how they're going to make any money." He gestures at a not-yet-hung sign that declares that network access here is free. "As long as my checks clear, I'm happy I guess."

"Checks? What's the name on the checks?" Max asks.

"Gibberish if you ask me," the worker says. "The Realtime Operating Node? Those ain't even words."

"I think the right customers will get the message," Max says. "When will it open?"

"No idea," the worker says.

"Tell you what, can you leave a message for whoever hands you the check? Tell them Max was here."

"I get the checks in the mail," the worker says.

"Then I'll make a point of stopping by when this place opens," Max says.

There's one more place left to check. It's fully dark by the time he reaches the public library. It's closed, but a light is still on by the administrative offices. Max bangs on the window until Miyamoto the librarian ushers him in.

"I'm honestly surprised you'd still speak with me," he says.

"Don't worry about it," Max says. "Hemera made lots of people do bad things." Miyamoto nods almost imperceptibly. "What do you know about my father?" Max asks.

"Ah, your father." Miyamoto gets a faraway look in his eyes. "He was a great man."

"Was?"

"I choose my words carefully, Max," Miyamoto says. "And the things for which your father is known to me, all of them are in the past. Thus my saying he *was* a great man."

"Have you heard from him?" Max asks.

"For you to ask that question, you must exchange information," Miyamoto says. "Did someone try to contact you in his name?"

"Actually, he did," Max says. "Or possibly an avatar acting in his name. But it felt like him. He knew things."

Miyamoto nods gravely. He turns and sifts through papers stacked on a shelf behind him. He looks through them, thoughtfully, one-at-a-time, licking his thumb repeatedly. He finds a page that meets his satisfaction. It's a small, torn strip of paper with spidery writing on it.

Miyamoto faces Max, and in his manner gets right in his personal space. "It so happens that I received an interesting phone call today." He hands the note to Max. "I didn't recognize the voice, but they said that if Max comes in and asks about his father, to give him this message."

Max starts to open his mouth with the first of a thousand questions.

"I know you'll have questions," Miyamoto says. "But this is all the information I have. Truly. Take your note. And once you resume your search, I wish you the best. I will always be here for you."

Resume the search? Max scans the note, then takes his leave before tears blur his eyesight too much.

Outside, under the light of a sodium streetlamp, he unfolds the note and reads it again:

Max, I know you're looking for me. I'd do the same in your position. You must know this: leaving you was the second hardest thing I've ever done in my life. I stand by my decision—it was the right thing to do—but it hurts me every time I wake up, every time I try to go to sleep and every moment in between. I realize I've left scars. I can't wave them away. At this point, a "normal" father-son relationship is out of the question. But I will make it up to you. This, I swear.

That said, in light of recent events, I have one final mission to accomplish. I'm not prone to dramatics, but it may be the most important thing I've ever done. Son, call off your search for me, at least for now. Your presence would only complicate what is a most delicate situation. I regret that I can't say more. Once this is accomplished, once the world is safe again, I will come find you. You've made quite a name for yourself. Locating you won't be hard.

I am so proud of you, Son.

HR

QUESTS:

* FIND HADLEY

Time passes. No word from Hadley Root, despite his promise. Not surprising, only disappointing.

Max switches off his implant, but it doesn't dull the pain. More time passes.

Then, one day, Max's implant switches itself back on. Max's HUD lights up with one final message.

WE NEED TO TALK

[The End][1]

---

1. Or is it?

GEEKS_

Read more: Join my mailing list!

Get These Free Books

As an indie publisher, I don't have the resources of the LevelUP megacorporation to help me promote my book. I rely on enthusiastic fans like you. Visit **8bitnovel.com** and sign up for my mailing list, which includes geeky behind-the-scenes peeks at upcoming projects and free books:

- Damage, a prequel to LevelUP
- Minds and Machines, a short story collection
- Totally '80s: inspirations for the LevelUP universe

P.S.: Uncover the mystery at levelupcorp.online for a special bonus....

SPECIAL THANKS_

How could I do this without the support from my family and friends? Thank you Ann, Anita, and Anežka. I don't know how you put up with me, but I'm eternally grateful that you do. I had all kinds of help from suggestions to proofreading from Fox, Adam, Tom, Dominique, Alida, John, Bryan, Terri, and and Eleanor. I was especially encouraged by Effie, Vincent, Tammi, Ric, Kate, and that one person who was especially enthusiastic at my FOGcon reading, but my social-anxiety-riddled brain refuses to recall their name.

Apologies to my time travel fans, because the next book in my time travel series took a backseat while I worked on this project. For that you can blame the Sterling and Stone crew, Johnny B. Truant, Sean Platt, and David Wright (but mostly Johnny) for convincing me to join the apprentice program, and power through it. It's coming yet, I promise. And if you look closely, there are hints that these two series may be more connected that it first seems…

At risk of repeating myself, there were many things that I technically first heard at Viable Paradise XIV, but only years later was able to fully appreciate. The ones that stood out most clearly to me during the writing of this story were from Elizabeth Bear, John Scalzi, Steven Gould, Laura Mixon, and Jim MacDonald. Thanks teaches!

Of course, I owe a huge debt of gratitude to Ernest Cline for completely blowing my mind with Ready Player One. I stand in awe of your accomplishment.

Most of all, I'm thankful for my readers. Thanks, you geeks!

FURTHER READING_

Like a lot of my AI-related stories, there are deep influences here from a number of sources, but mostly:

- Superintelligence: Paths, Dangers, Strategies by Nick Bostrom
- Pretty much anything from Eliezer Yudkowsky
- Better Faster Smarter by Charles Duhigg

There's lots of connections to my other books in various states of stealth. Check out my Comp-sci-fi stories for more on these ideas at http://micahjoel.info/comp-sci-fi/

And check out my time travel series starting at http://micahjoel.info/ixion/

Anyone who signs up for my mailing list at http://8bitnovel.com/ also gets three free books:

AUTHOR NOTES_

I'd love to hear what you think. Where would you like to see the next novel go? Were there any intriguing hints you noticed and wished you could hear more about?

C'mon by to http://8bitnovel.com/ and sign up for my low-volume mailing list and you'll join a growing tribe of like-minded individuals who get early access to new stories, trade reading suggestions, and share in other goodies.

P.S. Support independent authors. Reviews are so important for those of us without fat cat publishers. Before the day is out, leave a review for any indie book—it doesn't even have to be this one. Thanks!

Made in the USA
Las Vegas, NV
08 November 2021